T0193412

Critical Acclaim for Christine McGuire's Novels of Suspense

UNTIL DEATH DO US PART

"Starts with a bang—literally—and never lets up. . . . McGuire, an experienced criminal prosecutor, provides fascinating forensic details and juggles her plotlines skillfully, never sacrificing clarity, as the book speeds to its conclusion."

—*Publishers Weekly*

"A gripping drama. . . . Readers are treated to three-dimensional human beings filled with fears, doubts, and flaws."

—Amazon.com

"A vital, compelling read. . . . The reader gets top entertainment value for her dollar, so sit back and enjoy this absorbing, suspenseful tale."

—*Romantic Times*

UNTIL JUSTICE IS DONE

"What sets McGuire's novels apart from the pack is the level of realism she brings to the legal aspects of the story."

—*The Sentinel* (Santa Cruz, CA)

UNTIL PROVEN GUILTY

"A tense, nerve-jangling thriller that should satisfy fans of *The Silence of the Lambs.*"

—Peter Blauner, author of *The Intruder*

"Gripping. . . . This unrelenting . . . account of a vicious serial killer all but commands the readers to burn the midnight oil. . . . [The] pathological details and criminal profiles unfailingly rivet the attention."

—*Publishers Weekly*

This book is a work of fiction. Names, characters, places and incidents are products of the author's imagination or are used fictitiously. Any resemblance to actual events or locales or persons, living or dead, is entirely coincidental.

An *Original* Publication of POCKET BOOKS

POCKET BOOKS, a division of Simon & Schuster Inc.
1230 Avenue of the Americas, New York, NY 10020

ISBN: 978-1-4767-9693-2

First Pocket Books printing October 1998

10 9 8 7 6 5 4 3 2 1

POCKET and colophon are registered trademarks of Simon & Schuster Inc.

Cover photo by Peter Lopez Photography

Printed in the U.S.A.

This novel is dedicated to
The Victims and Survivors
of domestic violence
and their Advocates

Acknowledgments

With deep gratitude to my literary agents Arthur and Richard Pine and their assistant, Sarah Piel, and with special appreciation and thanks to my editor, Julie Rubenstein, her assistant, Leslie Stern, and to Max Greenhut.

UNTIL THE BOUGH BREAKS

PROLOGUE

THE NIGHTMARE NEVER CHANGED. IT EMERGED as tension and irritation, a festering sore that wouldn't heal without erupting. Escalating into anger over nothing, it evolved into a simmering rage and exploded into confrontation and violence. She walked a razor's edge of defiance and submission.

"Please," she pleaded, more sad than afraid, "listen to me. Let's talk."

"Fuck you, bitch, I'm sick of talkin'."

They had argued for hours. Always the same words. Always the same result. Like a runaway train on a dead-end siding, racing toward a violent end. She had stood up to him for once, which just provoked greater hostility. She just wanted it to be over but knew it would not be until the cycle ran its course.

"I can't take any more of this," she told him. "No more. I want you to go. Get out and leave me alone. I won't let you beat me again." Her voice possessed a

strength she had not previously known and a calm she did not actually feel. "I can't live like this anymore. I can't do it. I want you out of my life."

"You want? Who gives a fuck what you want, you ungrateful bitch!" Before she could react, he struck her with a roundhouse right hand that slammed her against the refrigerator door.

Instinctively, she scuttled across the kitchen and tumbled onto the deck. She got quickly to her feet and dashed toward the concrete walkway that ran along the side of the house to the sidewalk and street. She had to make it to the street, where she might be seen or heard by a neighbor or passing car.

But, still woozy from the blow to her head, her legs responded sluggishly. Suddenly she felt the heavy weight of his hand on her shoulder, the strong insistent grip spinning her around.

"No . . . use . . . bitch," he panted. "You can't . . . run away."

"Please," she begged, looking at him as she fell to the cement, surrender in her eyes. "Please just . . . I'll go away. Just let me up and I'll leave. I won't take anything. I'll just go away. Please."

Contemptuous, he yanked her to her feet and hit her again, this time with his closed fist, low down in the abdomen. She sank to the ground blinded by pain.

He sat astride her, grabbed her face in one rough hand and smashed her head against the cement walkway. Sweat and spit dripped from his face and mingled with her blood. "I think this time I'll fucking kill you!"

Teetering on the verge of unconsciousness, she

managed a scream which seemed to her to emanate from a distant place. He grabbed her by the hair and smashed a fist into her face. She heard a bone crack. The last sound she heard was the faint wail of a police siren. As it grew nearer, she wondered if there was an accident someplace.

1

THE FOURTH OF JULY CROWD LINING VILLAGE Road was noisy, boisterous, and happy. The Stars and Stripes flew proudly on bicycles, baby carriages, street signs, and building facades. Some stood, some sat on folding chairs or the grass strip separating the sidewalk from the pavement, while the more adventurous perched on the roofs of their cars or tailgates of pickup trucks whose rear ends faced the street. Small children were hoisted onto their dads' shoulders, legs wrapped tightly around their necks. Older kids crouched in front of the adults, waving their little flags.

"Here they come," Emma shouted excitedly to no one in particular. "Here they come." A true patriot at age nine, she waved the Stars and Stripes for emphasis.

Faintly audible John Philip Sousa marching music preceded the first float as it crested the small hill near the shopping center. It carried the Laguna del Mar High School Marching Band, which on this occasion was definitely not marching.

The ancient blue Dodge truck towing the float was decked out in red, white, and blue balloons and bunting. The all-girl wind section sat in front. Boys clad in identical red, white, and blue T-shirts immediately behind blared away on an array of trumpets, trombones, and tubas, while at the back of the float rode identically dressed students pounding away on drums and cymbals.

If it wasn't perfectly performed, the march was at least played loudly and enthusiastically, and the spectators lining the early parade route expressed their appreciation by cheering, stamping their feet, and clapping their hands in time with the march.

Not to be outdone, the drum majors and majorettes of the Española Middle School strutted in their maroon-and-yellow uniforms immediately behind the band in more-or-less perfect unison. No one noticed or cared about the occasional dropped baton as the procession approached the railroad underpass.

Immediately after the drum corps an antique tractor wheezed and chugged along pulling an equally old rubber-tired wagon stacked with gaily decorated apple crates on which sat pretty high-school girls dressed as Uncle Sam throwing kisses to their appreciative audiences.

Two elderly men wearing overalls, checkered shirts, and straw hats sat high on the wagon's driving bench. One had a piece of straw clamped in his teeth.

Following the wagon, firefighters of Laguna del Mar County Fire District Station Two crept along on

Engine 3552. The fire engine—gleaming red and spotlessly clean—sounded its siren periodically to the delight of the younger spectators. One of the fully regaled firefighters clinging from the engine spotted Dave Granz and pointed his finger at him, cocked his thumb, and fired an imaginary round straight at Granz's chest.

"Hey, Granz—bad guys taking today off?" he shouted above the din.

"Nope," Granz shouted back, "but the DA's office is."

"I guess so! The lead investigator's out playing, and I see they let the Top Gun prosecutor out for fresh air, too," he shouted back, acknowledging Kathryn Mackay—Kate to those who knew her—with a friendly smile. The fire truck disappeared around the turn into the old section of the village.

"Mom, look!" Emma yanked on Kathryn's arm and pointed to the road where a keeper led a small herd of serene, haughty-looking animals down the middle of the road. "Llamas! I heard they were going to have llamas. Aren't they beautiful, Dave?"

Dave struck a thoughtful pose, scratched his chin, and studied the strange animals who could best be described as a curious and not totally successful cross between a camel and a goat. One was a whiskey-brown color and the other off-white. "Don't know I'd call them beautiful exactly. Interesting, maybe. Next thing you know they'll be bringing elephants to our parade. It's downright un-American, I'd say."

"Oh Dave," Emma squealed in delight, knowing Dave was, in his terms, 'yanking her chain.' "We shoulda brought Sam. I saw a booth where anybody who enters their pet in the parade gets a prize and a ribbon."

Sam was Emma's golden Lab, the dog Dave gave her right after Emma's father was killed in a courtroom shooting. She and Sam were inseparable, Sam believing he was a sixty-five-pound lap dog, and Emma indulging his delusion.

"Too late now, sweetie. Maybe next year," Kathryn answered.

Changing the subject, Dave's attention turned to the area near the parade's starting point. "I'll bet Hal's having a great time up there sitting on the back of that Cadillac convertible," he said to Kathryn, only partially in jest.

Kathryn smiled. Her boss, District Attorney Hal Benton, had reluctantly agreed to preside as grand marshal of the Fourth of July Grand Village Parade and Extravaganza, proudly referred to by its organizers and local citizens alike as the World's Shortest Parade.

It began in the parking lot of the Wells Fargo Bank at the intersection of Village Road and the freeway interchange, wound about a mile through Laguna del Mar and terminated at Village Park. No one associated with the event took themselves very seriously, but everyone took the parade and the ensuing festival very seriously—it was an important regional event, and not one to be missed if you wanted to mingle with the movers and shakers.

"He'll cope," she replied. "He'll have to. Besides, where else could he get all this free publicity?"

Dave, Kathryn, and Emma had arrived at the

parade site early to assure a prime spot to observe the action.

Waking at five-thirty in the mornings was such a pattern for Kathryn that she never considered it unusual anymore. Emma, however, preferred to sleep late and lounge in bed watching cartoons on her own Panasonic TV-VCR which occupied the place of honor on the dresser in her bedroom. The TV-VCR, an indulgence from Kathryn, was an effective baby-sitter when Kathryn spent hours on the phone with police or other prosecutors.

By the time Emma awoke each morning, Kathryn had normally completed her morning household chores and spent half an hour on either the Stair-Master or stationary bicycle. Their routine was to have a light breakfast and orange juice together, chatting about the matters Emma found important, before leaving the house for school and work.

This morning was different. They walked up the short, steep hill to meet Dave at the pancake breakfast being served by the volunteer firefighters alongside the old Seacliff Hotel outside the entrance to Village Park.

They found him standing outside by the coffee bar. Kathryn had smiled inwardly, knowing that Dave couldn't start the day without his "caffeine kickstart." He was wearing a black T-shirt that said "Turn on Your Own Thunder" in bold red letters over the Harley-Davidson logo, with Levi's and black Nike Airs. With his beach-bum blond hair and youthful good looks, he couldn't have looked less like a cop. But, as an experienced investigator in the District Attorney's office, that's what he was.

Kathryn, as senior trial attorney prosecuting only the most serious felonies, harbored a deep and abiding respect and gratitude for Dave Granz's professional skills. She also cared deeply about him personally.

"Hi gang," he greeted them, snapping to attention and saluting Kathryn, who wore white jeans and a blue T-shirt with an American flag silk-screened on the front. "You guys ready to eat? I'm starving."

"What kind of pancakes do they have?" Emma inquired. She loved pancakes.

"Well, let's see," Dave thought aloud. "They have buttermilk pancakes with maple syrup. Or you can have buttermilk pancakes without maple syrup. Or you can have maple syrup with buttermilk pancakes. Take your pick."

Emma only ate pancakes so she would have someplace to pour her maple syrup, and Dave knew it. "I think I'll have buttermilk pancakes with maple syrup. Lots of syrup, please."

"Your wish is my command." He turned to Kathryn. "And what is your desire, ma'am?"

"I'll just have coffee, I think."

Emma rolled her eyes at Dave conspiratorially and pointed at her hips. "She thinks pancakes end up in the wrong spot. I'll eat hers."

"E-m-m-m!" Kathryn arched her eyebrows in feigned indignation. She loved it when the two of them ganged up on her. Her two favorite people together.

After they ate, they picked their spot alongside the road opposite the shopping center, just before the railroad underpass, from which they now watched the parade. Dave had brought a couple of folding chairs—Kathryn reclined in one, while Dave shared his with Emma. Kathryn had brought a thermos of cold orange juice, but no one was interested in it.

As another band strutted past in colorful uniforms playing "The Battle Hymn of the Republic," Kathryn inquired rhetorically, "How did this thing get started, anyway?" Right then a clown sauntered past with his spotted mongrel dog who wore a miniature harness and pulled a red rubber-tired Radio Flyer wagon. Another man costumed as Paul Revere roared past riding a mini bike trailing an obnoxious cloud of exhaust.

Dave, the local resident historian, began, "It started back in 1962. Some local ladies won a zoning decision barring the building of a cement plant near here. It was just before the 4th, so they thought a parade was a good way to celebrate. Back then it was even smaller than it is now. But it sorta . . ."

"It just growed," Emma interrupted, emphasizing her point, as she often did, with intentional bad grammar. She was waving to Grandpa and Grandma riding on a stack of straw bales in the back of a Model A Ford truck. A banner on the side of the truck read "Born on the Fourth of July. Grandpa—July 4, 1923. Grandma—July 4, 1926." The straw bales were entirely surrounded by fresh fruits and vegetables arranged to spill out of large baskets. Grandpa and Grandma waved back at Emma.

"Boy, if the Rose Parade organizers could see this," Kathryn mused.

"They'd die laughing," Dave responded, "but I'll bet we have just as much fun."

A 1957 red Cadillac convertible crawled past, its driver wearing a Bill Clinton mask. A banner on the windshield read: "Whitwater? I cain't even spel it." Hal Benton smiled and waved from his perch on the back deck. He flashed a wink to Emma and a thumbs-up to Kate and Dave.

In the middle of the parade rode a squadron of two dozen or so Harley-Davidson motorcycles flying banners declaring their membership in the local chapter of the Harley Owners Group.

The machines—mostly black, and all cleaned and polished to perfection—crept along so slowly it seemed impossible for them to remain upright. The big, powerful engines roared as their riders cranked the throttles to impress the bystanders.

The riders represented a cross-section of motorcycle enthusiasts. Some wore black leather vests, black T-shirts, black Levi's, and black boots, and sported long hair, beards, and mirror shades. Others, many riding "dressers," were a bit more sedate. But they all smiled and waved, especially at the kids along the route who were, Kathryn observed, properly impressed and envious.

Dave was in obvious pain. "Aren't those V-Twins music to your ears?" he asked Kathryn. "Can I have one for Christmas? I'll take a small one to start—a Sportster'll do fine."

"I thought you were saving up for another new Jeep."

"Yeah, I guess I am." He grinned. "But I'll tell you something. Those scooters bring out the cowboy in me, and those guys are the last of the American cowboys. Besides, I was thinking maybe I'd find one in my stocking if I came over to your place this Christmas."

Hearing all this, Emma couldn't resist. "Oh, Dave, you're too old for that stuff."

"Thanks a lot. See if I take you for a ride."

For the next forty-five minutes or so, the parade rolled past: the Rotary Club, the Boy Scouts, and a red Miata with the top down carrying George Washington and Betsy Ross. Next, a little guy on a tricycle passed by towing a two-wheeled wagon with a little girl and a huge bunch of red balloons which looked capable of lifting the wagon off the ground. They were followed by a row of vintage cars in various stages of restoration.

The last float, bearing the sign "End of Parade" and carrying a banjo band and barbershop quartet singing "Down by the Riverside," finally inched past the spot Dave, Kathryn, and Emma had claimed. Bringing up the rear, not official but equally enthusiastic, came a group of preteenagers on skateboards, bicycles, and rollerblades.

Finally, Dave picked up the chairs and folded them. They followed the crowd under the railroad bridge to Village Park, where the bunting-draped stalls, booths, and sideshows were set up in the parking lot. It looked like a carnival midway, with the aroma of hot dogs, hamburgers, onions, pizza, and hot grease mixed with the pungent tang of barbecue fires being stoked up to cook chicken and steaks. Nearby, the sounds of a bluegrass band had everyone tapping their feet.

Too full to eat, they wandered around for awhile,

although Dave had extracted Kathryn's solemn promise that they could eat "carney food," his favorite cuisine, for supper. They shopped the arts and crafts booths. Then, while Emma tried to win a stuffed animal at the Coke-bottle ringtoss, Dave's pager beeped.

"Oh, crap," he moaned as he checked the number display. "County Comm." At that moment, Kathryn's pager also sounded and hers, too, was requesting response to County Comm.

Kathryn was always on call for homicides and other serious crimes, and whenever she was on call, she requested Dave as her investigator. She knew it was serious, or they wouldn't be paged. "Why don't you call us in," she asked Dave, "while I go break the news to Em. She's going to be really upset. You know, except for Christmas, the Fourth is her favorite holiday."

"Okay, babe." Dave wandered away in search of a pay phone. "Meet me here. I'll be right back."

When he located them about five minutes later, Emma was consuming a huge chocolate ice-cream cone, her mother's only effective means of apology. It wasn't working entirely, Dave noted, judging by the frown on Emma's face. "Where's mine?"

Emma held it out to him for a lick but didn't smile. Kathryn waited in anticipation.

"House fire in Mission Heights," he reported. "A bad one. Looks like arson."

Before Kathryn could ask why they were being called out for a house fire, he continued.

"They recovered a body from the site. Looks like

14

more than an accidental fire. We're supposed to meet Dr. Death—woops, sorry—Dr. Nelson at the morgue." Morgan Nelson was a forensic pathologist who functioned as the coroner. Nelson was the best.

"M-o-o-o-m! Do you have to go? This is a holiday." Emma protested, but with little hope of winning her case. She'd done this many times before.

"You know I do, sweetie; I don't have any choice. I'll come home as soon as I can, and we'll go to the beach after dark to watch the fireworks. I promise."

Disappointed, Emma accepted this as the best she could expect.

"I'll go get my car," Dave suggested. "I'll pick you up here. Do you want to ride down together, or do you want to drive your own car?"

"No, I'll drive my own. But you can take us home. I'll call Ruth to watch Em, then meet you there." She saw a strange look on Dave's face. Noticing the direction he was looking, she realized what was bothering him.

They stood in front of the old turn-of-the-century Seacliff Hotel, a local landmark and historical structure recently renovated and converted to a restaurant and bed-and-breakfast by an English couple.

Just behind it lay the parking lot where, a few years ago, a serial killer dubbed by newspapers the Gingerbread Man had lured Dave to a meeting and almost killed him with a medical scalpel.

Kathryn no longer noticed the faint scars on his face and neck, although they were plainly visible if one looked for them. "Oh, Dave, why did you park there? I know it still bothers you."

He shrugged with more indifference than he felt. "Only place to park when I got here. Doesn't bother me except I get mad as hell. Mad at myself for being so stupid. That's all. Don't worry about it."

Turning away to hide his feelings, he headed off to retrieve his car. Jesus, he thought, maybe I ought to buy one of those Hogs and ride away. Be easier than this and a lot more fun.

2

IF THEY BROUGHT ME HERE BLINDFOLDED, I'D still know I was at the morgue, Kathryn thought as the elevator doors retracted and the familiar, pervasive odors assaulted her senses. Morgue odor was a distinctive fetid marriage of antiseptic and death, which the cooling units, exhaust fans, and deodorizers never fully dispelled or neutralized, despite their best efforts. It was a smell that once experienced was never forgotten, as was the inherent silence and stillness.

No matter how many times or how often she came here, Kathryn always sensed that this was a place for the dead, with their unseeing eyes and silent voices; any living thing, even the beat of a heart, was a foreign and intrusive presence.

At the end of the corridor was the cold-storage vault

where bodies were refrigerated and preserved before and after autopsy. Next to it was the staging room in which bodies were weighed, measured, and photographed before being transferred to gurneys and rolled to the autopsy suite.

To her immediate right as she exited the elevator waited the largest of the autopsy suites. It comprised three autopsy stations, each fully equipped with stainless-steel tables, scales, lockers, sinks, and sluices enclosed in soundproof booths designed to permit the pathologist to dictate notes.

Across the hall was the isolation suite, which was utilized to examine bodies in states of advanced decomposition or suspected of carrying infectious diseases. The suite was fitted with high-powered, high-velocity, high-capacity extraction fans that directed noxious and offensive gasses to an incinerator.

Down the corridor on the right was the VIP room, where cases requiring special or extended study were examined. Morgan Nelson awaited Kathryn at the open door. Dave Granz stood beside the forensic pathologist, having arrived shortly after dropping Kathryn at her condominium. The familiar bulky figure of Lieutenant Walt Earheart, the sheriff's chief of detectives, leaned against the doorjamb alongside Dave.

Earheart held his hands up palms out to Kathryn in mock surrender. "I know, I know," he apologized, "it's a holiday. But this couldn't wait."

Kathryn smiled in spite of herself. She and Earheart had a friendly and mutually respectful professional relationship of many years' standing.

"You think you're in trouble with me, wait till Emma gets hold of you," she replied. Emma had spent plenty of afternoons in the company of Walt and other sheriff's deputies while Kathryn conducted business at the Justice Center. Baby-sitters weren't always available on a moment's notice.

She reflected that Emma probably had more friends that were police officers than most police officers. She could do worse.

"Pretty scary thought," Earheart replied. "Remind me to come bearing gifts next time I see her."

Morgan Nelson was almost as fond of Emma as he was of Kathryn. He smiled and asked, "She still learning violin?"

"Onward and upward. She's playing Mozart."

He shook his head. "I'm impressed." Then more seriously, "Where does the time go, Katie?"

Nobody else ever called her Katie. It was Morgan Nelson's special dispensation as her very special friend. In his late fifties and tall, his gingery hair was close-cropped. Not one to be rightfully accused of being vain, his eyes were red behind his wire-rimmed glasses.

She wondered when he last slept. Eighteen-hour days weren't unusual; sometimes he worked around the clock. Unlike other workaholics, with Nelson it wasn't for lack of outside interests. He was a true renaissance man who knew more about more subjects than any person Kathryn had ever known. He was a renowned firearms expert often consulted for his expertise in that matter rather than his medical skills which were generally considered unsurpassed. But, the physical labor of lifting and turning dead bodies eventually wore him down; it wasn't called dead weight for nothing.

"What do you have?" Kathryn asked.

"Enter," Nelson invited, stepping aside and swinging open the heavy door. A blast of cold air struck them full force like leaping into a cold pool.

"Damn," Dave muttered under his breath as the automatic door hissed shut behind them. "What a way to spend the holiday."

It was no secret that he hated the morgue, despite his fondness for Morgan Nelson. He stoically endured autopsies as his penance for being a senior investigator. The scars—internal and external—inflicted when the Gingerbread Man nearly killed him years before had sensitized him to the extreme tenuousness of life and the awesome finality of death. As a result, watching Doc Nelson's meticulous examination of corpses, often accompanied by morbid humor, was more than merely difficult.

"Be right back. I have something to show you," Nelson said to the group.

He strode across the room, rubber boots squeaking on the clean vinyl floor, and rotated a gurney on which rested the fire-ravaged remains of a human being.

The blackened shape looked like a huge piece of meat badly charred on a barbecue. The raised arms were held in front of the grotesque head in the defensive posture of a prizefighter. Chest and stomach cavities were already opened and emptied, the bright pinkness of the interior flesh in stark contrast with the charcoal shell. It had no discernable face—nothing but the general head shape with vague lumps where nose, ears, and eyebrows had once been. The top of the ruptured skull was a clotted honeycomb of chocolate-colored blood.

"From the house fire in Mission Heights," Earheart advised. "Nice big house on Twin Oaks Drive. Just about burned to the ground. Firefighter named Steven Edwards found this in the rubble. I don't think he's ever seen something like this before. He was a little green when I got there. Can't say I blame him."

Mission Heights was a well-to-do residential neighborhood that sprung up on the west side of unincorporated Santa Rita County when the population exploded due to the electronics industry over the Hill in Silicon Valley. It lay roughly north of County Hospital at the base of the foothills. Later, Silicon Valley expansion had pushed development even higher into the hills as electronics-industry executives and other professionals escaped the Santa Clara Valley where they worked but refused to live.

"Male or female?" Kathryn asked. It wasn't evident, given the condition of the body.

"Male," answered Earheart, "although it was impossible to tell at the scene. Edwards found the body under some debris in the family room."

"He the only one in the house?"

Earheart nodded. "Looks like it. They've searched it and haven't located anyone else. Can't say I envied them that job. Those firefighters are all a bit unhinged."

"Do we know who he is?"

"We've confirmed his ID as Lawrence Lancaster, owner of the property."

Kathryn was impressed. "That was fast."

Doc Nelson chimed in. "We got lucky. His hands were clenched tight into fists. The fingertips were hardly damaged, so we were able to roll them and obtain a good set of prints.

"In a residential fire, we usually assume it's the resident. Knowing he was an attorney, and that all attorneys have their fingerprints on file in Sacramento, I normally would have requested a set of prints from the State Bar for comparison. But, since today is a holiday, I knew I couldn't get them until tomorrow. Correct me if I was wrong, but I figured you guys were in a bigger hurry than that."

He smiled and continued. "So, I contacted a dentist friend of mine to see if I could find out who his dentist was so I could get his dental X rays for comparison. Got lucky. My friend had been his dentist for years. He had the X rays to me in a half hour. They matched. It's Lancaster, no doubt about it."

"What do we know about the fire?" Dave asked.

Earheart replied. "Scary. They had six engines up there. They were worried about it spreading into the dry grass and neighboring homes. They had pumpers all over the place hosing everything down. Most of those places have shake roofs. Built before the county code required fire-retardant look-alikes. They were worried for awhile but contained it without it spreading. Jesus, those firefighters may be a bit weird, but they've got balls and know what they're doing."

"Helluva way to die," Dave lamented softly. "Fried like an overdone weenie."

Morgan Nelson shook his head. "Not this one."

"What're you saying? He wasn't burned to death? Looks like it to me."

"Looks can be deceiving, my boy. Some fire victims die of burns, it's true. But many more die of other causes like smoke inhalation or other trauma—falling masonry, jumping from windows trying to escape, even asphyxiation from toxic fumes. My job is to look past the obvious and establish which it was. That's why I make the big bucks."

Nelson continued. "Burns inflicted on a living animal, a human in this case, stimulate a vital reaction. It's easily recognizable by the hyperemia—reddening in the floor and periphery of blisters. This is accompanied by congestion of blood vessels, small hemorrhages, and especially infiltration of polymorphonuclear leukocytes into the tissues and blister fluid. None of these indicators were present in this case."

"Indicating . . . ," Granz led Nelson.

"Death occurred before the fire. Postmortem burns are never accompanied by the vital reaction. They are hard and yellowish, like these." He pointed to the front of the blackened torso.

"Thanks for sharing that with us," Dave muttered.

Nelson continued unperturbed. "As soon as I saw the body, I knew he didn't die in the fire, so I ordered full-body X rays and opened him up. First place I looked to confirm my initial analysis was the air passages—trachea and windpipe. There was a total absence of soot. If he were alive during the onset of the fire, he would have inhaled smoke."

"So what, then?" Kathryn inquired. "Did someone take an ax to him?"

Nelson looked confused momentarily, then understood. "Oh, you mean his skull. It does look like someone took a meat cleaver to him, doesn't it? But, there's no indication of blunt-force trauma. It's what's called a heat hematoma. It only occurs when the head is exposed to intense heat."

"So," Kathryn continued with a rising inflection of her voice, "the cause of death was . . ."

"When I examined the head X rays I spotted what appeared to be a bullet. I think Walt already sensed something more than an accidental fire death, or he wouldn't have responded to the scene. He was right, I'm afraid."

"No chance it was self-inflicted?"

Earheart answered. "No weapon found within arm's length of the body. In fact, so far no weapon recovered at the scene at all."

"What's the caliber of the slug?"

"My guess from the X ray is that it's a twenty-two. I'll know for sure in a few minutes, now that we're all here for the opening." Nelson bent over the body and switched on the bone saw. The high-pitched whine slowed slightly as the blade bit into the cranial bone. A faint mist of powdered bone and smoke rose from the circular cut across the skull.

As Kathryn watched, obviously less uncomfortable than either of the two men, she asked Walt Earheart, "The crime scene is sealed, I assume?"

It was an unnecessary question, she knew. Earheart was the best and did not miss a trick. It was a bad habit she intended to break, always assuring that other perfectly competent people had done their jobs.

Some might have been offended, but Earheart accepted the query in the nonoffensive spirit it was made. "Yep. Dispatched a team out while I was driving in here. Figured I couldn't lose. If it turned out to be nothing, it didn't cost anything but a little overtime. If my hunch turned out right, as it did, I couldn't afford to do otherwise.

"CSI is at the scene as we speak, standing by for your OK to enter the crime scene. They won't do anything except secure it without your say-so." CSI stood for the sheriff's Crime Scene Investigation Unit, a team of expert criminalists with varying specialties.

"Kathryn," Dave asked, "do we need a warrant?"

"We probably do in this case. After a fire is extinguished, we can enter to investigate the cause, even if it has to be delayed a few hours due to some condition that renders an immediate investigation impractical. It's a bit less clear as time passes. When the interruption is for a more substantial period of time, such as what we've got here, the original emergency—so to speak—ceases, and we need a warrant before conducting the search."

"Damn," Earheart cursed, "that could set us back hours."

"No problem. I've got blank search-warrant forms in my car along with my laptop and portable printer. We can do the warrant here, and I can fax it to the on-call judge from Morgan's office. I'll name you as the affiant."

"Let's do it," Earheart said.

While Kathryn prepared the warrant and affidavit in Nelson's cramped and cluttered office, Earheart called CSI on his cell phone to be sure they were standing by and to advise them of the plan to obtain a warrant.

Meanwhile, Dave Granz stood by to offer whatever support he could to the sheriff's investigators, who were the lead agency in the investigation until it was officially submitted to the District Attorney's office for prosecution.

As a practical matter, since Granz would assume investigative responsibility after the DA received the case from the sheriff's office, he needed to be in the loop from the beginning to avoid duplication of effort and overlooked information.

No animosity existed between the senior investigators of the two agencies, who understood the overlapping jurisdictions perfectly, although occasional territorial disputes arose among younger officers.

Within thirty minutes, the affidavit and warrant were faxed to Judge Jon Stevenson, who swore Earheart as affiant by telephone, signed the warrant, and faxed it back to Kathryn at Nelson's machine. From start to finish, less than an hour elapsed.

Kathryn wrote the words "duplicate original" on the document and turned it over to Earheart. The actual original would be obtained later and filed in court.

Earheart phoned the CSI Unit again to say they were enroute to the scene and asked that they hold off the start of the investigation until the three of them arrived to observe.

As they prepared to leave, Kathryn told Dave, "I'll just let Morgan know we're on our way." As she spoke, Morgan Nelson entered his office. Between the thumb and forefinger of his right hand, which he held aloft for theatrical effect, dangled a clear, sealed Ziploc evidence bag. It contained a lead bullet. "A twenty-two," he confirmed.

Walt Earheart volunteered to dispatch a patrol unit to pick up the evidence and transport it to the crime lab for examination. "Let's see if they can tell us anything about the weapon we should be looking for."

"Oh, Morgan, can you run a tox screen on the blood?" Kathryn asked as an afterthought. "I'll need that."

"No problem. Now you kids run along and have fun. And guys . . . ?"

They all turned simultaneously.

"Happy Independence Day. God bless America, land of the free and overworked."

They were still laughing when Dave punched the elevator button.

3

TWIN OAKS DRIVE RAN NORTHEAST BETWEEN bordering rows of century-old white oak trees, off Juan Cabrillo Avenue, about a mile above the hospital. In a sales brochure, realtors would once have described the four-bedroom, three-bath, 2,800-square-foot house as "offering a panoramic ocean view from the elegant master suite with cathedral ceilings." Not anymore. Now it was nothing more than a burned-out, soot-streaked shell like those visible from video-cam shots of war zones.

While firefighters saved surrounding structures and vegetation, they were unable to control the inferno before it destroyed the roof and second-floor structure of the house, which collapsed inward and ignited the ground floor and garage. The fire was extinguished before the entire ground floor was consumed, but it, too, was a total loss due to fire, smoke, and water damage.

The gutted hulk of a new Mercedes-Benz C-280 in the remains of the garage stood in mute testimony to the incredible intensity of the conflagration. Heat still rose from the distorted metal and melted tires.

Kathryn parked her red Audi behind one of the green-and-white sheriff's patrol cars and climbed out, still wearing the jeans and T-shirt she wore to the Village Parade. The stench of ruptured sewer lines and ozone from burned electrical equipment assailed her senses. The darker, woodier odor of burned furniture and the damp earthiness of scorched masonry and cement overlay it all, along with something faintly reminiscent of burned, wet wool blankets.

A sheriff's deputy raised the yellow tape demarcating the crime scene boundaries to permit Kathryn to duck under. As she headed toward the smoldering rubble, she spotted Dave's Ford Explorer pull to a stop behind her Audi. He hustled over to join her and Earheart.

"Hey, Jack," Earheart called. A slender, handsome middle-aged man in full yellow turnouts looked up at the sound of his name.

Jackson Rudisell nodded acknowledgement. His job was to investigate the cause and origin of the fire. He was reputed to be good at his job, although he was a bit short on interpersonal skills and tact. Neither Kathryn nor Dave had ever worked with him. "I hear we've got a homicide here," he said, speaking directly to Earheart.

"Looks that way," Earheart responded. "Coroner found a twenty-two slug in the victim's brain."

"Who's the victim?" Rudisell inquired.

"Lawrence Lancaster, owner of the house," Earheart said. "He was an attorney."

"A lawyer? No big loss," Rudisell muttered in disdain.

Ignoring the insult, Kathryn inquired, "Inspector, what can you tell us about your investigation so far?"

"Well, the escape routes weren't blocked. None of the exterior doors were locked and they weren't obstructed, so I concluded he didn't try to escape the fire," replied Rudisell.

Kathryn was beginning to doubt the validity of at least the expertise portion of Rudisell's reputation.

"We already know he was dead before the fire started," she said. "Unblocked escape routes doesn't add much.

"When you found the body, Inspector, was it face up or face down?"

Rudisell's face reddened. "The body was on its back. Why?"

Kathryn knew that in most cases a fatal-fire victim will be found face down. A fire victim found face up normally alerts fire investigators of the possibility of a homicide or suicide.

"Wouldn't the fact that the body was found in a face-up position have alerted you to the possibility of foul play, Inspector?"

Rudisell bristled. "What, do murdered stiffs have a preference for certain body positions? What difference does it make? The body was burned to a crisp."

"The difference, Inspector, is—"

Dave interrupted. "When we saw the body at the morgue, his arms were raised in front of his face like this," Dave demonstrated. "Could he have been fighting someone off?"

Rudisell shook his head knowingly, relieved to be asked a question whose answer and implications he was sure of. "What you saw is fairly common in fire victims. I'm surprised the coroner didn't explain it to you. It's known as the 'pugilistic stance,' or what we refer to as 'boxer's pose.' It's a contraction of the joints and large muscles of the body under extreme heat, resulting in a fist presentation of the hands and elbows."

"Inspector," Kathryn said, "could you run down what you did before you moved the body to the morgue?"

"We photographed the body where it was discovered and drafted a rough sketch of the scene. Standard procedure."

"Did you search the area immediately beneath the body once it had been removed?"

Clearly uncomfortable, Rudisell shook his head. Kathryn wasn't sure whether the discomfort resulted from his lack of attention to detail, or the fact that it was a woman questioning his competence. It didn't matter, as far as she was concerned.

She turned to Earheart. "Walt, would you please have CSI examine the area where the body was found? Then, have them X-ray and sift the debris for foreign objects that may have fallen from the body as it desiccated. We could get lucky and find something we can tie to the perpetrator."

"You bet." Then Earheart turned to Rudisell. "Okay for us to go in now, Inspector?"

"Sure, just watch your step," Rudisell answered, attempting to salvage a semblance of authority. "My people will show you where and what to avoid. And everyone wears protective gear and hard hats, okay?"

"Don't worry, I like my head just the way it is," Earheart replied lightly, attempting to dispel some of the tension. Always the gentleman, Kathryn mused. We could all take a lesson in tact from Walt.

They logged into the crime scene with the cop at the door and donned bright yellow coveralls, slipped clear plastic bags over their shoes, then filed into a hallway. The waterlogged sheetrock wall reeked of smoke and soot. Underfoot, hardwood floors were brittle charcoal.

In what was once a dining room, the spaces once filled by graceful arching windows gaped vacantly toward the street, remnants of drapes fluttering in the on-shore breeze. The dining-room floor lay buried under piles of rubble and the charred remains of second-story floors, furniture, and ceiling joists. A buckled spiral staircase lay collapsed to one side of the door like ancient dinosaur bones.

"Jesus," Dave murmured, "Rudisell was right. This place is a mess. Watch out for the holes there."

Kathryn nodded, careful to avoid stepping outside the taped safety walkways established by the fire department. Directly ahead, in what had once been an elegant sunken living room, she saw the ruins of a baby grand piano and broken bookshelves sagging away from the walls. What remained of the books lay piled in soggy mounds on the cracked floor tiles. Steam rose from the wet walls as they absorbed the July sun. Through gaps in the walls, Kathryn could see arson investigators working in the next room.

"Let's go next door," Kathryn suggested. "I want to see where they found the body."

Floodlights were rigged on looped cables, bathing the family room in a harsh halogen-white light. Kathryn stood next to a remarkably undamaged pool table, surveying the room.

A half-melted, imploded big-screen TV rested against the far wall, on top of which had fallen a melted lump of plastic that apparently had been a mini stereo and CD player. These were alongside the ruins of a wet bar whose contents of bottles and glasses had exploded and scattered their contents about the room. The heavy stink of burned fabric and wood was heaviest in this room.

A fire investigator was meticulously locating, notating, and logging the positions of light switches, electrical appliances, and wiring devices, while another examined flooring and wall cracks for traces of chemical reactions or unusual burn patterns, paper, rags, sponges, towels, or anything that might divulge the fire's origin.

"Over here," Earheart called out. He was standing beside the buckled frame of what had once been a sofa bed. Charlie Yamamoto from CSI knelt beside it.

"This where the body was found?" Kathryn asked.

"Yep." Earheart replied.

"Hi, Charlie," Kathryn said. "You have something?"

Yamamoto, a man of few words, nodded without looking up. "It's been heavily diluted by water, but I'll bet my paycheck this is blood."

"Dead bodies don't bleed," Dave observed. "Doc Nelson's right. He died before the fire started."

Knowing the answer instinctively, Kathryn nevertheless mused aloud, "So, why the fire?"

Rudisell, who had followed them into the family room, seized the opportunity to assert himself. "Fire is sometimes used as a means to create the appearance of accidental death by fire.

"Sometimes it's done to make identification of the victim difficult or impossible. Other times, to destroy evidence or cover up an injury to the victim's body." He paused for effect. "The perps don't know it, of course, but it's almost never successful."

Kathryn was about to ask Rudisell which, in his opinion, was the case here, when a commotion in the street outside the house attracted her attention. She watched as a slender, attractive woman with dark hair collapsed on the sidewalk just outside the yellow crime-scene tape.

4

ANNA LANCASTER LAY IN PARTIAL REPOSE IN the back seat of Walt Earheart's car, a late-model Chevy Blazer. Despite her disheveled long, dark hair, makeup smeared by tears, and obviously distraught condition, she was a strikingly attractive woman.

After introducing themselves and providing a brief overview of the situation to Anna Lancaster, Kathryn deferred to Earheart to commence the interview of the deceased's wife. Earheart began gently and quietly.

"We need to talk to you about your husband's death," he began. "Can you answer a few questions?"

Anna Lancaster pulled herself upright in the rear seat, drew a deep breath and expelled it slowly, then nodded her assent. "I'll do my best," she answered.

"I know you will," Earheart said. "Let me know if you need to stop for awhile. Now, I'll be taking notes while we talk. Don't be distracted by it; it's just how I make certain I don't forget what we've talked about. Okay. Now, can you tell me your full name and how you were related to Lawrence Lancaster, please."

"Yes, of course. My name is Anna Marie Lancaster. Lawrence Lancaster is . . . was . . . my husband." She sobbed softly but was in control.

"And your birthdate, ma'am?"

"I'm thirty-two," she answered. "November 30, 1964."

"Thank you. Mrs. Lancaster, can you tell us if your husband was alone in the house."

"As far as I know he was," she replied. "He wasn't feeling well this morning. He planned to stay home and relax, and I don't know of any plans to have visitors."

"Okay. Can you tell me where you were during the fire? It appears to have started midmorning, probably around ten o'clock."

"Lawrence and I had planned to celebrate the Fourth with friends over the Hill. They were planning a barbecue and fireworks after dark for the kids—their kids. We don't have children."

She sobbed again, softly, but continued. "When Lawrence woke up this morning feeling ill, he encouraged me to go over by myself. I left around eight and drove over. They live in Saratoga."

"So, you probably got there about nine o'clock?" Kathryn interjected the question softly to establish that it was a joint interview. She was turned sideways in the right-front bucket seat, looking at Anna Lancaster over the center console of the Blazer.

Anna looked at Kathryn as if noticing her for the first time. "No, I didn't go directly to their house. Macy's was having an early-morning sale and I stopped at the mall. I got there a bit late. The mall was packed."

"Did you buy anything?" Kathryn asked.

"Yes, I bought a Gianni suit."

"How did you pay for it?"

"What do you mean?"

"Did you pay cash, or did you charge it?"

"Oh. I charged it on my Visa card. I rarely carry enough cash to make major purchases. I think I kept the receipt, but I don't have it on me."

"That's okay," Kathryn said. "We'll ask you for it if it seems important. I'd appreciate it if you'd hang onto it awhile, though."

Walt resumed. "Can you tell me your friends' names and address, Mrs. Lancaster?"

"Sure. John and Clare Moody. He's a partner in Lawrence's law firm. We've known them for years. I'm not sure of the exact street address. I know exactly how to drive there but never mail anything to them. I'll get that for you later, if that's okay."

"That's fine, I can look it up. You say you had planned to spend the day and evening with them. Why did you come home early?"

"Well, I felt a little guilty. Lawrence and I are very close. I thought he might appreciate some attention, so I came home to be with him. But . . . when I pulled up . . . outside . . . I . . . I . . ." She couldn't continue as she sobbed.

Kathryn felt an overwhelming empathy for this woman. Her own sense of loss on learning about the murder of her ex-husband—Emma's father—Jack in a courtroom shooting years ago had been unsettling, even though they had been estranged for years. She couldn't imagine what it must be like to lose someone to whom you were still married and completely committed.

"Mrs. Lancaster—Anna—may I call you Anna?" Receiving assent, Kathryn continued, "Anna, we know this is extremely difficult and we appreciate your helping. We'll make this as brief as possible, but we really need to ask a few more questions if you are able."

Again, Anna Lancaster nodded rather than verbalized her assent.

"Thank you," Kathryn replied. "We'd like to know a bit more about Mr. Lancaster. You say he was an attorney. Where did he work? Was he in private practice?"

"Yes, he was a partner at Lancaster and Young in Santa Clara. Maybe you've heard of them. Lawrence was once a very successful computer-systems engineer. But he believed that once systems development peaked, the real money would be in litigating hardware and software disputes. So he went to law school. When he finished law school, he decided to practice law full-time.

"That's when he founded Lancaster and Young. They specialize in intellectual property and environmental law. They also do some professional malpractice work, you know, accountants, doctors, and even other lawyers. It's a big firm."

"I see." Walt took over the interview seamlessly. "And do you work, ma'am?"

"Yes, I'm an administrative assistant for Lawrence's firm." Despite her distress, she managed a small self-conscious smile. "That's a legal secretary in everyday English. In fact, that's how I met Lawrence. He hired me himself five years ago." She appeared to be holding up much better than at the beginning of the interview, answering questions with little difficulty.

Walt Earheart began the next phase of the interview carefully. The questions got tougher as they proceeded. "Mrs. Lancaster, I need to ask some questions that may be difficult for you. I apologize, but I promise you they are absolutely necessary.

"We know Mr. Lancaster was several years older than you. Did he have any serious physical problems? You said he was sick this morning."

"No, he just had a summer cold. He was in excellent health. Why do you ask?"

Ignoring her question, Earheart inquired, "What about emotionally? Was your husband experiencing any serious problems—business or financial, or maybe personal problems over which he might have been depressed?"

Anna expressed overt surprise at this line of inquiry. "No, not that I'm aware of." She looked pleadingly at Kathryn, perhaps expecting another woman to understand her confusion better than a man.

Kathryn's response was soft and understanding, but insistent. "You're sure your husband wasn't experiencing any business or professional difficulties, Anna? With a litigation practice, it's possible he angered someone. Are you aware of anyone, perhaps a defendant in a case he was litigating, or maybe a disgruntled client, who might have been angry with him? Any serious disagreements with his partners or associates in his law firm?"

"No-o-o, not that I can think of, but—"

Before she could complete her thought, Walt Earheart asked if her husband had experienced any recent financial setbacks, declining business profits, or gambling losses. She answered in the negative.

"Okay, Mrs. Lancaster, if I may, I'd like to ask a couple of questions about your relationship with your husband." Earheart paused before going on. "Were there any problems between you and your husband? Had you recently fought, or argued?"

She sat up absolutely straight and frowned. "Mr. Erhard—"

"Earheart, ma'am. Walt Earheart."

"Yes, Earheart. Mr. Earheart, my personal relationship with my husband is none of your business. But, no, we did not fight or argue. Lawrence was an extremely kind and gentle man. We rarely have—had—disagreements of any kind, much less fight. We are financially well off. Last year the firm brought in gross fees over forty-five million dollars.

"Not that it's of any concern to the sheriff's office. Neither Lawrence nor I gamble, drink excessively, and before you ask another offensive question, neither of us uses drugs of any sort. Now, frankly, I'd like to know why you're asking these questions. You make it sound as if something happened besides a fire. Didn't my husband die in the fire?"

Kathryn said, "Mrs. Lancaster, it appears your husband was dead before the fire started. A bullet found in his body appears to be the cause of his death."

Anna Lancaster appeared to faint. She collapsed against the back of the seat, her eyes glazed over, and she turned pale. "No, that can't be. You're wrong Ms.

Mackay. Lawrence didn't have any enemies and he certainly didn't kill himself. Someone is mistaken. Maybe it wasn't Lawrence's body that was recovered, at all. I'll bet that's it. When you locate my husband, you'll see I'm right."

"I'm sorry, Anna. We have positively identified your husband's body. He was shot and killed before the fire began."

Kathryn paused. "I know this is a lot for you to deal with right now. I think we can continue this later if we need more information. May we arrange for a police officer to take you to your friends' home in Saratoga?"

Anna Lancaster remained stoic. "I can manage. If I may leave, I'll drive my own car."

Walt Earheart arranged to interview her the following day at Kathryn's office. After she drove away, he turned to Kathryn. "Strong woman. I don't think I'd hold up nearly as well as she did in the same situation."

5

THE COUNTY GOVERNMENT CENTER BUILDING would never win any prizes for architectural beauty. Built in 1966 at the height of the Cold War paranoia, its uncompromising gray concrete construction suggested that its main purpose was to withstand nuclear attack, and it probably had been. And probably would. Five stories high, squat and square, it housed the offices of the Santa Rita County Sheriff, the District Attorney, Environmental Health, the Planning Department, the County Clerk, and various other lesser government functions.

With wide stone-floor corridors, flat white fluorescent light, and public hallways featuring ever-changing art exhibits of talented local artists which few people ever looked at, it was a place to work and nothing more—functional, cold, unwelcoming, and unloved.

Just before 10 A.M., Kathryn ran up the stairs to the second floor, as was her usual practice, to get whatever modicum of exercise they afforded, and turned left toward the District Attorney's office. The receptionist sitting behind the bulletproof glass saw her and buzzed her in before she reached the electronically controlled door. "Hi Kate, banker's hours, huh?"

Kathryn wrinkled up her face and answered, "Yeah, right! Emma was late again this morning. By the time I dropped her off at school, I didn't have time to come to the office before that sentencing hearing at eight-thirty, so I went directly to court without the file. Got reamed by the judge when I couldn't respond to his questions. Kids!"

The receptionist, a single mother with four children, smiled sympathetically. "Tell me about it," she said. "You've only got one."

Dave awaited Kathryn's arrival outside her office door. "Thought you'd like one of these," he said, proffering a cup of coffee. He glanced furtively around, knowing that she avoided shows of affection at work, and then kissed her on the cheek and flopped into one of the leather armchairs facing her desk.

Kathryn's office was her personal statement, and she had long ago discarded the government-issue metal office furniture. She had spent her own money to acquire a tasteful executive desk, leather interview chairs, a couple of end tables, and tasteful artwork. Even the computer and printer were her own. Hanging from the steel-wall partitions on magnetized hooks were a half-dozen sedately framed newspaper clippings from her most famous courtroom victories.

Some had unknowingly criticized the display as rampant egoism, but that was far from the truth. The clippings were her assurance to all who entered her office that *she* represented the frequently overlooked and forgotten crime victims and their families; *she* who was the public's advocate. In her mind, despite the misnomer commonly applied to court-appointed defense attorneys, it was she who was the "public defender."

"You must be a mind reader," she said gratefully. "The coffee, I mean, not the kiss. You know how I feel about that." Her tone was kinder than her words.

Dave grinned like a wicked, spoiled little boy. "Thought maybe I'd better take a kiss when and where I can get one these days. I was hoping for a real one yesterday—maybe a little extra to go along with it after the parade—but that didn't work out. Can't remember the last time, you've been so damned busy lately."

Kathryn was uncomfortable but knew he was right. She couldn't recall the last time they'd indulged in a leisurely evening of lovemaking, either. "Let's talk about it later, okay? What's on your mind besides sex?" she asked in an attempt to lighten up the situation.

"Rudisell just called me," Dave began reluctantly. "Looks like the fire was started by a gas explosion. His investigators uncovered evidence that someone left a candle burning on a plate in the kitchen, then turned on the stove. When the kitchen filled with gas, the candle ignited it and . . . boom!"

"I'll be damned. How did they figure that out?"

"They located traces of beeswax near the fire's point of origin, which they determined to be the kitchen. That's right next to the family room, you might recall. The wick of a candle leaves a particular kind of residue. You have to be looking for it, though."

"How long would it take for a sufficient accumulation of gas to create that kind of explosion?"

"Hard to calculate, apparently," Dave answered. "According to Rudisell, it's a complex equation made up of a series of variables: how powerful the gas jet was, gas-line pressure which can vary, the cubic capacity of the room, how many doors or windows were open; even the amount of air leakage around doors and windows. Too many variables to calculate with any precision."

"Well, that doesn't help much. Any outside parameters?"

"I asked him that. He didn't want to be pinned down, but he said it could be as long as an hour and a half after the gas jet was opened, but probably considerably less."

"Whew," Kathryn whistled. "Central Fire logged the 9-1-1 call just before 10 A.M. And we know from Lancaster's statement that she left around 8."

"So, either someone broke into the house after Mrs. Lancaster left, put a bullet in her husband's brain, turned on the gas, and lit the candle, or . . ."

"Or," Kathryn finished the thought, "Anna Lancaster did it herself before she left and is lying slightly about the time."

Neither needed to say more; each knew what the other was thinking.

"Yeah," Dave said. "I called the Moodys last night. Spoke with the husband; his wife and Lancaster weren't there when I called."

Kathryn raised an eyebrow. "That's a little strange."

"She took Mrs. Lancaster out to get a few personal items, you know, toiletries and stuff. Apparently she's gonna stay with them awhile. Anyway, he didn't know exactly what time Anna got to their place yesterday. Says he was at his office picking up a file he needed to review later that evening. When he got back, Lancaster was already there. While I had him on the phone, I got him to agree to have his firm's personnel office fax me over a list of company employees this morning. He's pretty efficient. It's already on my desk, twenty or thirty pages of it."

Kathryn frowned and sipped her coffee from the paper cup. "That's a good place to start, but damn, we need to know what time Anna Lancaster got to their place."

"I know," Dave agreed, "so I called back over about an hour later and caught Clare Moody right after they got back from shopping."

"And?"

"According to her, Anna arrived at their place at eleven-thirty," he answered.

Kathryn pondered the time frame for a moment. "That's only a forty-five minute drive, tops. Add another three-quarters of an hour at Macy's, and it's still less than two hours, total. A lot less if she bought the suit in a hurry. She could have left as late as nine-thirty or even ten o'clock and still made it."

"Kate, you know as well as I do that no woman on earth can look at suits, find a few she likes, try them all on, check herself out in the mirror, try them on again, pick one out, pay for it, and get out of the store in three-quarters of an hour. Not possible."

"Sexist pig," Kathryn accused him with a tolerant smile. "I could do it in half that time."

"Yeah, but that's because you'd return it later, like you always do."

Kathryn grinned. "You know me too well. Seriously, though, it would depend on how motivated she was, I'd say."

"Yeah, you're right. The time frame works. Add ten, maybe fifteen minutes for a gas stop, and . . ."

"Dave, she didn't mention she stopped for gas."

"I know. Clare Moody said Lancaster called her from Macy's around nine-thirty. Said she was running late but was leaving in a few minutes and was going to stop for gas on her way out of town. She was ticked off that she was driving her husband's BMW instead of her Mercedes.

"That was her Benz in the garage," he continued. "She said Lawrence never gassed the damned thing and always told her to drive it when it needed to be filled."

"I'm not sure this washes," Kathryn contemplated aloud. "Have we tried to verify what time she left the house?"

Dave checked his notebook. "The neighbor who called in the fire was . . . Elizabeth James. She lives across the street from the Lancaster house. I called her. She told me she thought Anna left about nine-thirty or so. Unfortunately, Mrs. James has a slight alcohol problem. She sounded soused already this morning. I asked her if she was sure."

"Was she?"

"Well, she told me she had a couple of drinks yesterday morning when she got up to start off her July Fourth celebration. Irish coffees. Finally said it could have been as early as eight or as late as ten o'clock when she saw Anna Lancaster leave the house. But she did see her leave. I know that."

"How do you know? If she's an alcoholic, she could be remembering a month ago."

"I know, I thought of that, so I asked her how she was so sure. Remember the bright red blouse Lancaster was wearing yesterday? She described it. And there's another thing."

"David! Don't play games. What?"

"She noticed that she was driving the Beemer. It's white—hard to mistake for a black Mercedes. Black Mercedes and white Beemer. Must've looked like a checkerboard in their garage when they were both home." He paused as if waiting for the grand finale, then, seeing the look of exasperation on Kathryn's face, continued.

"Another thing. I called Macy's this morning right after they opened. Kinda curious how their firecracker sale went yesterday morning. I talked to a saleswoman who had to work yesterday morning when she'd rather have been out boating on the bay. Asked her how many Gianni suits they sold yesterday morning during the sale."

Although Kathryn spent enormous amounts of emotion trying to appear calm on the outside, on the inside she always got nervous when she believed she was about to learn a significant new fact about a case. She even tried, often unsuccessfully, to hide this part of herself from Dave. She felt her palms grow moist and wiped them casually on the napkin he gave her with the coffee. "Damnit, Dave, don't keep me in suspense. What did she say?"

"She said people are weird as hell. They didn't sell a single suit during the two-hour sale, never mind a Gianni. But later in the day, an attractive woman with dark hair came back in and bought a Gianni suit for twice what she could have got it for that morning. She said the color wasn't right for her at all." He looked at Kathryn, genuinely perplexed, and asked, "What does that mean, anyway?"

"Men! It means she bought a suit that didn't look good on her. A woman like Anna Lancaster would only do that under extreme circumstances."

"Meaning?"

"Meaning she was in a big hurry to buy that suit and get out of there. What time was that?"

Dave made a big production out of checking his notebook. "'Bout forty-five minutes before Anna Lancaster showed up at the house and collapsed in grief. I'll bet she had the damn suit in the trunk of the Beemer. Oh, and I checked—Macy's charge slips are dated but don't show the time."

"Curiouser and curiouser," Kathryn said. "Does Anna Lancaster own a gun?"

Dave shook his head. "Nope. One of the first things I checked this morning. That's the bad news. The good news, if your warped sense of values sees it that way, is that Lawrence Lancaster had one registered in his name. A Walther PPK/S."

Kathryn smiled, despite herself. "A Walther PPK/S can fire long-range, standard-velocity twenty-two rounds. Doc Nelson said it was a twenty-two slug in Lancaster's brain."

"I called him. He says it could have been fired from any one of a half dozen weapons."

"Including a Walther PPK/S?"

"Yep, that's one of 'em. But unless we recover the weapon, not much chance of an ID. And no gun was recovered in the search of the house or either of their cars."

"So, where is it?"

He shrugged, a gesture he often made when asked a question for which he had no answer. For some reason, Kathryn found it appealing. She got up and crossed to her office door and closed it, then walked over to where Dave sat and planted a kiss on the top of his head. Before he could respond, she reopened the door and sat down.

"What was that for?" he asked.

"A reminder that you'll get lucky eventually, if you're patient. And an incentive."

He grinned again and said, "Takes more than a peck on the head to convince me I'll ever get close to you again. But I'll take it. Incentive for what?"

"We need to find that gun, Dave."

"I know, but Christ, if she ditched it, it could be anyplace. In the ocean, down a mountainside, in the dumpster behind Macy's. Any damned place."

"Anywhere between Mission Heights and Saratoga, I agree, but that narrows it down."

"Wait a minute," he said, "wait just a damn minute. That's why she didn't mention it."

"Didn't mention what?"

"Buying gas. It's because she didn't. Let's say she took Highway 9 into the back side of Saratoga. There's a lake along there at Las Casitas. Little bitty bass-fishing lake. She could have ditched the gun there. If so, she'd need a reason for the extra time to toss the gun and drive Highway 9. That'd add half an hour, tops, at that time of morning, but enough that the Moodys might notice.

"So, she tells them she wasn't quite finished shopping at Macy's and needed to stop for gas before she left. That would add just about the right amount of time to ditch the gun and make up for the slower drive over the back side into Saratoga."

"It's a long shot, but it fits the time line," Kathryn answered. "It fits tighter than O. J. Simpson's glove. But what makes you think she ditched the gun up there?"

"Dunno. A long shot." He grinned. "I'll call Walt from my office."

She thought it over and decided a hunch was the best they had. "Tell him we'll need a couple of divers, grappling hooks, metal detectors . . ." Dave looked at her and shook a forefinger in her direction. She realized she was needlessly making sure the other experts did their jobs right, again. She held her hands up in surrender.

"Sorry. Just tell him what we think; he'll do the rest."

Fifteen minutes later, Dave was back in her office. Her coffee was cold. "What, no coffee?" she asked.

"Forget it, not enough time. S.O. is putting a team together," he said. "Walt said you can ride with him if you want. I told him you never accept rides from men. Want to be as independent as possible. He said to meet him there in a half hour."

She took a sip of the cold coffee and made a face like she was about to retch. "God, that's good. Let's roll, Granz."

"Nope," he answered, "Earheart says one of us is enough. More than enough. You go; I'm gonna stay here and peruse Lancaster and Young's employee list. I've got to develop a list of files we might want to see besides Lawrence and Anna Lancaster's. Maybe I'll spot something. Let me know how it goes at the lake."

Kathryn grabbed her purse from the leg space under her desk and headed for the door. "Catch ya later," she said and was gone.

6

Dave Granz sat in the tiny partitioned alcove that passed for an office. He felt frustrated to be stuck inside instead of at Las Casitas Lake looking for evidence, yet at the same time strangely glad to not be with Kathryn. Although said mostly in jest, he was growing increasingly alienated by her lack of availability and inattention to their relationship. He had told her the truth when he said he couldn't remember the last time they'd shared a satisfying intimacy, and professional duties aside, he questioned whether he was important enough to her that she would make time for him even if it meant letting something else go.

He shoved those thoughts to the back of his mind and cleared a spot to work on his desk by shoving file folders, police reports, interoffice memorandums, empty coffee cups, and sundry personal items aside, excavating a crater in the center, into which he slammed a stack of about twenty-five 8½ × 11″ fax pages. He was thankful the county had converted from thermal to the newer plain-paper machines, otherwise this stack would look more like a mass of curly snakes.

The computer printouts he studied had been extracted from a sophisticated personnel data-base program at the law firm of Lancaster and Young. They listed every partner, associate, investigator, paralegal, and staff person employed by the firm for the past five years.

Dave agreed to limit his investigation to no more than two dozen individuals, with whom the firm would schedule interview times in their conference room, so as to minimize the disruption of company business.

He was looking for two types of individuals with whom to conduct interviews. Senior partners who had been with the firm long enough to know Lawrence Lancaster intimately were first on the list. From them, Dave hoped to learn whether Lancaster had expressed private concerns over financial, personal, or marital difficulties that might lead to a fatal confrontation with his wife or someone else.

He also searched for private secretaries and personal assistants to those senior firm members, knowing they probably belonged to a small but tight clique that exchanged intimate information about their bosses' as well as their own personal lives. He was certain that Anna Lancaster being married to her boss would not alter this aspect of their behavior.

Halfway through the "S" listings, he had accumulated ten names; five partners and five assistants. Then, in amazement, he read the entry: SOTO, JULIA, SpanLang (Int'l), 570222, 941610, *.

Dave flashed back to an intense but short-lived romantic relationship he had with a woman named Julia Soto a few years ago. A native of Cuernavaca, Morelos, Mexico, she was a court-certified Spanish-language translator whom Dave met during a trial. On the rebound from his recent divorce, he became more involved than he intended.

The affair ended abruptly when Julia was summoned to her home in Cuernavaca. As the elder of two daughters, it was her duty to attend to her terminally ill mother.

For a few months, Dave and Julia communicated regularly by phone and mail. Dave grinned ruefully at the memory of his gigantic telephone bills. Abruptly, however, she stopped calling and writing. Dave tried to contact her a number of times, but each time her father refused to allow him to speak with her.

Eventually, as brief intense romances are inclined to do, its urgency diminished in Dave's mind, and he moved on to other relationships. Then he became involved with Kathryn Mackay and wasn't interested in other women.

Now, with a certain trepidation, Dave dialed the Lancaster and Young's phone number. The receptionist connected him with Julia Soto's extension.

"Yes, this is Julia Soto, may I help you?"

Dave had not forgotten the sultry voice or the clipped Mexican diction. "Good morning, Ms. Soto. This is David Granz calling from the Santa Rita County District Attorney's office?" It sounded more like a question than a statement of fact.

Silence. Then, "David? . . . David?"

"Yes. Julia, is that you? I couldn't believe it when I saw your name. I . . . ."

"I was expecting you to call, David. You are calling concerning Mr. Lancaster's death, correct?"

"Yes, Julia, but . . . I had no idea you were back in

the United States. I haven't heard from you for so long. Your personnel records say you've been there for two years, but . . . ?"

"I wanted to call you, David. I thought about it many times but could not. I am sorry. I moved back to California late in the summer of 1994. I couldn't work at the courthouse with you still there, so I looked over here. I was finally hired here in October."

"What do you do there?"

"I am a Spanish-language liaison. The firm has a growing clientele in Mexico, with companies who manufacture computer components and assemble processors. Most of them are located in Monterrey. It's an industrial city about five hundred miles south of Houston, Texas. There are four of us who regularly travel between Mexico and Silicon Valley to help translate technical manuals, contracts, and legal documents. It's more interesting work than court translating, and it pays a lot better." She laughed nervously.

"I see. I'm sorry if I sound disorganized, but I'm still in shock. It's nice to hear your voice. What I called about was to ask for information concerning Mr. Lancaster's death, but I'm afraid I got a little sidetracked."

"That's okay, David, I am a little upset, too. I'm terribly busy at the moment translating a set of interrogatories for one of the partners. I wonder if we could talk later, when I have more time. It would give us both a chance to pull ourselves together."

"Sure, that's a good idea. When . . . ?"

"I live in your county. I bought a condominium on the north side of Santa Rita. If I give you the address, maybe you could come by this evening and we could talk there. I'll be home by six o'clock. Why don't you come at six-thirty or so. Is that all right?"

She dictated her address, which Dave wrote on the back of a used pink While-You-Were-Out memo.

"Okay, thanks. I'll see you then."

7

"WHADAYA THINK, WALT? A WASTE OF time?" Kathryn Mackay asked. She and Earheart stood at the foot of the narrow fishing pier which extended about twenty feet out into Las Casitas Lake, alongside the paved boat ramp.

"Maybe. It's a long shot. This lake's man-made. I remember when they dammed it up. Helluva political flap. The bottom's covered with dead trees, underbrush, and crap. Doesn't surprise me that they haven't found anything. The grappling hooks are pretty useless under those conditions."

Kathryn grinned and pointed at a small stack of wet junk piled on the pier. "What do you mean they haven't found anything?"

"Oh, yeah, 'scuse me, I forgot. A rusty lunch pail and a pair of bikini panties with a hole in the crotch are really significant discoveries." As an afterthought, he added seriously, "At least the water's clear and low this time of year. Makes it easier for the divers."

Fearing the search might stretch into the night, at about six o'clock the sheriff's watch commander, Sergeant McAfee, drove to the Mountain Store. In addition to buying food, one could rent videos, get palm readings, and have minor automotive repairs done, but McAfee only bought sandwiches and soft drinks for the search crew. In truth, he also bought a six-pack of beer, but that rang up on the store receipt as a box of cookies. Sergeant McAfee had learned long ago what the county controller's office would reimburse for and what they would not.

After a quick snack of sandwiches and alleged cookies, nondiving personnel rigged portable gas generators and floodlights at strategic points around the small lake. By eight-thirty, diving crews in scuba gear had searched about half the lake's bottom. In July, the sun didn't set until about nine-fifteen, and by eight-forty-five, the crew was prepared for an all-night vigil.

A small group of silent mountain residents drank beer and watched from outside the cordoned-off area.

At eight minutes after 9 P.M., a head burst from the surface of the lake about thirty feet off the end of the fishing pier. The diver tore off her mask and spit out her air tube, shouting to attract the attention of the command officers. Held high above her head, her right hand gripped a shiny metallic object which glinted in the artificial light. From her vantage point near the boat launch, Kathryn easily recognized the shape of a small-caliber handgun.

Before the diver could splash ashore, Walt Earheart sprinted around the foot of the pier and waded knee deep into the water of the concrete ramp to retrieve the weapon. He slogged ashore toward where Kathryn stood, flipped the safety on, and removed the automatic weapon's magazine. As he approached dry ground, he jacked the slide back to eject any live rounds and held the pistol backward to inspect the chamber and magazine well.

"Empty," he declared. "Walther PPK/S."

Earheart looked at Kathryn and asked, "You want to give me the serial number of Lancaster's piece, Kathryn?"

She pulled a notebook from her handbag and flipped it open. "S-Sam, 0-0-2-0-7-4."

"Bingo," Earheart shouted.

"Walt, what's the chance of getting a firearms examination tonight? In the next hour or two?" Kathryn asked calmly, which did not reflect how she actually felt. It was her "game face," as she had often been told by the 49ers fans in her office. "If I know anything, I know the quicker we get that evidence analyzed and nail the perp, the better chance I've got when it goes to trial."

The Department of Justice (DOJ) lab was the only place in Santa Rita County with the necessary equipment and expertise to conclusively match a slug with the weapon from which it was fired, maintain the chain of evidence, and provide expert testimony.

"I'll make it happen," Earheart promised. "I'll have County Communications contact the on-call DOJ criminalist and have him meet us at the lab within an hour."

By the time Kathryn climbed into her car, it was dark enough to require headlights. She realized it was past Emma's bedtime, and she would already have been tucked in bed by her baby-sitter, Ruth. She heaved a heavy and exasperated sigh. Another evening gone, without so much as asking Emma how her day went. She picked up her cell phone and punched in Ruth's phone number.

After telling Ruth that it would be another two or three hours, Emma came on the line. "Hello, Mother. Ruth says you aren't picking me up right away so I'll be going to sleep here. I'm already in my pajamas." It wasn't a question.

"I'm sorry, Em. I'll make it up to you, I promise," Kathryn said, ignoring the coolness in her daughter's voice, which she knew was totally justified. "This is really important, you know that, or I wouldn't need to stay so late."

Emma's little-girl voice cracked, and she sniffled. "Mommy, you promised that we could do something special together because you had to go to work during the parade. You promised!"

"I know I did, honey, and I meant it, too. How about if tomorrow afternoon I sneak away from work a little early and pick you up from school. We'll go home and put on our new bicycle outfits and helmets, and race down to the beach. If you beat me with your new bike, I'll take us out to dinner." She knew if this didn't work, she was in real trouble, because bicycling together was their favorite activity. Emma had barely learned to ride the new bike Kathryn had bought her when she outgrew her old one, which Em had dismissed as "that little-kid bike."

The phone was silent for a minute during which Kathryn assumed her daughter was contemplating the offer. "Okay, Mom, it's a deal. Can we go to Kentucky Fried Chicken?"

Kathryn smiled at her daughter's deal-making skills but turned up her nose at the choice of restaurants. "Sure, honey, your choice. But," she added, "you've got to beat me."

"No sweat, Mom. Remember, my new bike has eighteen speeds and yours only has sixteen." After a minute she said, "And don't worry, Mom. I understand why you're late. I love you. G'nite."

After Emma hung up, Kathryn punched the end button and slammed the cell phone on the passenger seat. She had a lump in her throat, and was afraid she might cry, as she swung her red Audi onto Highway 9 and headed for South County.

8

Kathryn turned into the empty parking lot of the Department of Justice lab and parked alongside Earheart's Blazer. Earheart was parked in the space marked "Reserved—Director—Unauthorized Vehicles Will Be Towed at Owner's Expense." This was as close as the sheriff's chief of detectives ever got to making a social statement.

"Kathryn, fancy meeting you here," Earheart said.

"Just like to watch the experts at work."

"Yeah, I can see that," he chided. "What else you gonna do on a beautiful summer evening?"

The DOJ facility was housed in a leased building at the extreme end of Research Drive, next to Federal Express. Discreet markings over the entrance to the long, low, modern structure identified it only as Building 46A. Among themselves, law enforcement often simply referred to the DOJ lab as "Building 46A." It backed against a steep hillside, with a spectacular view of the bay. The hillside provided absolute security, and the industrial neighborhood almost always bustled with activity, assuring a degree of anonymity for the police vehicles that frequented it, although on this night Research Drive was virtually deserted.

"So, who's on call?" asked Kathryn.

"Roselba Menendez. You know her?"

Kathryn nodded. "I could've sworn that up at the lake you said you'd have 'him' meet us here. What happened—no guys available? . . . Just joking," she added hastily. "Yes, I know her. She's as good as they come. Oh, that's probably her now."

They looked up to see a pale blue four-door Honda Accord swing past them and pull into a parking place next to Kathryn's Audi. Sixty-five empty parking spaces, and the three were lined up like holstein cows at a water trough.

The woman who exited the Honda was dressed casually in a faded yellow 1992 Wharf-to-Wharf Race T-shirt, cutoff jeans, and brand-new stark white Reeboks with blue-rimmed socks. She was Kathryn's height, about five-feet-three, slightly overweight but not fat, with dark hair and strikingly beautiful olive skin. Her fingernails were meticulously manicured and painted bright red.

"Hi there, Kate," she greeted, flashing perfect white teeth. "Haven't seen you in ages."

Kathryn couldn't have been more pleased to see her. Not only did she like Menendez personally, but she knew the criminalist was terrific technically and was probably the best witness among the two dozen who staffed the lab. "Sorry to break in on your weekend."

Menendez shrugged. "Part of the job. I don't mind. What's up?"

Kathryn indicated Earheart. "You know Walt Earheart, S.O. chief of detectives . . ."

They exchanged pleasantries, and then the criminalist observed, "I take it this must be important. Follow me. The security guard needs to let us in. We don't have keys to the lab. That way all access is controlled, and if some defense attorney wants to challenge the chain of custody, we can have the head of security testify to access procedures. But, you knew that already."

She spoke with impeccable diction and the slightest hint of a Spanish accent, which added immeasurably to the formality and credibility of her demeanor in court.

At the top of a five-step landing, she punched a button on an intercom next to the entry door and spoke briefly to someone inside. A minute or so later, a uniformed man appeared, checked their credentials, and permitted them to enter the foyer. There, they signed the log, which he countersigned with the time.

"Thanks, Richard," she said, then punched her Personal Identity Code (PIC) into the security door, which swung open to expose a wide, brightly lit corridor.

"Nice guy," she said, referring to the security guard. "Retired San Francisco PD patrolman."

She led them from the corridor through an open-plan office, past deserted rows of desks, and into another, narrower, corridor running perpendicular to the first. At the end, she pushed past swinging double doors into a spacious open area replete with scientific equipment. "Firearms examination area is over here," she advised them.

As they trooped through the lab, Kathryn recognized a big, boxy machine on one slate slab bench as a blood-alcohol tester. It looked like an overgrown toaster oven and hummed audibly.

"What's that thing?" Earheart asked, indicating a large technical looking gadget.

"Gas Chromatograph/Mass Spectrometer machine (GCMS). It can identify the molecular weight, size, and rate of movement of ionized compounds. We use it to identify illicit drug formulations."

She pointed to another. "That's our latest pride and joy. Can't even remember its technical name, but it uses vaporized gold in a vacuum to lift fingerprints off a piece of cloth."

"Amazing," Kathryn said, "that even with all this sophisticated hardware, law enforcement fails as often as it succeeds in bringing criminals to justice."

Menendez shrugged as if to say "whadaya gonna do?" When they got to her workbench, she turned to Walt Earheart, who handed her two sealed clear-plastic evidence bags, one containing the gun and the other the magazine he had removed from the weapon when it was recovered. She glanced at the weapon dispassionately. "Walther PPK/S."

The criminalist wrote something in a logbook, unsealed the plastic evidence bag, then removed the gun and magazine, laying them side by side on the lab bench. "About 70 percent of the weapons we test are automatics—semiautomatics to be technically correct—or single-shot handguns. Most of the single shots are Saturday Night Specials. Did you recover the casing?"

"Nope," Walt said. "Only the slug."

"Pity. Breech and firing-pin impressions, and ejector and chamber markings are easier to identify than rifling grooves and barrel markings. No problem, though; don't worry. I can do it. Where's the bullet?"

Kathryn handed it to Menendez.

Menendez eyed it carefully. "Twenty-two, copper jacket. Not too badly damaged. I can tell by the direction of the rifling twist that it might be a Walther slug. Can't tell you any more than that without a test firing and the microscope."

Kathryn and Earheart knew that, like temperamental artists, many criminalists prefer to work in solitude. Kathryn asked if they should wait in the employee lounge, but Menendez assured her that she welcomed company while she worked.

"How long will it take?" Kathryn asked.

"As long as it takes," Menendez answered. Her answer wasn't intended to be rude and wasn't taken as such.

"The firing tank is behind here," she said, indicating a soundproof partition. Menendez loaded three cartridges into the magazine and slapped the clip into the handle of the weapon crisply and expertly. "I'll fire three test rounds, then compare them under the micron microscope. Okay, here we go."

She inserted the barrel of the weapon into a rubber sleeve, cocked the weapon by pulling and releasing the slide, then fired the gun three quick times. Laying the gun aside, she grabbed a plastic dipper and fished the bullets from the bottom of the tank like dead guppies. Each was retrieved from the dipper with soft plastic tweezers and placed on a microscope slide under an optical comparison microscope.

She hunched over the twin lenses of the microscope, turning its knurled knobs slightly to rotate and align the bullets and adjust the focus to a sharp image. "It's a match," Menendez declared. "The bullet you recovered from the victim was fired from this gun."

While she spoke, Walt Earheart peered through the microscope's twin lenses and nodded his agreement.

Realizing she had been holding her breath, Kathryn expelled it audibly. Roselba Menendez turned to her and said, "There's no question, Kate. This is the murder weapon. Now, let's take a look at the gun itself."

As they walked back to the bench, Kathryn asked, "You think there might still be prints on it?"

"Hard to say," Menendez answered. "It wasn't in

the water very long, and water isn't a solvent for oil. If no one wiped it down, we might get lucky. Do you want to wait, or should I call you later?"

"We'll wait," Earheart interjected. He didn't need to ask Kathryn her opinion. He knew they wouldn't leave until the examination was completed. "Anybody interested in coffee? There's a machine in the employee lounge, right?"

"Yep," Menendez said. "I like mine hot and black."

"None for me," Kathryn said.

"I'll be right back," Earheart said.

When he returned, Earheart found Menendez and Kathryn side-by-side, hunched over a flat table, peering through hand-held magnifiers containing built-in halogen lamps. Menendez was dusting the gun handle and magazine for prints with a fine long-bristled sable brush loaded with dark gray fingerprint powder.

"Anything?"

The two women grunted in unison without looking up. "No prints on either the gun or the magazine."

The criminalist then placed one of the unfired cartridges recovered from the gun's magazine under the glass. She nudged Kathryn. "Can you see that, there, on the side of the shell?"

The loops and whorls of a partial fingerprint were clearly visible on the brass casing. "Absolutely. Can you photograph this for me?"

"Piece-a-cake. You want to look at this?" she offered Earheart.

"Not me," he replied, "but I want to know whose finger put it there."

9

LEAVING WORK EARLY, DAVE GRANZ DROVE
home, showered, shaved, and changed into a beige
Izod shirt and light tan slacks. He even shined his
shoes.

At exactly six-thirty, he stood outside Julia Soto's
front door in the expensive Casa del Norte condominium complex, ignoring the accumulating butterflies in
his stomach. Routinely calling on crime victims,
witnesses, and perpetrators was part of his profession,
and he knew his nervousness was unrelated to the
Lancaster case. He drew a deep breath, poked his
thumb into the doorbell button, and was greeted by
melodious chimes.

Waiting for the door to open, he reflected on what
he expected to see. In her mid-thirties when they were
involved, Julia was now approaching forty. He figured
she had probably grown fat and ugly. He heard
footsteps, then the door opened. She wasn't fat or
ugly.

"David, I am so glad to see you," Julia said,
extended her right hand to grasp his in a firm handshake.

"I'm happy to see you, too, Julia." He grasped her
hand. "You look wonderful."

She still wore her work clothes: a simple, straight ivory skirt and darker beige silk blouse which buttoned up the front, the suit coat having been discarded. The top three buttons of the blouse were open, offering a discreet but tempting glimpse of cleavage. A single strand of pearls hung around her neck. She was shoeless, stockingless, and he could hardly help but notice, braless. He wondered if she went to work that way, and if she did, how any of the men got any work done. Her dark hair was swept back tight against her head into a bun, and she wore no makeup.

Not classically pretty, Julia Soto possessed several individual features that, taken separately, were flawed but came together to create sultry good looks that took Dave Granz's breath away.

"Am I permitted more than a handshake after all these years?" she asked.

"Of course, I just wasn't sure . . ." Dave stammered.

She drew him to her in a tight hug. Dave felt her breasts press against his chest through her sheer blouse and his shirt, and wondered if she could tell how fast his heart was pounding. He returned the hug more enthusiastically than he expected; then she led him inside, closing the door behind them.

"I'm so glad to see you, David. I was afraid I would not be after we talked, but I am. I have thought of you often since I returned."

"It's been so long, Julia, and now just to see you so suddenly," he said. "How are you?"

They spent the next hour facing each other across a

coffee table, exchanging superficial personal information and filling each other in on the details of their lives. She made only a passing reference to her stay in Cuernavaca, concentrating on the period since her return to Santa Rita and her job. Dave told her about the cases he had worked, explaining his run-in with the Gingerbread Man that resulted in the scars she immediately noticed.

"Are you involved with anyone?" he blurted suddenly, surprising himself with the change in direction and the bluntness of his inquiry.

She arched a dark eyebrow and smiled but shifted nervously on the seat, crossing and uncrossing her legs seductively. Dave felt a stirring in his groin and hoped she couldn't tell. "Do you really care?" she asked.

Dave squirmed uncomfortably under her intense gaze. He thought about Kathryn and knew he shouldn't care but answered, "Yeah, I do." He paused, then persisted, "So, are you?"

She brushed a strand of hair from her forehead. "Not at the moment. I hardly have time; my job is very demanding. I saw someone briefly after I returned from Cuernavaca, but it meant nothing. Perhaps I should not tell you this, but . . . ," she paused, embarrassed. "I loved you more than you can know, but it turned out you cared for me less than that. I think perhaps I mistook your passion for affection. It has taken me a very long time to recover. I am not certain I have fully recovered yet."

"It wasn't that I cared for you less, Julia," he said softly. "But my wife and I had just separated; you knew that. I wasn't ready for a long-term commitment. I was a basket case. You deserved far better than I was capable of giving you at the time. That's why I didn't fly to Mexico to meet your family, I knew what that meant, and I wasn't ready to offer it to you. Our timing was so poor." He drew a deep breath and studied her stoic Incan face, but she offered neither encouragement nor discouragement, so he continued.

"I believed at the time that your being away for awhile was good. It would give us both time to work things out."

"I had nothing to work out, David. I loved you," she said simply.

"When you suddenly stopped writing and speaking with me, I assumed you were seeing someone else. So I went in other directions."

She smiled at him sadly, like a mother smiles at her small child whom she has just caught in a lie. "You cannot believe that. For five months we were inseparable. You were at my apartment or I was at yours. We ate together, we dressed together, we went places together, we slept together, we made love together. You were the first man I had ever been with. Did you know that?"

"I . . . yes, I suspected that."

"You knew that I immigrated from Mexico only two years before we met," she continued. "I grew up there, and in Mexico, a decent woman saves herself for her husband. That may seem naive to you, and perhaps it is, but that is how it was in my culture. I assumed we would be married. How could I have assumed anything else? You never led me to believe otherwise."

"Julia, I never said we would be married; the subject never came up."

"No, of course not; it was unspoken."

"But when you stopped writing and would no longer talk to me on the phone—"

"You dishonored me in the eyes of my family. I told my sister about you. She was the only person who knew about the depth of our relationship, although my father suspected. I spoke of you incessantly to them. He asked when you were coming to meet him. After my mother passed away, it was apparent that you were not. My father believed I was no longer suitable for marriage. There was no point in continuing."

"You could have at least told me," he responded lamely.

"No, I could not do that. An honorable Mexican woman does not pursue a man who is not interested." She paused, took a deep breath, expelled it slowly, and said, "Besides, something happened that changed everything."

Dave looked confused. "I don't understand. What do you mean, something happened? Something I did?"

"Nothing you did directly," she said, "although had you been there, had you come to meet my father . . . No, it is in the past now; there is no point in discussing it."

Several seconds of uncomfortable silence followed, then she asked, "And you, David, is there someone special in your life now?"

He paused. What about Kathryn? he thought. All I have to do is tell the truth. That isn't so fucking hard, is it? But what's the truth? That we love each other and she's just too busy, or that we're losing interest in each other and can't admit it? At one time, he admired her ability to focus entirely on her work, to the exclusion of everything else. Now that it was he who was so often excluded, that ability lost most of its appeal.

"I see someone, but we've made no promises. We don't live together." Sonofabitch, he thought, what was that all about?

"Perhaps we should change the subject," she suggested suddenly, sitting up straight and placing both feet flat on the floor. "What can I tell you about the Lancasters?"

Dave looked at her questioningly—disappointed but also relieved that he could not further pursue their personal feelings—then decided she was right. A change in the conversation was definitely a good idea.

"Did you know either of the Lancasters?" he asked.

She shrugged. "I rarely worked with him, since his practice was confined primarily to domestic law. Two Hispanic partners handle the Mexican connections, and I work almost exclusively with them."

"What kind of reputation did he have?" Dave asked.

"Well, from what I heard he was a nice man. A workaholic—he spent all his time at the office. Whenever I was there, he was working. He was always pleasant and polite to me, and that's what everyone else said, too."

"Temper?"

"What do you mean?"

"Did he have a reputation for being angry—violent?"

"Not that I ever heard. I do not think so."

The living room was arranged with a large fabric sofa with matching loveseat and chair around a glass-top black-marble table. The carpets were off-white, as were the walls. The artwork was all pastels, matted and framed in shades of white. Julia's dark Latin good looks stood out in stark contrast to her self-created, intensely feminine environment. Dave sensed a cool sterility in its design.

He sat at one end of the loveseat looking directly across the table at her. She adjusted herself on the sofa, pulling her feet back up to her left and tucking her legs under her body as women do.

"What about Mrs. Lancaster? Do you know her?" he asked.

"Barely," Julia answered, shifting positions again and flashing a generous portion of smooth brown thigh. "I have seen her maybe a dozen times but have only spoken with her once or twice, and only in passing. She is . . . maybe the best description is aloof. She is also very beautiful."

"Yes, she is." Dave appreciated the glimpse of Julia's bare thigh and imagined a more expansive and revealing view. "So, you don't know her well enough to give me any idea what she's like?"

"No-o-o. David, I know nothing about this except what was told to the staff this morning. We were told Mr. Lancaster died in a fire. Is that not correct?"

"According to the coroner, he died from a gunshot wound to the head, not from the fire. We're just beginning to piece it together."

"You think Anna Lancaster might have killed him?" she asked incredulously.

"Everyone's a suspect until they're eliminated," he hedged. "The spouse is always a prime suspect, but we don't know who killed him. That's what we're trying to find out. If you know anything, anything at all, it might be very useful."

"Who is the prosecutor, David? A man or a woman?"

"A woman. Kathryn Mackay. I know her very well." I'm a fucking master of understatement, he thought.

She paused and contemplated her response. "The rumors are that, how shall I say this—the rumors are that Anna Lancaster is something of a witch."

"A witch?"

"I am being delicate. The actual term is bitch. Many people in the office think so. She is quite irritable and unpleasant to the support staff much of the time. And . . . Mr. Lancaster's former secretary says she is a gold digger, that she married Mr. Lancaster for his money. But the secretary lost her job to Mrs. Lancaster, so perhaps she is biased. I only know what I have heard. I am sorry, I do not know anything more about either of them. I have not been much help, have I?"

"Yes, you have. Thank you."

She smiled at him. "You are being gallant, as always, David. Would you like a glass of wine? I certainly would."

"I don't know, Julia, I'd better—"

"Please? It's early. Have a glass of wine with me,

then leave. I will ask you to leave in an hour or so, anyway. I have some work to finish." She pointed at a pile of legal files on a corner table. "Translations. And I haven't eaten dinner. I'll be right back." She arose from the sofa and disappeared into the kitchen.

Why not? Dave asked himself. No harm to it. He heard her opening the refrigerator door and the tinkle of glasses, then wine being poured and the refrigerator door closing.

She walked into the room carrying two frosty-stemmed crystal glasses filled with a pale golden-yellow wine. "Riesling. I remembered," she said, brushing his arm as she handed a glass over his left shoulder. She walked around and sat on the opposite end of the loveseat, no farther than two feet from his left arm. "Please do not be uncomfortable. I apologize if I have spoken imprudently. It is just that the conversation became a little personal, and perhaps I am too emotional."

He imagined he could feel the heat radiating from her body toward him, causing a swelling in his crotch which he tried, unsuccessfully, to ignore. Was this intentional or inadvertent? Change the subject before it's too late, you idiot. "This is a beautiful place, Julia. I've never been inside the Casa del Norte before. How long have you lived here?"

She fixed her dark eyes on him, took a sip from her wine glass, then set it softly on the table in front of her. She slid gently down the small sofa toward Dave, lifted his glass from his hand, and set it on the table beside her own.

"I missed you, David. I missed you very much. I

did not realize how much until I saw you standing at my door. I tried to erase you from my memory after I . . . after returning from Cuernavaca. But I cannot ignore my feelings when I am with you. Do you think I am still attractive?"

"Julia, I . . ."

She turned her face upward toward him. He smelled the sweetness of the wine on her breath. Her left index finger touched his chin ever so slightly, rotating his head so he looked directly into her dark eyes. With her lips brushing his, she whispered, "Besa me, por favor. Kiss me."

Before he could react, her open lips pressed against his, her tongue caressing his lips and tongue gently. He was surprised by his own growing desires. The kiss extended, intensifying his passion, hastening the stirring in his crotch. Dave felt himself grow hard. "Julia, I, are you sure you want to . . ."

"Touch me, David, this way." She grasped his right hand in her left and, encountering no resistance, drew Dave's hand toward her slowly, and placed it inside her blouse, over her bare left breast.

Cupped in his palm, her nipple hardened to his touch. Dave moved his hand ever so slightly, tracing the hard circle of the areola with his fingertip, then squeezed and twisted her nipple delicately between his thumb and forefinger. She responded with a deeper, more passionate kiss which he returned eagerly. He slid his hand under her skirt past a silky thigh and gasped aloud when he discovered she wore no panties. She was hot and wet, and his finger slipped easily inside her.

She shuddered with a feral groan. "David. Amante,"

she whispered into his ear. He felt the zipper of his slacks slide open, and her soft warm hand encircled his swollen penis. She stroked slowly, insistently. "Amante. Amante."

10

"SHE'S DIRTIER THAN A BAG OF POTTING SOIL," Kathryn Mackay said to Walt Earheart.

He leaned back in the leather chair facing her desk and crossed his legs. "Yep. No doubt about it. Problem is, her story is good enough to fit the facts, and we can't put her at the crime scene when the fire started. I'll bet my paycheck that the partial fingerprint Menendez lifted off the bullet in the murder weapon's hers, but she's never been printed, so we've got nothing to compare."

"Yep, and without a match we don't have enough to take her into custody. A damn catch-22 if you ask me. Can't arrest her without a match, and can't get her prints to match until we arrest her."

Earheart stuffed half a raisin bagel into his mouth and chewed it. A small blob of cream cheese oozed from the corner of his mouth. When he swallowed and washed it down with a sip of his first coffee of the morning, he grinned sheepishly. "I'm starved. Didn't get anything to eat yesterday. Wasn't in the mood after we left Building 46A last night. Too late."

In contrast, Kathryn bit daintily from her multi-grain bagel, no cream cheese, and washed it down with coffee with Mocha Mix.

"So what's the point of talking to her?" He asked.

"Just to shake the tree and see what falls out," Kathryn answered. "I want to see what she says about the gun, and I'd like to get her to tighten up her time frame a little bit. If she did kill him, she'll say something to trip herself up that I can use in trial."

"We need to Mirandize her?" Earheart asked.

"Nope."

"Even if she's the focus of the investigation? You know damned well she did it, and so do I; we've just gotta prove it."

"Doesn't matter. Court cases make it clear we don't have to give her a Miranda warning as long as we don't tell her specifically that she's a prime suspect, and she agrees to the interview. We've just got to make it clear she's free to walk out anytime and stop cooperating."

"Your call, counselor," Earheart conceded. "You carry the ball and lateral to me whenever you think it's best. It'll be interesting to see if she shows up with a lawyer."

Kathryn's intercom buzzed and her secretary advised that Anna Lancaster was here for her nine o'clock interview. Kathryn glanced at Earheart, who gave her the thumbs-up. "Send her in," she said into the intercom.

Anna Lancaster sat in the other chair facing Kathryn's desk, about four feet from Earheart, half-turned to face Kathryn. She was alone and was dressed in an expensive gray business suit and low heels. Except that she wore no makeup, she could as easily have been headed for work as being interviewed about her husband's murder.

"Mrs. Lancaster," Kathryn began, "I appreciate your coming here this morning rather than making us drive to Saratoga. It saves us a lot of time."

Lancaster smiled nervously. "That's perfectly all right; I was happy to get out of the house for awhile. As you know, I'm staying with the Moodys, and they're both at work. I'm uncomfortable being there alone for too long."

"Well, we appreciate it. Also, I want you to know that you are entitled to have an attorney with you if you wish, and of course, you are free to go at any time. This is just an interview, which you may terminate any time you choose. Do you mind if I record our conversation? I'm not very good at taking notes." Kathryn fingered a voice-activated recorder on the corner of her desk.

Lancaster answered falteringly, "No, I suppose it would be okay to record it. Is there a reason I would need an attorney? I don't understand. Am I a suspect?" She looked first at Kathryn, then at Earheart.

"In the early stages of any homicide investigation, everyone is a suspect," Earheart told her. "That includes family members. However, we don't want to add to their grief, so we attempt to eliminate them as quickly as possible and go on to more productive leads."

"I see."

"So," Kathryn interjected, "it would be quite helpful if we could fill in some of the blanks from our discussion on Monday. You were justifiably distraught, and we'd like to clear up a few points. And we want to keep you apprised of all developments in the investigation. As I said, you are free to stop at any time and leave. We'll try to make it as quick as possible."

Lancaster was slightly ill at ease but clearly in control of herself. "Certainly, I'll help in any way possible, and I'm very interested in the investigation, as you can imagine."

Earheart pulled his notebook from his pocket and opened it. "As Ms. Mackay said, we only have a couple of things we'd like to clear up. Do you recall what time you arrived at the Moodys' on the morning of the Fourth?"

"Well, let's see. I don't remember looking at my watch; I'd have had no reason to do so since it was a holiday. But, I'd say it was around ten-thirty, maybe a little later."

"Do you remember who answered the door when you arrived?"

"Clare, I think. Does it matter?"

"Probably not. Was Mr. Moody there?"

"Of course. I told you they were expecting me. It was a holiday."

Earheart made a notation in his notebook and looked at Kathryn. "Mrs. Lancaster, you said you left the house about eight o'clock and went by the mall where you bought a Gianni suit. Do you remember how long you were there?"

"No, not exactly." She smiled at Kathryn. "You know how that is. It takes awhile to try them on, and I had a hard time deciding. An hour and a half, maybe slightly longer."

"I see. And did you take the main highway to Saratoga?"

"Yes. You know the old road is always so packed with tourists that's it's awful, especially on holidays. I stopped at the Shell station and put in gas first. They were packed, and I had to drive pretty fast over to the Moodys'"

Earheart made another note in his notebook and asked, "Mrs. Lancaster, did you know your husband had a twenty-two caliber Walther automatic pistol?"

She pursed her lips and looked irritated. "Yes, I knew about it. It was one of the few things we argued about. I told him I hated guns and didn't want it in the house. But he insisted it was for our own protection. I thought that was ridiculous, but he refused to get rid of it."

Earheart glanced at Kathryn, who shrugged slightly and arched an eyebrow questioningly. "Ridiculous? Your house is in a pretty remote area. We've had a number of burglaries and prowlers there over the past few years. Didn't he ever teach you to fire it, in case you needed it some night when he worked late?"

Anna Lancaster looked straight at Walt Earheart and in a steady voice said, "Mr. Earheart, it isn't the bad guys that are the biggest threat to a woman's safety. Everyone knows it's family members, and a gun is useless in those situations. I never fired that gun or any other, and I never shall."

"Do you know where he kept it?"

"I have no idea. All I know is that he kept it in the house against my wishes."

"Would anyone else have known where he kept it?"

"I'm not certain, Mr. Earheart. He probably told his friends about it. I believe they all felt the same way, and they all kept guns in their homes. I think it's a man thing. As I said, I never wanted to know, but there are probably half a dozen people who did. Why is it so important?"

Earheart and Mackay again exchanged looks. "The coroner has determined that your husband was killed by his own pistol," Kathryn told her. "We hoped you might know who had access to it."

"How can he tell that without the gun?" she asked.

"We found the gun, Mrs. Lancaster," Kathryn said, "but not in your home. We recovered it from the bottom of Las Casitas Lake. The crime lab has positively identified it as your husband's gun and established that it was used to fire the fatal shot. It's very important that we establish who might have known where he kept it."

Lancaster turned pale, flushed, then stood abruptly and walked to the window, her back to Earheart and Kathryn. Kathryn looked at Walt and raised her shoulders as if to say, I don't know what she's doing, do you? She stood looking out the window for a full two minutes, then turned to face them. Tears ran from her eyes and dripped from her chin.

"I'm sorry," she said, dabbing at her eyes with a tissue she pulled from the purse alongside her chair. She sat down and said to no one in particular, "It's just so hard. I think I'm under control, then something happens and . . . I can certainly see why it's important. Let me think about it. Perhaps I can remember something that will help."

"Fine," Kathryn said. "Are you okay to go on?"

"I'm fine. Let's continue. I know we have to do this eventually."

"I'm curious about something you said a moment ago. What did you mean that the real threat isn't the bad guys but someone in the family?"

Lancaster thought for a moment before answering. "I'm not sure I want to talk about it. It has nothing to do with this."

"That's okay," Kathryn answered. "As I said, you're free to stop this interview at any time. But I wonder if you could tell us again about the suit you bought. You said you bought the suit when you stopped at the mall on the way to Saratoga. Is that correct?"

"Yes, that's correct."

"Okay," Kathryn said, "perhaps this is a good time to quit." She looked at Earheart. "Do you have anything else, Walt?" she asked. He shook his head.

Kathryn stood and extended her hand to Anna Lancaster. "Thanks for coming in. I know how difficult this is. Would you mind if I called if anything else comes up? You'll be at the Moodys' you said?"

"Not at all. I want to help however I can, of course. If anything occurs to me about who might have known where Larry kept the gun, I'll call you."

"Oh, Mrs. Lancaster," Kathryn said just as Anna was opening the door to leave. Kathryn put the tips of her right fingers against her forehead, Columbo fashion. "Just one more question, if you don't mind. Was your marriage to Mr. Lancaster your first?"

Anna Lancaster's grip tightened on the doorknob until her knuckles turned white. "No, it was my second. I was married once before, as a very young woman. It didn't work out. Now, if you don't mind, I believe I will leave."

After she left, Earheart pulled his chair back to its usual place in front of Kathryn's desk. "Why didn't you call her on it when she said she bought the suit on the way to Saratoga? We already know she bought it on the way home that afternoon, not in the morning."

"I'm saving that for later," Kathryn replied.

11

"WHERE'S GRANZ?" EARHEART ASKED KATHryn.

She shrugged. "He took off without telling me where he was going. He was a bit mysterious about it."

"Damn! I told him ten o'clock sharp. No idea where he went?"

Even with a fresh coat of institutional tan paint, the sheriff's department conference room was most generously described as unattractive. It smelled faintly of cigarette smoke, despite the county's politically correct ban on smoking anywhere in the building. Its only redeeming feature was a view of the park, where senior citizens clad in stark white uniforms conducted a lawn-bowling tournament. The shabby plastic-covered chairs around the T-shaped conference table, the huge blackboard, which was actually green, and a map of the county were the room's only permanent furnishings.

"You know Dave. Remember the Gingerbread Man?"

"What're you guys talking about?" Yamamoto asked.

"The Gingerbread Man was a guy named Lee Russell. He was a teacher at one of the high schools who was fond of killing young women, scalping their pubic areas, then tanning them like leather pouches.

"We had a helluva time tracking this guy down until Granz initiated his own private investigation. Not illegal, but definitely outside the usual channels," Earheart told him. "And very effective, except it damn near got Granz killed."

Seated at the far end at the head of the table was Lieutenant Earheart. Charlie Yamamoto, of the Crime Scene Investigation Unit, sat at his right. Kathryn Mackay and Dr. Morgan Nelson sat to Earheart's left, facing Yamamoto. Racial stereotypes aside, Kathryn couldn't help but think the CSI man looked, well, inscrutable.

Yamamoto looked at Earheart.

He continued. "Late one night, Granz agreed to meet an informant behind the Seacliff Hotel. Instead, it was Russell waiting for him. Clobbered him over the head with a big wrench of some kind, then almost decapitated him with a scalpel. We caught him later, but Granz almost died.

83

Kathryn looked worried. "I'm afraid he might be impatient with how slowly the wheels of justice turn, again, and has gone out on his own."

"Goddamn," Earheart sighed. "Okay, while we're waiting for Granz to show up—assuming he does show up—Kate, why don't you brief Doc Nelson on what we learned at Building 46A."

"The bullet you removed from Lawrence Lancaster's head," she began, "came from a Walther PPK that Walt's team found at the bottom of Las Casitas Lake. Dead-bang match.

"Also, the criminalist lifted a partial print off one of the unspent rounds in the magazine. By the way, Morgan, she's going to call you for a consult."

Nelson nodded. "No problem. The likelihood of getting a print from a gun found in water is pretty slim."

"Pure luck," Kathryn replied. "There was a thin film of oil on the magazine, just enough to coat the shells and preserve the print."

"I'll take it," Earheart chimed in. "Offer me lucky or smart, I'll take lucky every time."

Earheart turned to Yamamoto. "Have you identified the print?"

Yamamoto didn't talk much or smile much, either. "I compared the partial to the print I rolled during the autopsy. Not Lancaster's."

"What about the wife?"

"No prints on file."

Kathryn shook her head. "CSI might not be able to match the partial even if we get her prints. They may not have enough. And even if they do, you can't age the print. It might have been on the casing for a long time. Weapons that are kept for self-protection are usually loaded once and stay put for years."

"She said she never fired the weapon," Earheart reminded her.

"Yeah, I know, but it wouldn't matter. She'd just say she forgot, that he showed her how to fire it just in case, and she went along with it to avoid another fight. All baloney, of course, but it'd create a doubt.

"Okay, assume we can't put the gun in her hand when we need to; let's put it together circumstantially. Let's see what we've got and figure out what we need. Maybe if we can't get in the front door, someone left the back door open.

"We know that for a smaller person, like a wife, to kill a larger person, like her husband, unless she poisons him or something, she needs something to equalize their strength."

"Yeah," Earheart agreed, "the overwhelming weapon of choice for wives to off their husbands is a gun. Often as not, it's the husband's own gun. And it's almost always a handgun, even if a rifle or shotgun is available."

"Okay, that fits." Kathryn thought for a moment. "But, why the fire? Why shoot him then set him on fire?"

Yamamoto spoke up. "There is no reason for her to have known, but it takes temperatures of eighteen hundred to two thousand degrees for up to two hours to cremate a body. It's rare for a house fire, even an intense one, to reach temperatures over about twelve hundred degrees."

"Meaning that, even in a cremation, a couple of pounds of ashes, bones, and teeth are left over,"

Nelson said. "And without those sustained temperatures, the body recovered is much better preserved. She no doubt figured the body would be destroyed so we couldn't pinpoint the cause of death."

"Yeah, but the bullet would still be there," Kathryn observed.

"Not necessarily. Bullets are made of lead, and lead melts at a temperature much lower than cremation temperatures. The lead would liquify and disburse. Probably be overlooked unless someone expected to see it. Of course, this fire never even got that hot."

Kathryn nodded. "Let's get back to the victim," she suggested. "Are we sure he had no worries—no financial problems?"

"I don't know about everyday worries," Earheart said, "but he certainly didn't have financial problems. Last year, his firm generated over forty million in fees, and get this: according to John Moody, Lancaster accounted for almost ten million himself.

"His expertise is putting high-tech companies together with venture capitalists, structuring the deals, and protecting their intellectual property rights after they start making money.

"He's got an international reputation, according to Moody. The partners split the firm's profits based on a productivity formula. Moody wouldn't say how much, but I'd bet Lancaster took home seven or eight million bucks last year before taxes."

"Okay, I guess we can all agree that money wasn't causing him undue stress," Kathryn conceded. "How about other women?"

"Don't think so. He was an incorrigible workaholic, according to Moody. Channeled all his energy into practicing law and making money. Pretty good at it, too."

"Sounds like someone we all know and love," Nelson said, patting Kathryn on the arm affectionately. "All except the money part."

Everyone at the table smiled, but before they could resume the discussion, Dave Granz slammed the door open and entered the stuffy room. "Hi, gang. Nice day."

"You were supposed to be here an hour ago," Earheart said.

"Sorry, Earheart," Dave said without meaning it. "I went up to Las Casitas Lake. Fish weren't biting, so I decided to interview a few neighbors."

Kathryn was visibly upset. "Damnit, Dave, you promised me. . . . Some of those people up there aren't altogether friendly toward cops. Damnit, Dave." She met his eyes squarely and held his gaze.

"Okay, I'm sorry, Kathryn." This time he meant it. "I just thought about it at the last minute and figured to be back before the meeting. It took a little longer than I figured. But it paid off."

Dave had everyone's attention. "Go ahead," Earheart encouraged.

"I remembered a little cabin up on the ridge. It's one of those little weekenders, and it has a full-on view of the fishing pier.

"Took a chance and drove up there. Found a couple of rednecks who went up the night before the Fourth, planning to go fishing early the next morning. They got a little drunk and went skinny dipping that night. Woke up late the next morning with big heads and fuzzy tongues. Decided to watch the Giants-Marlins game on TV, instead. So, they were sitting on the front porch around ten-thirty on the Fourth drinking coffee."

Dave paused, looking around. "Didn't you guys get coffee?"

Kathryn still wasn't happy with Dave's procedural failings but knew he was onto something important. "Get on with it, please."

"Okay, okay. You're not going to believe what I found out. They both saw a car drive up and park at the head of the pier. A woman gets out of the car, looks around, and walks down to the end of the pier. Then she takes something out of her purse and heaves it out into the water. She looks around again, then hauls ass up to her car and takes off."

"What direction?"

"North. Toward Saratoga. And guess what kind of car? A white, late-model Beemer."

"Didn't she see them from the pier?" Kathryn asked.

"Not a chance," he answered. "The place is so overgrown with poison oak, manzanita, and other stuff that you can hardly see it. And it's a ways from the lake. That's how I happened to gain the cooperation of these two fine, upstanding citizens."

Earheart said, "Goddamnit, Granz, if you threatened them or something, we'll all be in the shit up to our knees. Do we want to know what you did? I know those mountain folks aren't usually too helpful."

"Not to worry. They're buddies who own the place together. I just suggested that the county fire marshal might be interested to know about all that dead growth right in the middle of the fire season. The fines that go with those citations are pretty stiff. About five hundred bucks, and you still have to clear the growth out.

"I suggested that it'd probably be a good deal for them if the fire department didn't hear about it for a day or two, so they had time to cut it down. When I left, they were digging out the brush cutter and chain saw. I told 'em to have a really nice weekend."

"Excellent," Yamamoto said.

"Another funny thing," Dave added. "One of the guys had a set of those little Pentax binoculars. Says this woman was a real fox and wanted to get a better look. Got a good look at the license number, too, and wrote it down. I ran the plate already. Lawrence Lancaster's BMW."

He tossed a DMV printout on the conference table.

"Why don't you pick her up, Katie?" Morgan Nelson asked.

Kathryn shot him a warning look. It was one thing for him to call her that, but she didn't want everyone else developing the habit. "Not yet. Dave, did they get a good enough look at her face to identify her as Anna Lancaster, or were they looking at her other body parts? If they thought they could ID her, we could put her in a lineup."

"No need, I already thought of that. You'd have to get a lawyer involved and all. I put a photo lineup together. Used her driver's-license photo that DMV faxed me. Showed it to both of them separately. They both picked out number four without hesitation."

"And let me guess—Anna Lancaster's picture was . . . ?" Earheart urged.

89

"Number four," Dave stated.

"Can I see the lineup, please?" Kathryn asked. For a photo ID to be admissible, the others must be similar in appearance to the suspect. They were.

"Should we pick her up?" Walt Earheart asked her.

Charlie Yamamoto and Morgan Nelson stood up. Nelson spoke for them both. "Looks like you can get along without us, and not being men of leisure, we're going to leave. Give me a call if you need me."

"Okay, Morgan thanks for coming. You too, Charlie. Thanks a lot. I appreciate it."

Morgan patted Kate on the shoulder as he filed past. Yamamoto smiled inscrutably but only nodded.

"Okay, Walt, we could pick her up, but let's think this through first. We know she's staying at the Moodys'."

"Yep. So?"

"Then, why don't I get a Ramey warrant? You know she can't be arrested inside a house, even if it's not hers, without a warrant."

"We could wait till she gets in her car," Dave offered. "Then we wouldn't need a warrant."

"Yes, but that could be awhile, and we can't afford to wait. We don't want her to get remorseful or scared and take off or kill herself before we can take her into custody," Kathryn replied. "Remember, too, we haven't found the casing for the bullet that killed him. It's so small, it could be hidden anyplace. She may have it with her, and the warrant would allow us to search just about anyplace we want in the Moodys' house."

Agreed on this procedure, Kathryn drafted the

warrant and affidavit, naming Walt Earheart the affiant. They walked it to superior court, where they
found Judge Jesse A. Woods in chambers. He swore
Earheart, who affirmed the affidavit under oath, then
signed the arrest and search warrants.

Earheart, Granz, and Mackay walked out of the
court building toward the employee parking lot.
"Okay," Mackay said. "Let's pick up Anna Lancaster."

12

"MOM," EMMA CALLED AGAIN, THIS TIME
the inflection rising. "Mo-om!"

Kathryn Mackay awakened with a start, vaguely
disturbed but unable to determine if she was awake or
asleep. She glanced at the red digital-clock readout;
4:47 A.M. She put on a worn white terry-cloth robe
and hurried into Emma's room, stumbling over the
violin case and backpack piled in front of the bedroom door. Sam growled at her before he realized who
she was. "What is it, honey?" she asked, sitting on the
edge of Emma's bed. "What's wrong?"

The edge of the bed was warm, even though Emma
lay on the far side, next to the wall. So, Sam had been
sleeping with Em again, Kathryn thought. I'll have to

talk to them about that again, as if she could reason with a sixty-five-pound golden Lab and a nine-year-old girl who was his best friend.

"Mom, I feel terrible. I'm all shivery and my throat hurts."

Kathryn felt Emma's forehead. It was warmer than normal, but not hot. "Does your head hurt?"

"I hurt all over, Mommy."

"Okay, honey, I'll be right back," Kathryn said. She grabbed a thermometer from the bathroom and read it aloud after a minute under her daughter's tongue. "My diagnosis is that you probably have a cold and that, with proper medical care and bed rest, I think you'll live. However, I must order you to stay in bed today and avoid strenuous activities such as going to summer school."

Emma giggled. "Do I have to take any medicine?" she asked.

"Just a little Tylenol and some warm Ovaltine, sweetie. I'll go get it." When Kathryn returned, Emma was still in bed and Sam had crept back so that his rear end was sitting on the floor, but his big head was resting on the bed next to Emma. What're you gonna do? Kathryn thought.

Emma swallowed the medicine, distorted her face dramatically, then slurped a mouthful of the Ovaltine. "M-m-m, that's good."

"Okay, now you get some rest," Kathryn ordered, "and no TV."

Kathryn closed Emma's door and checked her watch. Almost five-thirty. She would be awake anyway. Might as well stay up. Glancing out the front window at the minimal ocean view her condo afforded, she saw the first golden rays of sunrise peek over the dark horizon, clawing their way into the July sky.

She started water for coffee, and when she had brewed a big cup and lightened it with Mocha Mix, she grabbed the Lancaster case file and climbed on the Stairmaster in the spare bedroom/office. Given a choice, she would have preferred to bundle up, climb on her bicycle, and ride along the beach in the cool ocean air. She had at least an hour before she could call her boss, District Attorney Hal Benton, to arrange for Benton to cover her court appearance.

Today, Kathryn was scheduled to arraign Anna Lancaster for the murder of her husband. She was still in custody at the women's detention facility. Now, Kathryn would need to brief Benton sufficiently so he could handle the arraignment himself.

At seven o'clock, Kathryn dialed Hal Benton's unlisted home phone number, which he answered on the second ring. "Hello, Hal, It's Kathryn."

"Good morning, Kate. Beautiful day outside." He said in his familiar soft voice, the faint southern drawl from his childhood only slightly diminished by a lifetime in California. Always a gentleman, if he was ever irritated by being called at home or at social events, he never indicated it.

"Got a small problem, Hal. Personal. Emma's sick. Nothing serious, but I need to stay home with her today and can't make it to court."

"No problem," he said, "but why—"

"I was scheduled to arraign Anna Lancaster today at eight-fifteen. It's got to be covered. Can you handle it for me?"

"Of course, Kate, no problem at all. Anything special I need to know?"

"Nothing. I reviewed the case file after I took care of Em. She woke me up before five," Kathryn said. "The court will appoint the public defender or put it over for her to retain counsel."

"Bail?" Benton asked.

"Five-hundred thousand. Woods set it at the statutory bail schedule. Wouldn't matter, anyway. They're so rich, if she can make half a million, she can make a million. Leave it as is."

"Okay. Anything else? What date do you want me to set for the preliminary hearing?"

"Well, it has to be held within ten days unless she offers to waive time. I'd like to use the prelim to get a peek at the defense strategy, but it's not likely the defense would demand a prelim within ten days on a murder case. But just in case she does, have the judge set it as close to the last day as possible. I'm swamped."

"All right, anything else?"

"No, Dave will be there and can fill you in on the details. My secretary has a copy of the case file if you want to look through it."

"I'll take care of it. Don't worry, and give Emma a hug for me. I hope she feels better soon."

"Me too. Thanks, Hal."

"No problem," he said and hung up.

Immediately after speaking with Hal Benton, Kathryn called the DA's office and arranged for someone to deliver files for her other cases to her condo. After talking to her secretary, she showered and put on a pair of faded Levis and a loose gray T-shirt that Dave had given her. She wore no shoes and was braless under her shirt, as she almost always was at home. The T-shirt bore the logo of the local Harley-Davidson dealership and read, "If I have to explain, you won't understand." She smiled, knowing how badly Dave wanted to buy a motorcycle. Then she settled in for a long day. Staying home with Emma due to illness wasn't exactly the same as spending quality time together.

Since Emma would be sleeping and watching TV off and on all day, it was a perfect time to make some headway on her other cases. Within an hour, Kathryn had a banker's box full of case files. Before she could make any headway on her cases, the phone rang.

"Hi, babe," Dave said. "Is Emma okay? Benton just told me you had to stay home today because she's sick."

"Just a little cold. Nothing to worry about. She's asleep."

"Well, give her a hug for me when she wakes up. And tell her I'll call her tonight."

"I will, Dave. Thanks for calling. Maybe we'll get to spend some time together this weekend."

"Sounds good to me, Kathryn. It's about time we had a chance to be together. A man has certain needs."

She smiled. "It's been too long."

"Okay, babe, I'd better run. Gotta get some work done. Talk to you later."

Ignoring her growing libido, Kathryn hung up the phone and attacked her case files. Before she realized any time had passed, she looked at the clock and was startled to discover that the afternoon had slipped away and it was after five-thirty.

Although not hungry, from habit she made herself a sandwich and heated a can of Campbell's chicken-noodle soup, Emma's favorite food. She carried the sandwich and soup, and two glasses of fresh-squeezed orange juice into Emma's bedroom, where she found Emma engrossed in an episode of *Sister, Sister* on television.

"Is this over at six o'clock?" she asked.

"Yes, Mother," Emma answered, already feeling well enough to be a young woman again. The transition did not escape her mother's notice. "It's over now. It's on again at eight."

"Would you mind terribly, then, if we watched the Six O'Clock News?"

"Okay," Emma agreed readily, picking up the remote control. "What channel?"

"Seven, please."

Emma scrolled the new Panasonic through the channels until she found the Channel 7 News logo filling the nineteen-inch screen. Despite her normally generous and sharing nature, Emma reserved all rights to her new TV for herself.

The Channel 7 News logo faded to the Kewpie-doll-perfect images of Channel 7 News Co-Anchors Steve Wallace and Arliss Kraft.

As she always did, Arliss began the newscast with teasers of the day's lead stories. Despite several important Senate subcommittee hearings, and major brush fires along the tinder-dry West Coast, today's major breaking story was a sports special.

"Minutes ago," she intoned, "in a surprise announcement, San Francisco 49ers management announced the resignation of their head coach and the hiring of his replacement. We'll have more on this development in the sports segment with Rob Schmidt on the quarter hour." She smiled sweetly and turned to Steve. "Steve?"

If a computer could be human, it would look and sound like Steve Wallace.

"Here in Santa Rita," Wallace said, "famed San Francisco Defense Attorney Angela Bickell argues that her client, currently in custody in the Santa Rita Women's Detention Facility, is a victim of the judicial system. Let's go to the County Building, where James Walter is standing by. What do you have, James?"

The image of a young man in his late twenties, handsome, but not in the perfect Ken-and-Barbie manner of Steve and Arliss, focused on the screen. Behind him, a flamboyantly dressed, very large woman with frizzy black hair wearing a canary yellow suit was answering questions into a forest of microphones.

"Steve and Arliss," Walter said softly, "Channel 7 News is here on the steps of the County Building, where Attorney Angela Bickell has just agreed to speak with the press. As you know, she's as notorious for her ferocious fist-pounding as she is famous for her successful defense of many high-profile murder cases. Let's listen." He thrust his microphone toward the lawyer.

Speaking through lips caked with a thick layer of purple lipstick, Bickell was saying, ". . . and here in the United States alone, nearly four million women are viciously beaten every year. In our society, domestic violence is the single leading cause of injury to women."

Bickell ran her fingers through her hair, frizzing it even further. Her fingernails were extremely long and painted high-gloss black. Before reporters could ask more questions, she continued: "Six out of every ten women who are murdered in the United States suffer that fate at the hands of someone they know; half of them are killed by their spouse or lover. That cycle of violence and destruction cannot continue. If our system won't put a stop to it, the victims will."

Kathryn had never met Bickell personally, although they had attended various conferences at the same time, but she knew Bickell to be a daunting adversary in the courtroom. Shrewd and smart, she played the media for all it was worth and pushed the legal system to the limit. She was probably accused of more ethical violations with the state bar than any lawyer in California, but none of the charges ever stuck.

She was, Kathryn thought, with a growing sense of unease whose cause she could not identify, a helluva lawyer and an even greater feminist. What was she doing in Santa Rita? There were no cases in process that would interest Angela Bickell.

A reporter with his back to the camera shoved a microphone in Bickell's face. "Ms. Bickell," he asked, "are you saying your client was the victim of domestic violence?"

"Damn right."

Another unseen question. "Then why is she being held in jail and charged with murder?"

Bickell flicked her left hand as if discarding a

cigarette butt. "A ridiculous miscarriage of justice. She's a victim, not a criminal. My client didn't murder anyone; she defended herself. She was in mortal fear for her life. Her husband threatened to kill her. Given the history of abuse, she believed him. She had no choice but to kill him or be killed."

Kathryn felt a lump growing in the pit of her stomach. Emma sensed it instantly. Scared, she asked, "Mommy, what's wrong? Do you know that lady?"

"Shush, honey, please," Kathryn said, putting her arm around Emma's shoulders. "I need to listen to this."

Bickell was answering a question that Kathryn hadn't heard but knew from the answer what it had been. "Yes, that is exactly what I'm saying. Battered Women's Syndrome. Recent court rulings have finally legitimized it as a defense by allowing juries to consider expert testimony establishing that when a woman is battered enough, it leads her to a state of mind of perpetual victimization, from which she can only escape by killing her abuser."

"So, you admit your client killed her husband?" James Walter asked.

Angela Bickell looked squarely into the lens of the Channel 7 News cam. Her eyes were the deepest, coldest, most beautiful blue Kathryn Mackay had ever seen.

"Absolutely. Anna Lancaster finally put an end to the cycle of violence and abuse inflicted on her by her husband; something our system refused to do on her behalf. We have waived Mrs. Lancaster's right to a preliminary hearing in the interest of seeing my client freed as quickly as possible by a jury, and the prosecutor has agreed. We'll be in trial as quickly as we can get it on the calendar."

Stunned, Kathryn heard James Walter sum up the press conference. "What may have looked like an open-and-shut case this morning may become the biggest trial to hit Santa Rita in decades. Back to you, Steve and Arliss."

Kathryn was dialing Dave Granz's phone number before Ken and Barbie reappeared on the screen. She got his answering machine. "Leave a message. I'll get back to you as soon as possible."

"Dave," she dictated, her voice an octave or two higher than normal, "what the hell happened in court today? Call me!"

13

"GOOD MORNING, KATHRYN. MAY I COME in?" Formality to this extent was a dead giveaway that something serious was amiss. "How's Emma?" Hal Benton was uncomfortable. Very uncomfortable. A handsome man, he normally exuded an aura of competence and self-assurance that was palpable. Not today. In a dark blue pin-striped suit and navy blue and red striped tie, his dress was typical but his demeanor was not as he stood uncertainly at the door to Kathryn Mackay's office. When meeting with his deputies, he preferred to summon them to his office. To consult in the deputy's office was a sign of respect he extended to only the most senior and successful trial lawyers on his staff. He waited until Kathryn looked up.

"What happened, Hal?" she asked bluntly.

"I take it Emma's better." Hal had his ways of maintaining decorum even in difficult situations.

"I'm sorry," Kathryn said. "Yes, she's feeling much better. Her fever went down nicely over the weekend. I suspect a three-day absence from summer school had something to do with it."

"We need to talk," Benton continued, satisfied that the tone of the conversation was appropriate. "Is now a good time?"

"Now is fine; have a seat," she answered, indicating one of the leather chairs and placing a case file on the corner of her desk.

It was eight o'clock on the Monday morning following Angela Bickell's news conference. Hal Benton had been away on business the entire weekend, and Kathryn hadn't reached him until Sunday night to apprise him of the latest development in the Lancaster case.

"Thank you," he said. "What a screwup. I'm really sorry, Kathryn."

"Hal, please call me Kate. I worry when you call me Kathryn. Tell me what happened," she said, trying to make him feel more comfortable.

"When I talked to you Friday morning, I planned to handle the Lancaster arraignment myself. But, when I got to the office, Rose reminded me that I was due in Sacramento by noon as keynote speaker for the Governor's Task Force on Gang Violence. I forgot all about it. So, I asked Heinz to take it." He made no attempt to explain his absence for the remainder of the weekend, and Kathryn did not presume to inquire.

"Jeez, Hal, if you don't mind me asking, what were you thinking? Greta Heinz hasn't ever handled a superior court jury trial, much less a murder case. Why her?"

"My mistake," he answered. "She was available and I didn't have much time. It was set for eight-fifteen. And I figured she couldn't screw it up too badly with Granz there."

"So, what on earth possessed her to waive prelim and agree to set the trial date in less than sixty days? Why didn't Dave stop her?"

"That's where it finished unraveling. I'm sure Dave told you he got called out at the last minute. Heinz was on her own. When Bickell offered to waive prelim, Heinz thought she'd save you the trouble of putting on a prelim or going to the Grand Jury. She didn't count on this. Don't be too hard on her."

"No, I won't. None of us figured on Battered Women's Syndrome as a defense. I didn't anticipate that myself."

"I hope this isn't screwed up beyond your ability to salvage it, Kate. Now what? If you need my help, just holler."

"No, it's a setback, but nothing I can't handle. I was down here all weekend researching the law on the BWS defense. And at no small cost, I might add. It's all pretty recent law, but I've got a handle on it. They're tough cases to prosecute because of the emotional issues, but it's just as hard on the defense, especially if there're no recent physical injuries to the woman to validate her claim that she believed she was in imminent danger and had to defend herself." She paused. "Hal, I need some coffee. Have you had coffee yet this morning?"

"No, I haven't. Didn't have time. Hand me your phone." He dialed a four-digit interoffice number which his secretary answered on the first ring. "Carol, would you mind running down to the cafeteria and grabbing a couple cups of coffee . . ." He held his hand over the mouthpiece and raised his eyebrows.

Kathryn said, "No sugar, and a little nondairy creamer."

Benton spoke into the phone. "Carol? One with no sugar, with creamer; you know how I like mine. Thanks, I hope you don't mind. Oh, and cancel any appointments I have for the next hour. I'll be here with Mackay." He turned to Kathryn and asked, "What did you mean you were down here all weekend and at no small cost?"

Kathryn knew she could be honest with Benton. "Dave and I haven't been seeing much of each other lately. I've been so busy. We had planned to spend last weekend together, hopefully to make up for a little lost time. After the unexpected blowup in the Lancaster case, I had to cancel." She looked at her desk and said softly, "He was pretty upset. Said maybe I should rethink my priorities. I told him if he was going to be involved with a prosecutor, he needed to get used to it. I didn't handle it very well."

Benton eyed her kindly. "Don't think I don't appreciate the work you did, but maybe he's right. Maybe you need to strike a better balance, Kate." He held up his hands, palms outward. "None of my business; just a friendly observation. Continue, please."

Kathryn sighed deeply and settled back into her chair. "Well, there are two dangers in cases where a woman kills her alleged abuser. One is that she might fabricate a BWS defense, since like rape cases they're almost always her word against his, and he's dead. If it's a fabrication, we attack it that way. The other risk is that we might prosecute a legitimate victim. If she actually is a victim, we've got to know that right away and decide if this is truly a case for the criminal justice system."

Kathryn paused and sipped her coffee. "I confess to the Christopher Darden Syndrome. Where he had a difficult time prosecuting a black man, I will not be able to prosecute a battered woman who kills in legitimate self-defense. You know I have intense feelings on this, Hal, or I wouldn't have founded the County's Domestic Violence Commission and dedicated all that time to helping the high schools and community colleges develop their curricula on domestic violence."

"Yes, and I respect that, Kate. I don't want to prosecute a legitimate victim any more than you do. So, how do we ferret out the truth; was Anna Lancaster a battered wife who is entitled to claim self-defense, or is she a murderer who saw an opportunity and seized it?"

"Well, the first step is to prepare this case more exhaustively than any I've ever handled. I gather evidence with an open mind. Since no one probably saw the beatings themselves, we look for the next best evidence."

Hal Benton drained his coffee. "Where do you start?"

"I already have. I've got a motion on tomorrow's calendar to compel a physical and psychological examination. I'll ask for a full physical examination to establish if there is any bruising or scarring. Also, I'll ask the court to order full body X rays. If there's a history of violence, there may be broken bones that have healed. I also intend to ask the judge to order her to submit to a mental exam, but I'll probably lose that."

"How about her medical records? Since there's no physician-patient privilege in criminal proceedings, she'll have to instruct her personal physician and gynecologist to release her files."

"Yeah, that's in the motion already." She thought for a moment. "Violence like she's claiming can't be hidden entirely. I'll have Granz check family-law court filings, and medical insurance records if we can get them. Something's got to turn up if she's really been abused. We've just got to find it."

"Better get on it, Kate. I'll reassign some of the other cases you're working on. We can't let this one fall apart. I know I can count on you. You want me to swing by the investigators' offices and send Granz down?"

"Yes, thanks. And Hal?"

He looked back at Kathryn.

"Don't worry. I'll handle this."

14

"ALL RISE," THE BAILIFF COMMANDED. "Superior Court of the State of California, County of Santa Rita is now in session, the Honorable Judge Jemima Tucker, presiding."

Judge Tucker seated herself at the bench and smiled at the courtroom, which was filled to capacity. "Please be seated."

Judge Jemima Tucker was a tall, slender black woman with jet-black hair, flawless chocolate-brown skin, and perfect features. She was, in a word—albeit inadequate—gorgeous. But her beauty-queen good looks wasn't what startled first-time attendees in her court most; it was her name.

She was the daughter of rural Texas parents, both of whom possessed Ph.D.s, who felt she might benefit from a little outside motivation. Her name was the Tucker family's equivalent of Johnny Cash's "A Boy Named Sue."

Whether the name accounted for her incredible success was greatly in doubt, graduating as she had number one in her class at Bolt Law School, and ascending meteorically to judgeship through the ranks of the attorney general's office.

Notwithstanding her professional status, she invariably introduced herself at social and professional functions not as Judge Tucker, but as Jemima Tucker. She wore her name proudly, like a badge of honor.

Any preconceived notion that owing to her race, gender, or prior prosecutorial affiliation, she could be pigeonholed as liberal, racially sensitive, anticrime, or otherwise predictable, was quickly dispelled. Her grasp of legal concepts was rivaled only by her social and political acumen. She was a woman on the rise, no doubt about it, and she tolerated no nonsense in her courtroom. Kathryn Mackay admired her.

Judge Tucker's inclination, if indeed she possessed one, was that she determined early in a trial which attorney she liked and which she did not. That initial determination impacted the entire course of the trial. Kathryn had been on both the good side of Judge Tucker and the bad, and vastly preferred the former to the latter.

Judge Tucker surveyed the entire courtroom before establishing eye contact with the defendant, the defense attorney, and the prosecutor, in that order. "Good morning Ms. Mackay. Ms. Bickell, welcome to Santa Rita." She turned to Kathryn and waited.

"Good morning, Your Honor. Kathryn Mackay appearing for the prosecution. This morning I filed with the court clerk three motions in the case of the *People* v. *Lancaster*.

"I apologize for giving the court so little notice, but the prosecution wasn't apprised that the trial was to go out in two weeks until last Friday. Nor were the People aware that the defendant planned to assert a Battered Women's Syndrome defense until hearing about it on the Six O'Clock News Friday evening.

"As Your Honor knows, bruises that might prove the defendant's claim of physical abuse dissipate quickly with the passage of time. It is crucial that Your Honor order the defendant to submit to an immediate physical examination, including radiographic skeletal survey to establish the presence or absence of skeletal injuries."

"Go on, Ms.—"

Angela Bickell leapt to her feet. "Your Honor, really, this is outrageous. My client is a victim, not a criminal, and we resent—"

With more kindness than she was noted for, Judge Tucker cut the defense attorney off. "Ms. Bickell, I know that in San Francisco, with their docket of important cases, judicial proceedings may be handled differently than here in Santa Rita, where we don't even have a professional sports franchise.

"However, we find it works very nicely here on the outskirts of civilization if the lawyers allow the judge to finish her comments before interrupting. I hope you understand this simple courtesy, Ms. Bickell, because if you suffer any further lapses of memory, you will find yourself facing a contempt proceeding. Now, would you mind if I continued?"

Angela Bickell, accustomed to controlling the courtroom rather than vice versa, flushed as red as her double-breasted jacket.

"Of course, Your Honor," she apologized and sat down. The surliness in her voice and the glare she shot the judge portended future confrontations between the two.

"Very well, then, Ms. Mackay, you were saying?"

Grateful that it might be someone besides herself who might incur Judge Tucker's wrath for this trial, Kathryn continued.

"In addition to the physical examination, Your Honor, the prosecution seeks an order to compel the defendant to undergo psychological testing and discovery of the defendant's medical records. Again, Your Honor, the People apologize for the short notice but remind the court of the short setting."

Judge Tucker turned to Angela Bickell. "Ms. Bickell, do you have any objections to the prosecution motions?"

"Absolutely, Your Honor," Bickell said, rising from her seat. "Psychiatric exams only reinforce the stereotype that women who kill their abusers are hysterical or crazy, rather than acting under a reasonable belief that deadly force is necessary to prevent their own death. As for the request to compel a physical examination, such would constitute an unreasonable and therefore unconstitutional bodily intrusion and must be denied."

"Very well, thank you, Ms. Bickell. Give me a few moments to review Ms. Mackay's moving papers." She placed a discreet pair of reading glasses on her nose and studied the documents before her.

After a moment, the judge removed her Dr. Deane Edell glasses and sat back. "The court is prepared to rule on the prosecution's motions. The court will grant the prosecution's motion for an immediate physical examination including the radiographic skeletal survey by physicians chosen by the prosecution, and it is so ordered."

She turned to face the defense table. "The defendant is, of course, entitled to have her own physicians present, if she so chooses.

"The court further orders defendant to instruct her personal physician, including her gynecologist if she has one, to immediately make full and complete copies of defendant's medical files available to the prosecution." She turned again to the defense table.

"Does defense counsel understand the court's direction? The court is aware that defense counsel has in the past misunderstood discovery orders and wishes to avoid such misunderstandings in this case."

Bickell nodded.

"Defense counsel will need to make an audible response so the court reporter can record her answer. Please speak up, Ms. Bickell."

"I understand, Your Honor."

"Very well. As to the prosecution's motion for psychological testing of defendant, the court is aware that five other states have ruled that prosecutors can demand a psychiatric examination of a defendant who intends to bolster a self-defense claim with testimony about Battered Women's Syndrome.

"However, given that Battered Women evidence was developed to describe the experience of being in a battering relationship and not the mental condition of the woman, the prosecution's motion is denied without prejudice to bring the motion again upon an additional showing of good cause. Is there anything further?"

Seeing nothing, Judge Tucker arose, and the bailiff shouted, "All rise," and Judge Jemima Tucker's court was adjourned.

15

"WELCOME TO 3COM PARK, LADIES AND gentlemen. Please rise for the singing of "The Star-Spangled Banner," which will be performed this evening by Mr. Huey Lewis, who is standing behind home plate."

Dave Granz did not rise as the announcer instructed, instead popping the top on a wide-mouth Miller Lite and swallowing half of it in a single gulp. While Huey belted out his stylized version of the national anthem, Dave nuked a Sophie's chicken burrito in the microwave and plopped on the sofa in his living room. He was dressed in a pair of old Levis that had been washed so many times they were off-white and soft as a cotton ball, an L.A. Dodgers T-shirt, and thongs.

He propped his feet up on the coffee table, grabbed the TV remote, and turned up the volume in anticipation of the first pitch of the first game of the San Francisco Giants' seven-game home stand against the Colorado Rockies. A major Western Division confrontation, the game was a sellout and therefore not blacked out on local television.

When Huey finished singing, Rod Beck began his warm-up tosses in an unusual appearance as a starting pitcher. Dave was relieved he had the evening to himself. An avid Giants fan, he looked forward more to an evening of solitude to contemplate the recent complication in his life—in the person of Julia Soto—than the ball game itself.

Dave felt guilty because that afternoon Kathryn called him to her office to apologize for canceling their weekend plans and invited him to watch the game with her at her place. She bought beer and peanuts, and promised to watch the whole ball game with him, although he knew she hated baseball and football. She also promised more primal pleasures afterward. He saw the hurt in her eyes when he declined, offering a lame excuse about not feeling well and wanting to watch the ball game and turn in early. In truth, he didn't know how to face her after his sexual encounter with Julia exactly one week earlier.

Since that night, he had avoided both women, hoping to figure how to deal with this unexpected turn of events. He spoke with both of them on the phone each day, generating serious guilt pangs, duplicity being contrary to his basic nature. Yet he feared he would be unable to let either of them go voluntarily.

On one hand, he and Kathryn never formally committed, but it was tacitly understood that they were a monogamous couple. On the other hand, Kathryn was incredibly busy since the Lancaster killing and had no time for him at all. This was an increasingly common complaint. Plus, Julia Soto excited him sexually like no woman he had ever known.

Four beers, a burrito, a bag of chips, a large container of salsa, and three innings later, the Rockies were ahead eight to one on the basis of six home runs, dispelling the notion that their batting prowess derived from the thin mountain air of Coors Field in Denver. At nine-fifteen, the phone rang.

"Shit!" Dave muttered to himself. The answering machine was off. It rang twelve times before he answered. "Hello?"

"David, it is I, Julia. What are you doing?"

"Watching the ball game," he answered. "What about you?"

She purred, "If I told you, you would become aroused. If you will come over, I will permit you to do it for me."

Dave's crotch immediately stirred. Jesus, what is it about her? he wondered. "I don't know, Julia. I'm watching the ball game. I just drank several beers, and I have to get up early in the morning for work, and—"

"David, you make me laugh," she chuckled. "Okay, you come over and I'll turn on the ball game on the television. You can just ignore me while I do whatever I do, and we will see how great your powers of concentration and your love for baseball are."

Dave thought it over for at least three seconds. "I'll be there in fifteen minutes."

"David?" she said.

"Yeah, babe?" Oh, shit. He had never called anyone babe except Kathryn. What the hell was happening?

"Bring your toothbrush. You'll need it in the morning, and I have no spare."

Fourteen minutes later, he rapped softly on the door of unit twenty-three at the Casa del Norte. Julia opened the door instantly, wearing a silk dressing gown in a bright Mexican floral print. It didn't look like there was anything underneath. She stood aside, grabbed him by the arm, and ushered him through the door. He could hear the Giants game on the television. On the drive over, Dante Bichette blasted a three-run homer, and the Rockies now led eleven to one. Maybe he didn't need to watch the entire game, after all.

Julia sat near him on the sofa, which was turned slightly to face the entertainment center. She tucked her legs and feet under her right hip and picked up a glass of white wine. "Would you like a glass of wine or a beer?" she asked.

"No, thanks, three is my limit." What the hell's wrong with me? he thought. I just lied about the number of beers I drank, and it's none of her business.

"I missed seeing you this past week," she said, then quickly added, "It is all right; I know you are busy. I have been, as well. But I had hoped to do more than talk on the phone after last Tuesday night." She dropped her left hand casually onto his left thigh in the familiar manner of a long-term lover.

"Yeah, I was pretty tied up," he said, sneaking a glance at the television. Larry Walker had just blasted another solo home run. "But, I—"

"I know," she interjected, "me too. It was so sudden, I've been confused all week, and I haven't been totally effective at work." She stared at him intensely, then asked, "Were you with another woman?"

Before he could stop to think about it, which would no doubt have led to resentment at the question, he answered defensively, "No, I worked every night this week. I haven't even seen . . . I haven't been with anyone. I missed you, too."

Julia slid her hand slightly higher on Dave's thigh and squeezed affectionately. It was now perilously close to his most private part. *Jesus, if she doesn't move her hand in a minute, I'll expand to meet it.*

"Good. I do not share well, as I am sure you know." Her hand inched barely higher and rested against his penis.

She moved her hand from his leg and untied the belt on her robe, allowing the front to open slightly but not enough to reveal anything vital. He was right, there was nothing underneath. Then she raised and crossed her arms slowly, hooked her thumbs into the opposite sides of the top of her robe, and slid it off her shoulders. "Look at me."

"Look at me," she said again, softly. Dave's eyes dropped hungrily to her generous breasts. While he watched, she grasped each nipple between a thumb and forefinger and pulled softly, until they stood erect. "Here," she urged, placing her right hand gently behind his head to draw it toward her, guiding her left nipple into his mouth. He sucked first one, then the other, and she moaned softly.

"You could do this every day if you wished, Amante. Do I taste good?" she asked in a husky voice. She placed her hand in his lap and found him swollen.

Dave leaned back to look at her. She was more beautiful than he remembered, her smooth dark skin flushed with excitement. Julia reached down and parted the skirt of her robe. With her forefingers, she spread herself for him to see. She was pink and wet and inviting. He leaned over and kissed her. She smelled of lust. He teased her with his tongue.

She raised his head and said, "Come with me." She

stood, her robe falling to the floor, and led him to her bedroom. She removed a condom from the night-stand and opened it, then pulled his T-shirt over his head, and sat on the edge of the queen-size bed. She unbuttoned his jeans, pulled them to the floor with his shorts, kissed his stomach, and rolled on the condom.

She lay back on the bed, pulling him onto her, then rolled them both over so he lay on his back, and knelt astride him, her knees alongside his chest.

"Oh, God, Julia, that . . . I . . . oh God," Dave groaned.

Reaching down, she grasped him and guided him into her. He watched himself enter her slightly. She moved her hips gently, positioning herself so he was fully available to her, then lowered herself slowly, totally consuming him.

She arched her head and trunk backward and grasped his ankles for leverage. Her long black hair cascaded down her back. He thrust and she responded. Finally, unable to contain himself, Dave spasmed, grabbed her hips, and spent himself into her.

Afterward, they lay on the bed, her head in the crook of his arm, and she asked, "Are you going to smoke a cigarette? That is what you used to do after we made love."

"I quit. Smoking, that is," he said as he got up to go to the bathroom.

When he returned, she said, "Now it's my turn. I'll be right back." She got up and went into the bathroom and closed the door. Dave heard water running, then the toilet flushed. When she came out wearing a white flannel robe, he was sitting on the edge of the bed with his clothes on. She crossed her arms over her chest in a defensive posture and said, "David? What are you doing?"

"Julia, this has happened so suddenly. We need to think it over."

"Think what over, David? It was good, as it was before?"

He stood and patted her shoulder, obviously uncomfortable. "Yes, it was wonderful. Better than I remembered. But I'm confused."

Julia sat on the bed. "Confused? About what? I love you. You love me, that is obvious. We are together again. It's a very simple matter. Come to bed. You will feel better tomorrow morning after a good night's sleep."

Dave shook his head. "I can't, Julia; I can't spend the night. I have a lot to think about. Maybe I made a mistake coming here tonight before I worked it out. Maybe we shouldn't see each other again until I decide how to handle this."

"Handle what? Oh, God, David, don't do this again. Please!" she pleaded. Tears welled up in her eyes, spilled over, and ran down her olive cheeks. "I cannot handle it again. Please! We belong together. You know that. At least promise you'll be faithful to me. Promise me!"

"I can't promise that. Julia, let me go home and think about this, okay? I'll call you tomorrow night or the next. Then we'll talk." He turned and walked into the living room. She did not follow. As he opened the door, he heard her wail from the bedroom, "Not again. Oh God, not again." He closed the door softly behind him.

"Jesus Christ, Granz," he said aloud, "what have you done?" What about Kathryn? he thought. Did he love her or not? What the fuck was going on?

16

KATHRYN RUSHED INTO HER OFFICE, COFFEE cup in hand, bent over and kissed Dave on the cheek despite her feeling about such behavior at work, and plopped down in the chair behind her desk. She was becoming increasingly aware of the strain on their relationship and thought a show of affection might help. "Why so morose, babe?" she asked.

Dave sat stiffly in a leather client chair facing her desk, eating a bran muffin. "It's nothin'," he replied quickly, avoiding eye contact. "I was up late last night interviewing a witness. Turned out to be useless. Just a little down, I guess."

She looked at him skeptically but did not pursue the matter. "That's my role on the eve of trial. Yours is to keep me pumped up." Only a few days remained before opening statements must begin in Judge Tucker's court in the Lancaster murder trial.

Kathryn requested the meeting with Dave, her investigator, at eight o'clock Wednesday—the morning following her more-or-less successful motions heard by Judge Tucker—to discuss the state of his investigation.

"That's what I wanted to talk about, to see if you've made any progress, I thought you might be working. I tried to call you several times last night at home but gave up about ten and went to bed. Fill me in."

Dave explained the personnel lists, including the names of the employees he submitted to the personnel department. He was to begin interviewing Friday morning.

"Why so long?" Kathryn asked. "Couldn't you start this afternoon?"

"Personnel director says he needs a little time to sanitize the files. You know, remove the payroll information and other confidential stuff before I can see them. Can't violate their privacy, counselor. Anyway, it takes a while."

"Who did you talk to last night?" she asked.

He checked his notes, then replaced the notebook in his inside coat pocket. "Julia Soto. Said she was leaving on business and wouldn't be back for awhile," he lied. Well it wasn't entirely untrue, he thought, it was just a week earlier that he had that conversation, and she didn't have anything useful to say, anyhow. "If I wanted to talk to her, it was last night or nothing. Lives in Casa del Norte."

Kathryn raised her eyebrows in appreciation. "Well paid, I take it."

"I suppose. A foreign-language expert, works in the international division. Turned out she barely knew either of them. Wasn't any help."

"It took you till ten o'clock to find that out?"

Dave shrugged. "Didn't get to see her until almost nine."

"Well, what did she say?"

He again withdrew his notebook from his pocket and flipped it open. So far, he had not made eye contact with Kathryn since she came in. "Said Lawrence Lancaster was acknowledged by pretty much everyone as a nice guy. Workaholic, but everyone liked him. Had a slightly different take on Mrs. Lancaster, though."

"Like what?" Kathryn asked. She wondered if he was sick. She knew something was wrong but knew better than to ask again. Dave would only talk about something that bothered him when he was ready.

"Well, she said she doesn't know Mrs. Lancaster, so she was only passing along rumors. But, according to the rumors, her behavior is pretty erratic. One day she's aloof but pleasant, the next she's irritable, withdrawn, and bitchy. Apparently, she's a bitch more often than not."

Kathryn's eyebrows raised with interest. "I don't know that it means anything, but that sort of erratic behavior and personality shifts are pretty common with abused women," she said. "Anything else?"

"Not really, let's see, oh yeah, a gold digger. Some of the staff seem to think she married him for his money. God knows he has plenty to go around."

"You mean, had. I'd say she's the one with plenty of money now, wouldn't you?"

He grunted, still not making eye contact. "Anyway, maybe I'll pick up something when I interview the secretaries."

"How about the personnel files on the Lancasters?"

"Yeah, those were the first two I asked for. The personnel guy said he'd have to clear it with his boss. He thinks they might want them subpoenaed just to protect themselves, even if they're cleaned up. Said he'll let me know as soon as they get it sorted out with their lawyer. I can start on the others and look at those last."

"I suppose so, but don't overlook them, especially hers. There should be family information in there, you know, next of kin, emergency notification, that sort of thing. If she was a battered wife, she may have confided in a sister or her mother. Even a brother, but that's less likely."

For the first time since Dave had entered her office, he met her eyes. His voice was hard. "Damn right. If some guy was beating up my sister on a regular basis, husband or not, I'd kick his ass for sure."

"So would most brothers, I imagine. That's why she probably wouldn't tell him. The last thing a battered woman wants is to make her abuser angrier than he already is."

"I suppose. Anyway, that's all I've got for now. This morning I'm going to talk to the neighbors around their house, out to about a three-block radius. Walt talked to the nearest neighbors, but someone farther away might have seen or heard something. Pretty slim, but it's about all I've got."

"Slim ain't the word," Kathryn answered. "It's downright emaciated."

"Anything more from Building 46A?" he asked, referring to the Department of Justice lab.

"What more is there? They couldn't lift any more prints from the cartridges. The gun and the magazine were clean. I can't see it matters, anyway. She admits to shooting him, so who the hell cares if her prints are all over everywhere. It wouldn't change anything."

"What about the medical exams?"

"Judge ordered a physical exam and full-body X rays. Denied the psychological testing, but I expected that. The physical is scheduled for late this afternoon at County General."

"That'll help."

"I don't know," she said. "The presence of fresh bruises or injuries, or old healed injuries which would show up in the X rays, might help establish that she *was* battered, especially if they appear in typical abuse patterns. But the absence of injuries doesn't prove she *wasn't*. Who's to say he didn't hit her where it wouldn't break a bone? I'm not sure we're going to get much help."

"Okay, listen," he suggested. "I'll call back over to Lancaster and Young. I'll ask around and see if she was especially close to anyone, maybe one of the secretaries that wasn't on my list. If I find someone, maybe I could schedule an interview away from the office. Go to their house tonight after work. I'll let you know."

"Sounds like a good idea. Try to call me before ten o'clock, though." As an afterthought, she said, "You all right? You don't look too good."

Just as Dave started to rise from the chair, Nancy, the receptionist, stuck her head around the corner of Kathryn's door. "Can I interrupt?"

122

"Sure," Kathryn answered. "Do you need me?"

"Not you. Dave. There's a guy at the front counter from Jerry's Floral. Says he has a delivery for you. He's got a dozen roses. I never get roses."

Dave jumped from his chair like he'd been shot from a cannon. "Gotta be a mistake. Who the hell'd be sending me flowers?" He laughed nervously. "I'll take care of it. Talk to you later, Kate."

Kathryn stopped him before he got to the door. "Dave," she asked softly, "what's going on?"

"Nothing, really. Gotta be a mistake, like I said," he answered and rushed out.

"I hope so," Kathryn said to herself.

The card Dave Granz withdrew from the envelope stuck in the flowers from Jerry's Floral read: "Thank you for last night. I love you. Check your voice mail." It was signed simply JS.

Cautiously, he picked up the phone on his cluttered desk, dialed his own extension—2815—and entered his security code—5735. A computer-generated officious machine-woman advised him, "You have four messages: Press One to listen; Two to erase; Three to save. Press Nine to exit."

Careful that the speaker phone was deactivated, he punched One.

Beep. "Granz, Earheart. Where the fuck are you? Call me."

"Tuesday, 4:50 P.M.," Machine Lady droned.

Beep. "Mr. Granz, this is Lou at West End Ford reminding you that we have your . . . your Explorer scheduled for service tomorrow morning. If you need a ride to work, please let the service technician know when you drop off your car. Thank you." Shit, Dave thought, missed another one.

"Tuesday, 5:17 P.M."

Beep. Then a sultry female voice with a Mexican accent. "Buenos tardes, David. I know this has all happened so quickly that you are afraid. I am too. Please call me as soon as you get to work tomorrow morning."

"Tuesday, 11:45 P.M."

Beep. "Good morning. I guess you aren't in your office yet. I sent a gift to your office. I hope you don't mind. Call me as soon as you get this."

"Wednesday, 7:37 A.M."

Beep. "That was your last message. To save your messages, press Three. To erase your messages, press Two. After you have made your selection, press Nine. Thank you."

"Fuck you, you robot," Dave shouted, pressing Two, to erase.

His phone rang immediately. It was Kathryn. "Dave, maybe it's none of my business, but you know how direct I am. Who sent you the flowers?"

"Just a grateful victim, Kate. Nobody important."

She swallowed hard. "Dave, we work almost all our cases together. Flowers for you but none for me?"

He laughed nervously. "Kate, am I being interrogated?"

She couldn't say anything for a minute and didn't think she wanted to hear his explanation. "Of course not. I'm sorry I asked." She dropped the phone into the cradle harder than necessary and stared out the window for several minutes before returning her attention to the case file on her desk.

17

DAVE GRANZ INTERVIEWED TWO DOZEN NEIGH-
bors in the Lancasters' neighborhood, where neighbors minded their own business and expected
everyone else to do the same. He found no one who
knew the Lancasters well enough to add any new
information to his investigation.

He returned to his office just before five o'clock and
dialed up his phone messages.

"David, it's me. Are you upset? Perhaps I should
not have sent the flowers to your office. I know you
like to keep your personal life separate from your
work. It was thoughtless of me. I apologize. Please call
me." The message was time-stamped just before 11
A.M. The second message was recorded at six minutes
past one. "Are you avoiding me? Maybe you are
embarrassed. Don't be, please! I'm waiting to hear
from you."

The third and final message was short and to the
point. "If you are avoiding me, please stop. Call me."
It arrived at 4 P.M.

Dave grabbed the phone and dialed Lawrence and
Young. Another voice-mail system answered. Her
outgoing message went as follows: "Hello, you have
reached the office of Julia Soto. Due to illness, I left

the office early today. Please leave a message, and I shall return your call as quickly as possible." Pause. "If this is Inspector David Granz calling, please call me at my home tonight."

Immediately, he dialed her home number, which likewise greeted him with an electronic answer. He left a terse message telling her he would return her call later from home. After wrapping up a few chores and slamming things around in frustration, he left the office. He stuck his head cautiously into Kathryn Mackay's office to say good-night; she was still hunched over her desk.

"Oh, Dave," she said. "Are you feeling better?" What she wanted to say, but would not, was: If you don't tell me where those damn flowers came from, I'll never see you again, you S.O.B.

"No, I'm not. I think I'll turn in early tonight and try again tomorrow. I'll fill you in on what I did this afternoon first thing tomorrow. Is that okay?"

"Sure, no problem. Dave, I'm worried about you. Are you sure you're okay?"

"Yeah, I'm fine, Kathryn. Really."

She looked at him skeptically but knew to not press the issue. "Okay, but take care of yourself." She wanted desperately to get up and take him into her arms and ask what was going wrong between them, but she knew she could not.

He took the stairs to the ground floor, exited through the large double doors on the parking-lot end of the building, and walked to his car, which was parked in a red zone in front of the building with "Police Vehicle" written on a business card lying on the dashboard. As he unlocked the door to the Explorer, he spotted a pink envelope under the windshield wiper.

The greeting card was mildly aromatic. Before opening it, he started the Explorer and pulled into his assigned parking space. He opened the envelope and removed a pink, scented greeting card with blue flowers scrolled around the outer edge. The transparent, ivory-colored rice-paper cover was cut out in the center of the card, revealing the words "Thinking of You" in gold script.

Inside, the card was devoid of a printed message.

In blue ink, it was signed simply, "Julia."

"Hello?" She answered on the first ring.

Jesus, he thought, she must be sitting on the damned phone. "Julia? Dave."

"Oh, David, I am glad to hear from you. I was worried."

"Julia, what's going on? This has to stop."

"Stop? I do not know what you mean. What has to stop?"

"The phone calls, Julia! The phone calls and the flowers and the damn notes. All of it."

"Please do not be profane, David." Her voice changed perceptibly. "It is not necessary. I can understand you perfectly well."

"I'm sorry," he answered, trying to calm himself. "Last night I told you I needed to think about all this and work things out. I told you I'd call you in a day or two. Maybe we made a mistake getting so involved so fast. If so, I'm sorry."

"*We* did not make a mistake. *I* did not make a mistake. If you are now sorry for what we did, that is your problem. I did not make a mistake." She paused before continuing. "David, if you believe you can come back into my life after all these years and take advantage of me, only to abandon me again, then you are very much mistaken. In that case, you have made a mistake, as you say."

Dumbfounded, Dave could hardly speak. "Wha . . . Julia, what are you talking about, abandon you? Again?!"

"You know what I mean, David. You were not there when I needed you. Now you expect to drop into my life, make love to me like I am a whore, then walk away. I will not permit that. I will tell her about you and me."

"Her? Her? What the fuck do you mean, HER?"

"Stop swearing David, or I will hang up the phone. You will be very sorry if I do that, I promise you. I called your office several times. After getting only your voice mail repeatedly, I called your receptionist."

"Julia, for Christ's sake—I'm sorry—you did what?"

"I talked to your receptionist. I told her I needed to reach you very badly on a personal matter. I asked her if maybe I could talk to your girlfriend, that I couldn't remember her name. She connected me with Kathryn Mackay's extension."

"You talked with Kathryn? What did you say to her?"

"I didn't talk to her. I hung up when she answered. She sounded very nice."

"I'll say this once more. Maybe we made a mistake getting so involved so fast. I need time. Meanwhile, don't call me. Do you understand?"

"Yes, I understand very well." Julia Soto hung up her phone and did not answer it again, although it rang repeatedly.

The next morning Dave found his Ford Explorer, which was parked outside, resting on four flat tires. A vandal had slashed them and broken the windshield. On the windshield was a scented pink greeting card with blue flowers scrolled around the edge. It was not signed.

18

LATE FRIDAY NIGHT—ACTUALLY 12:45 A.M. Saturday morning—Walt Earheart's phone rang, waking him out of a sound sleep. Unceremoniously, he growled into the receiver, "Earheart. It's the middle of the damn night. This had better be the state lottery calling with good news."

"No, sir, it isn't," dispatcher Laurie Sweeney answered. "It's County Comm. About fifteen minutes ago a woman walked into the emergency room at County General Hospital and reported that she was just raped in the living room of her home. They transferred her to the Sexual Assault Nurse Examiner room. There's an advocate from the rape crisis center with her now. We need you to respond."

"Aw, shit! Okay, I'll be on my way in twenty minutes. Anybody else been called?"

"Yes, sir, the on-call SANE nurse is on the way. One of them's on call twenty-four hours a day. She'll probably be there before you. She said for you to ring the buzzer, and she'll let you in."

Dressed in faded Levi's, a Sierra Pale Ale T-shirt, and beat-up Sperry Topsiders with no socks, Earheart approached the electronically controlled security door that accessed the SANE exam room. A small wire-reinforced opaque window, about a foot square, was cut into the door at eye level, and a buzzer button was set into the door frame. He punched the button briefly.

Access to the exam room was through a private entrance from the hospital's emergency room, or an unmarked exterior door. The exterior door opened to a secluded but brightly lighted, secured section of the hospital parking lot. It served SANE personnel and designated medical staff only.

Momentarily a female voice asked through the intercom, "Yes?"

"Lieutenant Walt Earheart, sheriff's office."

The security door swung open. "Hello, Walt, surprised to see you here," said Jane Ostheimer. Jane had been a SANE for almost a decade. "I'm taking the calls for my scheduled sexual-assault investigator. She was called away on a family emergency."

"Can't remember the last time I got called out on a rape," Earheart said. "I may need you to take the lead."

Earheart followed Ostheimer into a small waiting room that was set aside for spouses, mates, friends, and family of the victims, who are often severely traumatized by the assault of their loved ones.

While small, the waiting room was carpeted and decorated with comfortable chairs and a sofa. The walls were painted pastel green. Judiciously placed coffee and end tables offered innocuous reading material.

A single door led from the waiting room to the special exam room, which was subdivided into three distinct areas.

The first, into which the waiting room opened, contained spartan and utilitarian equipment available primarily to law enforcement: a gray metal desk, a chair, a telephone, a modem jack, and a file cabinet. It was used by police officers and prosecutors to conduct interviews and write reports.

Investigating officers are frequently male, and their presence, as well as the business they must conduct, is often disturbing to the victim, so the law-enforcement room was totally segregated from the medical area. Earheart's detectives had spent many hours in this room.

A second, partitioned area adjoined the exam cubicle itself in which medical staff—nurse examiners and doctors—dictated and wrote their notes and reports relative to the examinations and prepared evidence.

The medical-exam room occupied the innermost portion of the facility. For the victim's emotional well-being, it was as tastefully and soothingly decorated as possible. The institutional surroundings and imposing array of medical equipment confronting the victim were, for the most part, unfamiliar and intimidating. Their impact was softened somewhat by deeply upholstered chairs, plush carpeting, flowered wallpaper, and pastoral art work on the walls.

"Have you begun the exam yet?" Earheart asked.

"I just got here myself," Ostheimer answered. "The advocate has been with her since she was transferred here from the E.R."

"Do we know her name?" Earheart asked.

"Not yet," Ostheimer said. "Let's see what we can find out before I get started."

The nurse examiner entered first and motioned for Earheart to follow.

"Hello. My name is Jane Ostheimer," she said. "I'm a nurse. I'd like to talk with you about what happened and examine you, if you don't mind. If it would be okay with you, Lieutenant Earheart here would like to ask you a few questions. Do you feel up to it?"

The woman sat curled up in the upholstered chair. Although she was no longer hysterical, she was in obvious distress.

"Yes, I believe I can speak with you." She looked at Ostheimer. "Will he . . . does he need to be here when you . . . examine me?"

"No, of course not. When the examination is conducted, he will be in the other room. And your advocate will be with you the whole time, I promise. Will that be all right?"

"Yes, thank you." Looking at Earheart, she said, "I did not mean to offend you, but . . . nothing like this has ever happened to me before." She sobbed uncontrollably for a moment, then pulled herself together.

Earheart knew that rape victims often blame themselves for what happened. It is one of the most common reactions and must be dealt with carefully. "I'm not offended." Earheart replied gently. "You have nothing to be ashamed of. You have done nothing wrong. Any time you want me to leave, or you need to stop, just say so."

He pulled a tiny cassette recorder from his jacket pocket and set it on a small table. "Do you mind if I record our conversation?" he asked. "That way I'm sure I don't forget anything later."

"No, I don't mind."

As usual, he asked simple questions first: the victim's name, address, phone number, birth date, and so forth. She stated there was no one she wanted notified.

Then he made a notation in his notebook, and asked, "Ma'am, do you know the man who raped you?"

"Well, yes, but, I . . ." She looked about wildly, imploring the nurse to help her. It wasn't necessary.

Jane Ostheimer interjected immediately, "No, no, that doesn't mean we don't believe you, or that it's all right for him to rape you. It's just that we need a place to start. If you know who he is, it will be much easier to apprehend him."

"I understand. Yes, I know him."

"Do you know his name, or is he someone you've only seen?" Earheart asked.

"Yes."

"I'm sorry, ma'am, yes what? Do you know his name?"

She hesitated. "Sí. Yes. I'm sorry. Spanish is my first language, and when I am upset, sometimes I revert."

"That's all right. Do you need a translator?"

She smiled briefly. "No, that's what I do for a living. I will be more careful."

"How well do you know this man, ma'am?"

"I . . . we . . . I know him very well. We were . . . involved. But, I stopped seeing him only a few nights ago. He was angry."

"Will you tell me the man's name, please?" Earheart asked, pen poised over the notebook.

She didn't answer.

"Ma'am?"

"I am sorry, I cannot."

"Can you tell me why?" he asked.

She looked at Jane Ostheimer. "May I speak with you alone?" she asked.

When Earheart departed to get coffee, she confided to the nurse. "I'm frightened. What will the examination be like?" She began to sob quietly.

Ostheimer placed her strong arm around the woman's shoulders. "It sounds worse than it is, I promise. I must examine your vagina and cervix to determine if you have been injured and require medical attention. Of course, I am also looking to recover foreign materials, such as semen if it is present. Do you know if he ejaculated inside you?"

"I think so. Yes, I know he did. Will it hurt?"

"No, it's no different from being examined by a gynecologist. First, I'll dilate you with a warm speculum. You are familiar with them?"

"Yes."

"Good. It may pinch just a bit. Then, I will use cotton swabs to obtain samples for testing, to see if there is semen present. I will also swab you with a blue dye called toluidine blue. It will come off with your next shower."

"What is that for?"

"Well, sometimes with forced intercourse, small tears and lacerations occur that aren't visible to the naked eye and that aren't normally present with consensual sex. If lacerations are present in the vulva, the dye interacts with special skin cells found there, and the lacerations show up as dark lines, which I will then photograph with that camera there." She pointed to a Pentax MX mounted on a tripod.

Panic crossed the victim's dark face, and her eyes grew large and round. "You will photograph my . . . my . . . my vagina? Who would see them?"

"For now, only the police and the attorney assigned to prosecute the case. Usually, that's a woman named Kathryn Mackay. She's the best prosecutor in the office, and she helped set up this facility. You'd like her. I can arrange to introduce you to her, if you want."

She shook her head. "No, not now. Would they show these photographs in court if there is a trial?"

"Maybe. I'm not sure, but Ms. Mackay could tell you about that."

"You say the blue dye will not show injuries if sex is, how did you put it, consensual?"

"Sometimes, but not always. Did you resist when he raped you?"

"I was afraid. I did what he wanted."

Ostheimer felt she had entered the realm of the police investigation and was reluctant to continue without Earheart present.

"Have I answered your questions about the examination? If so, I'd like to have Lieutenant Earheart come back in so you don't have to tell your story more than once. It's hard enough on you as it is. Is that all right with you?"

She nodded her assent. Earheart returned, and Ostheimer filled him in on what the victim told her.

"Of course you were afraid. That's perfectly understandable," he told her kindly. "Did the man hit you?"

"I was afraid he would kill me. I wish he had," she sobbed. When she regained control, she added, "He had a gun."

"A gun? He threatened you with a gun? Ma'am, can you tell me exactly what happened, the best you can recall? Start from the very beginning, please. How did this man happen to be at your home?"

"I told you that we were once involved. As I said, I had decided to stop seeing him only a few nights ago. When I told him we could no longer be . . . that I no longer wished to be intimate, he became very angry. I had never seen him like that."

"When was that, ma'am, that you told him you no longer wanted to be involved with him?" Earheart asked.

"It was, let's see, it was last Tuesday evening at my home. He was there on business. I felt it was a good time to tell him."

"Did he threaten or hit you Tuesday evening?"

"No, but he was very upset, as I said. When he left, I did not believe I would see him again. When he left, he called me . . . a name."

Earheart encouraged her gently. "A name? What name did he call you?"

The woman appeared near panic. "He called me a . . . a . . . oh, God, I am not what he called me. I am not a whore, as he said," she uttered between sobs.

"Ma'am, I know this is hard for you. You said you had been intimate with this man. By that you mean you were having a sexual relationship with him? Consensual sex?"

"Yes. We were involved four or five years ago. We cared for each other deeply, but he took advantage of me by promising to marry me. When I learned he did not intend to do so, I stopped seeing him. Later, we started seeing each other again. He told me he loved me and once more promised to marry me. Once more, I was deceived."

"Go on, please. Take your time."

"When I discovered this second deception, I knew I must never see him again. When he was at my home last Tuesday, I told him of my decision. He asked why, and I told him I am an honorable woman. I cannot be intimate with a man whom I do not intend to marry. That is when he called me a whore. He told me that . . ." She sobbed, unable to continue.

Earheart waited until she collected herself, then nodded encouragement.

"He called me at work this morning—He apologized. He said he wanted to tell me in person and asked that I see him for only a few minutes last night. Although I knew better, I agreed. We had been so . . . so close."

"So he came to your home last night. Was it after work?"

"It was rather late. He said he had business and that he could not come earlier. He did not arrive at my home until about nine o'clock. When he first arrived, he was very polite. He apologized and said he would not contact me again after that. Then, he . . . he . . ."

"He what, ma'am?"

"He asked me if we could, if I would, if he could make love to me once more. He said it was for old times' sake."

"Did you agree?"

She shouted her answer, "No, of course not. I told him I am no whore. Then he said I had been his whore for a long time. He removed a twenty-dollar bill from his wallet and threw it on the floor. He said, 'There, take that, you whore, it's the least I can do. It's less than it costs to take you out to dinner.'"

"What happened then?" Earheart asked.

"I told him to leave. Then he became very angry. He removed his gun and set it on the table beside the sofa. I was afraid."

"Did he threaten to shoot you?"

"He did not say so, but I knew what he meant."

"Okay, ma'am, then what happened?"

She looked at Jane Ostheimer. "This is so embarrassing. I don't know if I can say."

"Go ahead," Ostheimer encouraged her. "I know this is difficult, but the only way the police can arrest this man is if you tell them exactly what happened."

"Yes, I understand. Then he stood up and unbuttoned his pants. We were sitting on my sofa. And he said, 'Come on, suck on this.' He said . . . he said . . . 'Give me some head. You can keep the twenty dollars, you whore.'"

"Okay, then what happened?"

"Before I knew what was happening, he grabbed my hair and pulled me from the sofa. He threw me against the wall. I think he hit me in the stomach, but I am not certain. Yes, I am sure, he hit me in the stomach, hard, with his fist."

"Jesus," Earheart said softly to himself, then to her, "Go on, please, if you can. Then what happened?"

"I think I must have blacked out. When I came to, I was on my back on the floor, and he was ripping off my clothes.

"I shouted, but it didn't help. He hit me again and again. I tried to crawl away from him, but he came after me. All the time, I thought he was crazy. He kept saying over and over, 'Twenty dollars, fucking bitch, twenty dollars, fucking whore.'"

Violent sobs racked her body. After several minutes, she regained control. No one spoke.

"I wanted him to stop hitting me, so I told him if he would not hit me again, I would do what he wanted."

Earheart asked, "You offered to have sex with him if he stopped hitting you? What did he say?"

"He said . . . oh, God, this is so hard. I'm so ashamed to say these words."

Before Earheart could offer encouragement, she said, "No, that's all right. I can continue. When I told him I would do what he wanted if he would not hit me again, he said, 'Fucking-A you will.' He got me up on the sofa, no, on the loveseat, and told me, 'Lie down and spread your fucking legs, you bitch. And lift up your ass.' "

Under control now and needing no encouragement, she continued, "Then he entered me and . . ."

"He penetrated your vagina?" Ostheimer asked. This must be established with certainty.

"Yes. He penetrated me."

"Then what happened?" Earheart asked.

"When he finished, he grabbed me around the throat. He said, 'You'd better keep your mouth shut about this.' "

"Those were his exact words?"

"No."

"What exactly did he say?"

"He said, 'If you breathe one fucking word of this, I'll come back and kill you.' Then he left."

"Is that when you went to the hospital?" Earheart asked.

"No. I lay there for about half an hour. I did not know what to do. I knew that the police would not believe me over him. So I ran a bath. Hot. Then, I thought, I cannot be treated as if I am a whore. I am an honorable woman. I cannot allow this man to treat me in this way. So, I drove myself to the hospital."

Almost in unison, Earheart and Ostheimer said, "You took a bath!?"

"No, I never got into the tub. I changed my mind. I got dressed in clean clothes. That was when I went to the hospital."

"And, ma'am, when this man threatened to come back and kill you, did he point the gun at you?"

"No."

"What did you mean when you said he threatened you with his gun?"

"He looked at the gun which was on the table beside the sofa. He smiled. I knew what he meant."

"Have you seen this man with a gun before?" Earheart asked.

"Yes. He always has it with him."

"Do you know why this man who raped you carries a gun?"

"He uses it in his work."

Earheart felt a sense of dark foreboding grow in his subconscious. "Ma'am, why does this man carry a gun? What sort of work does he do?"

"He . . . he . . ." she looked pleadingly at Jane Ostheimer. "Do I have to say? I am so afraid of what he might do to me. And no one will believe my word against his."

"Ma'am, is this man—"

"He is a police officer. Oh, God, I am so ashamed. I am afraid and ashamed."

Shocked, Earheart asked, "Ms. Soto, what is this man's name—this police officer who raped you?"

"David Granz," she replied reluctantly.

Ostheimer locked eyes with Earheart for a moment. Then, touching him gently on the arm and leading him toward the interview room, she said, "Lieutenant, we need to get on with the exam. I'll get with you as soon as we're through."

Two and a half hours later, Ostheimer walked into the interview room carrying a sealed forensic evidence box.

"The toluidine blue didn't pick up any injuries," she said. "But that's frequently the result we see where the victim submits to sexual intercourse because of threats or some other kind of intimidation."

"What else?" asked Earheart.

"I collected semen and examined the sperm. It was nonmotile."

A look of relief passed over Earheart's face. "That means the semen's not the rapist's, right?"

"Walt, I know you and Dave are friends, but don't get your hopes up. Motile sperm is evidence of recent penetration and ejaculation, but the absence of motility is not significant. Sperm can become immobile in the vagina within thirty minutes. According to Ms. Soto, she was raped more than two hours ago."

"How much semen did you recover, Jane?" Earheart asked.

"There's enough seminal fluid for a DNA profile of the rapist," she answered.

19

"WHO IS IT?" WAS THE SHOUTED RESPONSE from behind the closed door of Dave Granz's apartment.

Walt Earheart took a deep breath and answered, "Dave, it's me, Walt." Had Dave been suspicious, the fact that Earheart used both their first names would have alerted him to trouble. It was 3:45 A.M. The rape examination of Julia Soto was concluded, and Earheart had driven her home.

Dave opened the door and stood there in green Jockey shorts. "What's up? Did something break in the Lancaster case? Let me get some clothes on."

"Hang on, Dave. Where've you been this evening?" Earheart asked.

"Why, did you try to call me earlier? I had a little problem on my mind. Went for a drive, then walked on the beach. Did you beep me? I had my pager with me."

"Dave, something has come up that I need your help with. I think it must be a mistake somehow. I don't know how to do this, so I'm just going to come right out with it. Do you know a woman named Julia Soto?"

Dave blanched, answering his friend's question nonverbally. "Yeah, I know her. She's nuts. She's been harassing me all week. I can't prove it, but she's the one who slashed the tires on my car and broke the windows. Jesus, why? Did you catch her trying to torch it or something?"

"No, nothing like that. Have you ever been to her home?"

"What's going on here, Walt? Of course I've been to her home. She lives at Casa del Norte. I interviewed her there in connection with the Lancaster case. Why?"

"Have you ever had sex with her? Jeez, Dave, I just took her home from County General. She was raped last night."

"Oh, no! Are you serious? Do you know who the

son of a . . . Jesus, Walt, are you saying what I think you are?"

"She said it was you. Said you raped her last night at her home. I'm sorry, Dave."

Dave partially walked, partially stumbled, and partially fell away from the door, then collapsed on the couch in the apartment's living room, which adjoined the entryway.

"This can't be right, Walt. She's lying. I haven't seen her since last Tuesday. I wasn't with her last night and damn sure didn't rape her."

"Have you ever had sex with Julia Soto?" Earheart asked.

Dave didn't answer. "Walt, am I under arrest?"

"Not yet. I don't know."

"What is it you want from me, then?"

"We were hoping you would agree to submit voluntarily to a physical examination. Provide samples," Earheart said. "They recovered semen from her vagina and pubic hair from her sofa. That's where she said it happened. On the loveseat in her living room. If it wasn't you, the tests will prove that, and we can find out what's going on."

"What do you mean, we? 'We were hoping' . . . you want me to submit to a suspect exam? Walt!"

"I talked to Benton and the Sheriff. If you consent to be examined and provide samples, you won't be taken into custody. Otherwise . . ."

"Okay, okay, let me think a minute." An experienced police officer, Dave Granz knew that persons who have been placed under arrest do not have the right to refuse an examination for the purpose of collecting evidence. A suspect in custody must provide evidence such as hair, dried secretions, foreign materials, and even blood. If he did not submit voluntarily, he would be arrested, and the result would be the same. Besides, he thought, what did he have to lose?

"I don't have any choice, do I? All right, I'll submit. Right now! I want to do it right now. And, Walt, I'm not making any more statements or answering any more questions. If you want to ask me any more questions, I'll have to call an attorney. Agreed?"

"Absolutely, thanks. And Dave, I'm your friend. You're doing the right thing."

"Fuck you, Earheart. Some friend. Come in with me while I get dressed. You'll want to be sure I don't change my goddamn skivvies."

Walt Earheart pulled his Chevy Blazer into a reserved parking space behind the twenty-four-hour drop-in medical clinic usually referred to as the "Quick Doc Box" by law enforcement.

Dr. Roger Mayweather, a board-certified acute-care physician met them at the rear door to the clinic and led them to his private office. He and Dave Granz were well acquainted. No one spoke until they were seated.

"Walt. Dave." Mayweather looked at one, then the other. "I can't say I'm pleased to see either of you. Hal Benton called and asked for my help on this."

Turning to Dave, he said, "Dave, this is difficult for Walt and me. I can't imagine how it must be for you. You've seen these before, but it's not the same when it is you who is being examined. I'll tell you what I'm doing every step of the way. If there is anything you don't understand, tell me and I'll explain. Okay?"

Dave was perilously close to tears. "Okay, Roger. Let's get this done. Walt, could you stay?"

"You bet. I'll be here." Earheart made the promise as a friend, although established procedures require that during sexual-assault suspect exams, a law-enforcement officer remain with the suspect at all times.

Dave was asked, and agreed, to sign a consent form authorizing the search. The consent is provided on an OCJP (Office of Criminal Justice Planning) MEDICAL REPORT—SUSPECTED SEXUAL ASSAULT, Form OCJP 923. It was a catch-22, he thought. If he did not consent, he would be arrested. If he did consent, it might lead to his arrest. He signed the form. It was the most traumatic event in Dave Granz's life.

Mayweather handed Dave a hospital gown and asked, "Would you remove your clothing, please, and hand them to Lieutenant Earheart one article at a time?"

Earheart inspected each article of clothing, including Dave's undershorts, carefully looking for any rips, tears, or the presence of any identifiable foreign materials, such as fiber, hair, grass, sand, blood, or seminal fluid.

Each article was placed into a plastic evidence bag, sealed, dated, time recorded, and signed by Earheart. Later, they would be sent to the DOJ lab at 46A Research Drive for further examination.

Mayweather then placed a blood pressure monitor on Dave's upper right arm and measured his blood pressure. He also measured and recorded his pulse, temperature, and respiration rate. The doctor led him to another part of the exam room, within easy view of Earheart, and measured and recorded his height, weight, eye color, and hair color. He noted that Dave was right-handed. Each item was recorded in the proper part of OCJP 923.

Although the nature of the reported rape did not indicate its necessity, Mayweather placed Dave's hands one at a time under a desk light and carefully collected fingernail scrapings into a tiny plastic bag, which was documented and sealed identically to the clothing bags. It was the cleanest his nails had been in months.

A general physical examination followed. Before he began, Mayweather asked, "How are you holding up, Dave? You haven't spoken since I began."

"I'm all right. Let's just get this over with, okay?" he answered tersely. Irrespective of the outcome or manner in which the exam was conducted, and even knowing he was only doing his job, Dr. Roger Mayweather would never again be looked on as a friend.

"All right," Mayweather responded a little testily himself.

They had been in the examination room for slightly more than an hour. Sunrise in July occurs a few minutes after 5 A.M. The sky outside, visible through the exam-room window which faced Coronado Avenue, was brightening. Everyone's nerves were frayed to the limit.

"Remove your gown, please," Mayweather directed.

When Dave complied, the doctor recorded his

general physical appearance, noting the absence of any apparent indicators of drug or alcohol use, such as odor, needle puncture marks, pupillary reaction, slurred speech, or impaired coordination.

The coordination test was the "heel-to-toe-walk-the-white-line" test commonly known among police officers as a Roadside Sobriety Test. Dave had administered hundreds of them during his years as a uniformed patrol officer. He passed with no difficulty.

Form OCJP 923 is a six-page form, printed vertically on both sides of three 8½ × 11″ sheets of paper. Section E.7, at the lower two-thirds of page three, contains four rendered drawings of the human body, one from each side and one each from the front and back. At the bottom is a drawing of a human head.

This part of the form is used to indicate the location and nature of identifying marks such as scars, tattoos, birthmarks, injuries, dried or moist secretions or stains.

A long-wave ultraviolet light called a Woods Lamp was passed over Dave's entire body to locate secretions or stains that are invisible to the naked eye.

"Anything?" Walt Earheart asked.

"Fuck you, Earheart," Dave responded.

Mayweather shook his head. "No indications of staining. No scratches, bites, or other injuries. Not even a tattoo. Not much to write about. What's that scar on the inside of your right ankle from, Dave?"

"Dog bite. When I was about eleven, I was picking berries to earn a little spending money, and the owner's dog bit me. Took about twelve stitches."

"I've got to take three blood samples," the doctor said. Right or left arm?"

"Left," Dave answered.

Mayweather placed Dave's arm on a table, palm up, tied off his upper arm with an elastic tube, and slapped the inside of the elbow gently to raise the vein. It wasn't necessary. Dave donated blood regularly and his veins were easy to hit. His arm was swabbed with a nonalcoholic solution to avoid elevating the blood-alcohol level, and the needle slid painlessly into the arm.

Mayweather released the elastic. "I need three samples, Dave, bear with me," he said as he filled one vial, placed a gray top on the tube, and drew blood into the second.

"Three? Why so damn many?"

"One for blood-alcohol/toxicology. That's the one I just put the gray top on.

"This one," he said, removing the second vial and capping it with a yellow top, "is for blood typing.

"The third one is for syphilis serology. It gets a red top.

"There, all done. Hold this cotton ball on your arm for a minute or so."

"Open, please," Mayweather requested. When Dave complied, the doctor used a pair of sterile tweezers to place a gauze square under his tongue, left it there a moment to become saturated with saliva, then removed it and placed it into an evidence bag.

"We're almost done, Dave. How are you holding up?" Mayweather asked. "We could stop for awhile if you want."

"Anyone up for coffee?" Earheart asked with more spirit than he felt. "Jesus, it's almost seven already."

"Not for me, thank you," Mayweather said.

"Fuck you, Earheart," Dave said.

Earheart's patience was severely tested by the strain of the situation, but he knew that no matter how badly he felt, his friend needed compassion and understanding, not cynicism. "Granz, I'm getting a little worried about your vocabulary," he answered kindly.

"Fuck you, Earheart."

Head, body, and facial hair samples were collected next. Fifteen of each hair were plucked, not cut, since for DNA testing to be effective, the hair root, or follicle, must be obtained. For each type of hair, samples from various locations are obtained, so they represent the total range of length and color present.

"Fuck you, too, Mayweather," Dave snarled, more serious than joking. "That hurt. How the hell do women pluck their eyebrows every day. Bunch of masochists!"

After recording the samples taken on OCJP 923, Part E, Item #11, Mayweather looked at Dave apologetically. "This is the bad part, Dave. Are you ready?"

"Say what? The bad part? Lemme see if I've got this straight. Some guy that used to be my friend rousts me outta bed in the middle of the night and tells me some whacko accused me of raping her. He drags me out against my will, and I'm forced to submit to a physical exam. You steal my clothes, look into places no one's seen since my mother changed my last diaper, poke holes in me, suck out enough blood to feed Count Dracula for a week, and yank out all my goddamn hair. I'd put in a claim to be reimbursed for a supply of Rogaine to grow my hair back, but that bean-counter son of a bitch in the Controller's office would reject it. Now, you tell me the bad part is yet to come? Hell, I didn't even see the firing squad arrive. What, are they loading their M-1s outside? Shit!"

"Dave, I'm sorry. You know all this is standard operating procedure. You've seen it a hundred times."

"Hell yes, I have, but those assholes were criminals, Roger. Not me!" Dave's tough facade was increasingly difficult to maintain. "Aw, Jesus, what do you need?"

"Pubic hair. And I need to inspect your genitalia."

Walt groaned audibly in sympathy—or empathy—no one could tell.

"Fuck you, Earheart," Dave said. "Okay, let's get this over with. What do I do?"

He was directed to sit on an exam table, and Mayweather placed a sheet of white paper under his bare buttocks. The doctor gently lifted and inspected Dave's penis and scrotum, noting the absence of injury, trauma, abnormalities, foreign materials, or vasectomy scars on the OCJP form.

Next, he shined the Woods Lamp on the genital area, noting the absence of fresh or dried stains on OCJP 923. Two penile swabs were obtained, which were air-dried and placed in plastic evidence bags.

"This is the last thing I need to do," Mayweather told him. "Hang in there. Almost finished."

The doctor examined Dave's pubic hair, noting that no visible secretions were present. He then gently combed it, collecting loose hair and other materials on a clean white paper, which was dumped into the last evidence bag. Walt Earheart assumed custody of all evidence, which would be logged as part of the case file.

In all, more than four hours had elapsed since Dave Granz, Earheart, and Mayweather walked into Quick Doc Box. It was almost eight-thirty on a bright, sunny July day.

In front of the clinic, Coronado Avenue was already clogged with beach traffic. Most of the cars contained young people from over the Hill, coming to the beach and boardwalk for a day of carefree summer fun.

Dave Granz wondered if there would ever be another fun day in his life. He doubted it.

"Dave? Dave?" Mayweather interrupted Dave's thoughts. "Did you bring clothes to wear home?"

"Goddamnit," Earheart growled. "I forgot all about it. My fault. Dave, gimme your keys, and I'll run out and get you something to wear."

"Fuck you, Earheart. I don't want you in my place." Turning to Mayweather, he asked, "Can I get an outside line?"

"Sure," he said, punching a button on the desk phone and handing it to Dave.

"Who are you calling?" Earheart asked.

"Morgan Nelson," Dave said.

"Nelson? Aren't you going to call Kathryn?"

"Kathryn! Oh sure, you dumb motherfucker. Exactly what a guy would do who's just been arrested for rape. Call his girlfriend and say, 'Hi hon, just thought

I'd let you know I've been busted for rape. And by the way, could you give me a ride home?' You dumb asshole, just gimme the phone so I can call Nelson. He's the only friend I have left."

20

"THANKS FOR CALLING ME, DAVE. I'LL BE there anytime you need me. Get some rest." His usual insightful self, Nelson had learned what happened and spoke only once during the drive to Dave's apartment.

Against Dave's wishes, Earheart followed. After Nelson dropped him off at nine-fifteen, Dave went into his apartment. He did not invite Earheart inside, so the sheriff's detective waited in his Blazer, which sweltered in the hot July sun.

While Earheart waited, Dave took a shower, shaved, and pressed a clean pair of beige Dockers and a matching tan shirt. He shined his shoes, put a load of clothes in the washer, ground a batch of Starbucks dark French beans, and brewed a cup of coffee in his clear glass Mason Jar look-alike mug.

When he finished his coffee, he washed the cup and last night's dirty dishes, and put his clean clothes in the dryer. Then he walked to the parking lot outside his apartment looking fresh as a daisy. Earheart sweated profusely.

"Thanks, Granz, I nearly died of hypothermia."

"Fuck you, Earheart. And, it's hyp*er*thermia."

Earheart drove Dave to the County Government Center, where the meeting was to be held.

District Attorney Hal Benton, the sheriff, his lieutenant Walter Earheart, and District Attorney Inspector David Granz sat uncomfortably around the large wood-inlay conference table in Benton's office. It was 1 P.M., Saturday, July 16, eight and a half hours into Dave Granz's nightmare.

"Dave, you are not under arrest at this time. We do not intend to ask you any questions about the charges made against you, and you should not make any voluntary statements. Do you understand?" The tone of Benton's voice was considerably more kind than the words themselves might imply.

"I understand. Then why the fuck are we here? I'm tired, sleepy, and pissed off."

Ignoring the outburst, Benton said, "It is my decision, and Sheriff Purvis agrees," Benton glanced at Purvis, who nodded, "that while you are not to be arrested at this time, you will be placed on administrative leave pending the outcome of the sheriff's investigation of these charges.

"Of course, we will conduct our own internal investigation, as well. Lieutenant Earheart will personally handle the sheriff's end of the investigation. I will appoint an investigator in our office who will report directly and only to me."

"So, exactly what the fuck does that mean?"

"It means that as of now you are on indefinite paid leave, and you are relieved of all official departmental duties until you are otherwise notified. I'm sorry, Dave, but you will need to give me your shield and ID."

"Yeah fuckin' great. The American judicial process up close and personal. Guilty until proven innocent if you're a cop instead of a goddamn drug dealer or murderer. Well, you can have the motherfucker; I don't want it anymore. With friends like the three of you, I've got all the enemies I need." Dave removed the leather basket-weave badge/ID case and tossed it across the table, where Benton picked it up and placed it in his inside coat pocket.

Benton was the only man at the table formally dressed, the others being in their weekend casuals.

"What about my piece?" Dave asked, referring to his Glock automatic service weapon. "I'm not packing; I left it at home. And while you're at it, how 'bout a pound of flesh?"

"No, the weapon's your personal property. You keep it. But, you understand that you are not authorized to carry a concealed weapon while on administrative leave?"

"Why would I want to?" he asked sarcastically. "I've been tried, convicted, and executed already."

"Not true," Purvis interjected. "If these charges are false, we'll determine that. In the meantime, you have to hang tough and trust us to do our jobs."

Dave made a derisive snorting sound through his nose. He did not answer.

Benton continued. "And, Dave, I must tell you this,

considering your tendency to, shall we say, go off in your own unique direction at times, . . . leave this alone. Do not interfere or attempt to conduct your own investigation, officially or otherwise. That will lead to serious repercussions that none of us will be able to deal with. And one more thing."

"Let me guess."

"Stay away from Julia Soto. She is afraid of you. Do NOT go near her. Understood?"

Dave heaved a heavy sigh that originated someplace deep within his soul. "Hal, has anyone told Kathryn about this?"

"Not yet. I thought I'd let you decide how to handle that, as long as you understand you are not to discuss this investigation with her. She'll be given the same order. Now, how do you want to—"

"Could you call her, Hal? Ask her if it would be all right for me to call her later. I won't discuss the investigation with her, but I can't not speak with her at all. Call me at home and tell me what she says."

"Sure, I'll call her right away and let you know. You going straight home?"

"Where else would I go?"

"Okay. Anything else?"

"Who's going to take over for me on the Lancaster case? Kathryn's only a week away from trial."

"I've already called Jim Fields. He's standing by at home. He doesn't know why you've been pulled, but I told him not to call Kathryn until I give him the word."

James Fields was the inspector who was seriously injured in a courtroom bombing some time earlier.

Although he lost his right hand, he was a top inspector and one whom Kathryn Mackay trusted almost as much as Dave.

Earheart drove Dave home down Coronado and past the beach. It was a beautiful day. Neither said a word.

After Earheart dropped him off, Dave went into his apartment, removed his freshly washed and pressed clothing, and brushed his teeth. He felt dirty all over.

He dropped and broke the rinsing glass on the tile floor. While he cleaned up the mess, he stepped on a jagged glass shard, inflicting a deep cut on his right heel.

Climbing into the shower, he turned on the hot water full blast, watching his life go down the drain along with the bloody water, and cried like a baby.

Hal Benton called at about two-thirty to tell Dave that he had caught Kathryn Mackay just as she and Emma were going out bicycling. They had spoken, Benton said, for over an hour. Kathryn was extremely upset but eventually agreed to speak with Dave. Benton advised that it would probably be a good idea to wait an hour or so before calling.

He did. In fact, it was after five o'clock before he worked up the courage to complete dialing Kathryn's number. He tried but failed at least a dozen times before she finally answered.

"Hello." She sounded as if she had been crying.

"Kathryn?"

"Dave, why?"

"I don't know, Kate. I can't talk to you about it,

except I have to tell you: I didn't do this, Kate. I don't know what's happening, but I had to speak with you and tell you that. It isn't true. I love you, Kathryn."

The lawyer in Kathryn knew she shouldn't be quick to judge Dave before getting all the facts, but her emotions got the best of her. "I know our relationship has been on the rocks, Dave, and I don't know what to think. I want to ask you . . . but Hal told me not to discuss it with you at all."

"Kate, please. All I ask is that you, of all people, trust me enough to keep an open mind until the S.O. can straighten this all out. Please, Kate, can you do that for me? I don't know how I'll get through this if I don't have anyone who believes in me."

"I'll try, Dave, I promise I will, but—"

"There's something else. I need to see Emma."

"I don't think so, Dave. I don't think that's a good idea."

"You haven't told her!"

"Of course not, but—"

"Kate, I can't just disappear from her life for no reason. That's not fair to her or to me. Let me pick her up tomorrow. We could drive over to Monterey and go to lunch or something. She's been wanting to go to the aquarium. I could take her to the aquarium, then out to lunch. I'll tell her I've got to go out of town for a couple of weeks on an investigation. It won't take longer than that to clear this mess up; it can't. Then she won't worry that I've forgotten about her. Please, Kate?"

"I don't know, I don't—"

"Kathryn, you can't be worried that I'd do anything

to hurt her! Jesus, Kate, I love her. I can't just disappear from her life like a thief."

"I'll have to think about it, Dave. Let me call you back, okay?"

"Okay, sure. I'll be here at home. Kate?"

"What?"

"I love you."

Half an hour later, Kathryn returned Dave's call. More businesslike, she said, "Dave? All right. Pick Emma up around ten. That'll give you time to spend a couple of hours at the aquarium and have a late lunch on Cannery Row. Have her home by three, okay? She has homework to do."

She paused. "Be careful with my baby, Dave. She's all I've got."

"You've got me, Kate."

"I don't think so. Not anymore." She was crying when Dave heard the line disconnect.

21

"You hungry yet?" Emma asked. They were southbound on Highway 1 in Dave Granz's Explorer approaching the power plant in a thick July morning fog.

Emma was wearing new white sandals, blue shorts,

a blue-and-white V-necked blouse and an O.P. jacket. Her feet were propped up on the dashboard so she could appreciate her brightly painted purple toenails. Her dark hair was swept back into a ponytail and tied with a red bow. She did it that way on purpose because she knew that was the way Dave liked it best.

"Didn't you eat breakfast? It's not even eleven o'clock. I didn't think you became perpetually hungry until you reached the ripe old age of ten." In truth, Dave was finally hungry himself. He had not eaten a bite since being awakened by Walt Earheart . . . was it only thirty hours ago?

"Sure." Emma made a major production of rolling her eyes up into her lids and scrunching up her face. "You know Mom. She made me eat a low-fat muffin with that yucky sugarless all-fruit stuff on it. Just because everything goes straight to her hips, she thinks everyone should suffer."

"Yeah, she's really fat and disgusting, all right," Dave joined in, visualizing Kathryn's beautiful, slender body. "If you can keep from fainting from hunger for a few minutes, I'll spring for a cinnamon roll or two at that bakery next to McFly's."

Emma clasped her hand over her chest and swooned. "Oh, be still my heart. Real food! Can I have two?"

"You can have a dozen as long as you don't tell your mother. Tell her we had a . . . let's see . . . tell her we had a no-fat, eggless, wheatless, nondairy bran muffin and skim milk for a snack. She'll love that."

Emma giggled. "She'll love it. She won't believe it, but she'll love it. It's a deal." They pinky-swore to seal the pact.

Emma looked at Dave and said seriously, "You're a lot more fun than Mom. She makes me do homework and clean my own room, and she never has time to do fun things anymore."

Although he agreed about Kathryn's time limitations, Dave couldn't let the comment stand. "Your Mom does a very important job, Em, and she does it better than just about anybody. Sometimes things happen that she has no control over. When they do, she has to deal with them, even if it means she has to break a promise to spend time with you. It doesn't mean she doesn't love you. You know that. And you should be really proud of her." Dave made a mental note to talk to Kathryn about Emma, then realized he was unlikely to have that opportunity in the near future.

By the time Dave pulled his Explorer into the parking lot at the base of the Coast Guard Pier near Cannery Row, the sun had broken through the clouds. Fisherman's Wharf and Monterey were already packed with tourists, and so was the parking lot. He bought a long-term parking permit, tossed it on the dashboard, and they trooped off toward the aquarium.

"Are you sure we can get in, Dave? There's always such a long line on weekends you need reservations weeks in advance."

"Faith, my girl," he said. "It so happens that as an upstanding member of the community I am well acquainted with the aquarium's chief of security. Badgered him on the phone last night until he promised me free passes. They'll be waiting for us at the entrance. They're under the name of 'The Shadow.' I thought it best to disguise our true identities."

Emma giggled again. "You crack me up," she told him.

They strolled past the place that rents open roadsters, under the snazzy hotel breezeway, around the corner past the redwood burl and fountain store, and past the Ghirardelli ice cream parlor. "Remember that place," Dave suggested. "After cinnamon rolls, the aquarium, and lunch, we may need a bite to eat."

At the bakery, Dave bought four huge, gooey, icing-covered cinnamon rolls. They were heated in the microwave. Along with his double espresso and her milk, they carried the food to a table around the corner and sat in the sun to eat.

Halfway through her second cinnamon roll, Emma asked, "So, Dave, why did you bring me here? And how come Mom didn't come?"

"Well, toots, it's like this. Your mom is so wrapped up in that case she's working on that she just can't get away. I asked. And I knew you wanted to see the aquarium, so . . . here we are."

Only nine, Emma sometimes startled him with her mature insight. "That's not it, Dave. I thought you were working on that case with her. And, you coulda brought us over some other time. What's going on? Tell me at once, or I'll start screaming and tell everyone I'm a starving child and you refuse to give me anything to eat."

He held up his hands. "Got me. You're right. I wanted to talk to you about something. I've been assigned to a very important case and have to go out of town for a couple of weeks. Maybe a bit longer. I wanted to tell you so you didn't think I took off without saying good-bye. That's all. Your mom just couldn't get away."

She stuffed the final bite of cinnamon roll into her mouth and wiped her chin. She checked her milk carton, which was empty. It was all a ploy. She didn't believe him for a minute, but some inner sense told her not to question. "Okay, Dave, I believe you. Sort of. What time does the aquarium open?"

Dave checked his Swiss army watch, a birthday gift from Kathryn. Past a lump in his throat, he managed to croak, "Right about now, I'd say."

As they approached the aquarium, Emma yanked Dave's shirtsleeve and pointed across the street. "Hey, Dave, that looks like a good place for lunch after the aquarium. Whadaya think?"

"I think you've got a hollow leg that all that food falls into and disappears. Aren't you full yet?"

"Stuffed. But it's a couple of hours till lunch, right?"

Their tickets, entitling them to the VIP tour, were waiting at the main door under the name, as Dave had told her, of The Shadow. Emma couldn't believe her ears when he announced himself; she pulled her jacket over her head in embarrassment.

The tour lasted two hours. Emma's favorite display was the shark tank, although she clung to Dave's hand the whole time. Dave liked to think it wasn't entirely motivated by fear. Dave's favorite was the Sea Otters.

All in all, they agreed as they walked away, it was a wonderful tour, but they needed to come back several more times to really appreciate it all. They solemnly promised each other to do so, even if Mom couldn't make it with them.

True to form, by that time Emma was famished and couldn't wait to eat. She picked a little Mexican restaurant across from the wine-tasting room. Secretly, she wanted a hamburger but knew that Dave's favorite food was Mexican. After chips and guacamole, she had a taco, plain, with the fixings on the side, and a diet Coke. Watching her weight, she declared. Dave consumed a combination plate with chile relleno, enchilada, tamale, rice and beans, and a Corona Light.

After lunch, they stopped at the Ghirardelli ice cream parlor for dessert. Emma chose a medium-size piece of pure milk chocolate, while Dave had a piece of peanut-butter fudge. On the way back to the car, Emma commented, "I don't think I'll eat for a week."

"Don't tell me you're full, already," he chided her. "I was planning to stop in Castroville for ice cream."

"No, gracias."

"I'm impressed. Are you learning Spanish in school?"

"Yes, but that's about all I know how to say."

They chatted all the way back home. When Dave pulled into the driveway of Kate's condo, he did not turn off the ignition.

Emma asked, "Aren't you coming up to say hi to Mom?"

"I'd better not, toots. She's busy. Now, give me a kiss and run in. You're late, and I happen to know you've got homework to do."

She took off her seat belt and leaned over to hug

him tight. "Thanks, Dave, I had a great day. Only next time, don't be so stingy with the food."

"Me, too," he said. "Now, git!"

As she ran toward the condo door, she turned and yelled, "Call me, okay?" Suddenly, she turned and ran back to the car. "Mom wants to see you for a minute. She wants you to come up."

After Emma had gone inside with instructions to shower and wash her hair, Kathryn listened until she heard the water start running, then closed the door and leaned against the wall of the landing. She was wearing jeans and a chambray shirt. She was solemn and her eyes were red. "Dave, I had to talk to you. I don't care what Benton says. I can't just not know. Did you rape that woman? That Julia Soto? Jesus, you interviewed her as a witness. How could you?!"

Dave felt so weak he was afraid he would fall, so he leaned against the wall for support. "I swear to God, Kathryn, I did not rape that woman. I swear. That's the truth."

Kathryn eyed him skeptically. "I don't know whether to believe you or not. I want to, but . . . Why would someone you don't even know, that you've only seen once, accuse you of raping her? It doesn't make sense. There's something you aren't telling me."

Dave looked up at the ceiling and drew in a deep breath. He slid both hands into his pants pockets so she wouldn't see them shake. He said softly, "I knew her, Kathryn. A long time ago. We were . . . involved before I met you. It didn't last very long, and I hadn't seen her for years till she surfaced at Lancaster and Young."

"Damn you, Dave! You never told me you were involved with her once. Damn you."

Another deep sigh. "I know I should have told you, but it didn't change what she said. She didn't know anything about the case at all."

"So, you just saw her that once?" Seeing the look on his face, she said very softly, almost in a whisper, "You bastard. Those flowers! You've been seeing her, haven't you?"

Dave's eyes were moist. "I saw her twice, that's all. Once was the night you invited me to watch the ball game." He added quickly, "But that's not why I turned you down that night. I didn't even know at the time that I was going to see her. She called me and invited me over. But I didn't rape her, Kathryn, I swear to God! It was just sex. And the last time I saw her was Tuesday. I wasn't anywhere near her on Friday. I can't prove it, but Friday night I went for a drive, then walked on the beach. I wasn't anywhere near Julia Soto. You've got to believe me."

Then, Kathryn walked over and stood within six inches of him and did something she had never done before and thought only happened in the movies; she slapped his face, twice, as hard as she was capable of. He made no move to defend himself.

"I deserved that, Kathryn, I don't deny it," he said, his left cheek already flame red. "But no matter what, you have to believe two things. I did not rape Julia Soto, and I love you."

Kathryn shook her head. "Dave, we're finished. You lied to me. For what it's worth, I believe you that you didn't rape her, but that doesn't change things when it comes to us. Now, I'd like you to leave."

"Kate . . ."

"Please, Dave, just leave. I don't think I can hold up much longer, and if I'm going to fall apart, I'd rather do it alone." She turned and went inside without another word, leaving Dave standing outside the door to her condominium.

22

AT 8 A.M. ON MONDAY, JULY 18, EXACTLY seven days before opening statements were scheduled in the Lancaster murder trial, Harold Benton summoned Kathryn Mackay to his office. "Good morning, Kate. Close the door and sit down, please," Benton directed.

She assumed a position in front of Benton's desk, slid her chair close, and opened the sizable Lancaster case file on his impeccably clean desk. "I'm prepared to brief you on the Lancaster investigation, advise you on the results of her court-ordered physical examinations, and discuss trial strategy," she stated without preamble.

"Whoa!" Benton said. "No good morning, how are you, how's the wife, or anything?"

"I haven't much time, Hal," she answered. "We need to make some decisions now, and I need your input."

"Close the file, Kate."

"Excuse me?"

"Close the case file, please, Ms. Mackay. Now, please!" She closed the file and leaned back in her chair but did not speak.

"Thank you," he began. "I called you in to discuss the status of the case against Anna Lancaster and the mechanics of getting Fields up to speed. But I must confess that's not all that's on my mind."

She did not respond.

"There is no basis for a continuance in the Lancaster trial, as you know, nor am I interested in any delay," he continued. "If you are not emotionally prepared, I will take it over."

She stared at him in silence and he stared back, for what seemed an eternity, until she could no longer maintain eye contact and looked down. It was the opening for which he was looking.

"Are you okay?" he asked in a fatherly voice.

"Sure. I'm ready to meet with Fields. I've organized ev—"

"I don't mean the damned case, Kate, I mean you. Are *you* okay?"

"It was hard. I spoke with Dave on Saturday. He picked Emma up on Sunday and took her to the aquarium," she said.

He leaned forward, clasped his hands together in a steeple, and held them in front of his face. "You didn't talk with him about his situation?" It was more a statement requiring affirmation than a question.

"No, of course not." It was true. They discussed his sexual conduct, not the case. "But, we needed some closure. And he wanted to let Emma know they wouldn't be seeing each other for awhile. I didn't agree at first, but I'm glad I did. It would be devastating for Emma if he simply disappeared without an explanation."

"What did he tell her?"

"That he was called out of town for awhile on an important investigation. That he'd be gone two or three weeks. That he'd call her."

"It'll take time, Kate. You have to be patient and go on with your life, no matter how hard it is."

"I know, that's what I'm doing. I'm strong. Stronger than I look. I'll get past this either way. Please don't press me on this, Hal. I spent a lot of the weekend crying. I don't want to get weepy again, and I feel like I'm on the verge. I can't afford that; I'm too busy right now."

"I'm sorry, Kate, I don't mean to pry. I just want to help, if I can."

She nodded. "I appreciate it. I know I can always count on you. I also know Dave didn't rape anyone, Hal. I know that."

"How can you be so sure?"

"I know him. Better than anyone does."

Benton considered Kathryn his colleague, his friend, and his subordinate, in that order. He sat back in his chair and rocked it back as far as it would go, rested an elbow on each arm of the chair, and interlaced his fingers in his lap. He looked directly into Kathryn's eyes. She returned his steady gaze.

After a few moments, apparently satisfied with what he saw, he once again leaned forward, placed his hands side by side, palms down on his desk, and told her, "Get Fields in here. Let's see where we're at on this Lancaster thing."

Five minutes later, James Fields sat next to Kathryn. He was the flip side of the coin from Dave Granz. Where Dave was tall, slender, athletic, blond and fair, Fields was shorter, stocky, with dark hair and complexion. His face bore the aftermath of teenage acne, and his hair was thinning. Dave preferred casual dress and, even when wearing a coat and tie, always appeared ready to hop on a surfboard and catch the next big wave.

Fields was always meticulously dressed in a suit, never a sport coat and slacks. He shared one characteristic with Dave Granz. He was an extraordinary cop with natural investigative instincts that could not be taught at the police academy. You either had them or you didn't. He did.

Today, Fields wore a lightweight, pale-blue summer suit with a dark-blue shirt, baby-blue tie, and black tasseled loafers. The right sleeve of his suit coat was neatly gathered and tucked into itself where his right hand should be.

To casual observers, James Fields looked handicapped, and a lesser man would be. Loss of his right hand in a bomb blast during the opening of the Hudson murder trial was followed by a long, difficult rehabilitation period. And a successful one. Naturally right-handed, Fields taught himself to do everything left-handed: throw, write, eat, and shoot. His firing-range scores now consistently exceeded those he had achieved with his right hand.

Following rehab, he was restored to full duty as a

DA inspector. Kathryn loved working with him and knew that if anyone could pick up the ball and run with it in Dave's absence, it was Fields.

Fields addressed his initial comment to Kathryn. "As you know, Hal and I met here Saturday. He filled me in on what happened. Anything I can do to help you out personally, let me know."

She nodded. "I appreciate that, but I'm fine."

Turning to business, he retrieved the investigative file for the Lancaster case from his briefcase and pulled his own notebook from his right-hand coat pocket. "Fortunately, Dave kept good notes," he said.

"Okay, let's see. I spent Saturday afternoon going over the file. Looks like Earheart and Granz covered neighborhood interviews pretty well.

"But a few years back there was a string of home-invasion robberies up in that neighborhood. Always happened early Saturday, Sunday, or holiday mornings."

Seeing Kathryn's questioning expression, he explained. "Home-invasion robberies, you know, the burglar enters the house while the residents are inside, usually asleep. Anyway, we staked out up there for weeks." He noticed her eyebrows arch again.

"Ever catch the guy?" she asked.

"Nope, never did. He just stopped. But, I learned something that turned out to be helpful on this case. Every Sunday morning, rain or shine, no matter what, a couple dozen of the residents walk their dogs, jog, or just stroll up Twin Oaks, past Don Gaspar—it runs parallel to Juan Cabrillo—past that little cul-de-sac, and up into a tiny opening at the base of the hills.

"Dogs do their business, the joggers stretch and

cool down, the walkers sit on tree stumps. Everybody just sits around and chats for a half hour or so. Like a little social club."

Kathryn was all ears. "So? Did the Lancasters have a dog?"

"Nope. I checked SPCA licensing. But Larry Lancaster did have an interesting idiosyncrasy. Seems he was an early riser. Very early. Lady Anna Lancaster liked to sleep in. A basic incompatibility, I'd say.

"Anyway, he rarely missed a Sunday or holiday morning at 'The Meadow,' as one lady called it. Seems she and Lawrence struck up a friendship, and—"

Kathryn interrupted. "They were lovers?!"

"Nothing so sordid. She's in her late seventies—the matronly type. When I talked to her, she wasn't wearing her teeth. She said she saw Lawrence up there Sunday morning, the third. He told her he probably wouldn't be there the Fourth."

"Did she say why?" Kathryn asked.

"Didn't know. I asked. He didn't tell her. But she guessed he was going out partying the night before. According to her, he did that a couple of times a year. Stayed out all night partying and didn't show up on Sundays the day after. According to her, it was a regular thing, some kind of get-together with buddies or something. Apparently he never told her what it was, but she said as far as she knew, he rarely drank except for whatever those things were."

"Interesting," Benton mused. "Some kind of boys' night out."

"So," Kathryn mused, "maybe he came home drunk late Sunday night or early Monday morning, feeling his testosterone from a night out with the boys. They get in a fight, Lawrence threatens to beat the hell out of her, maybe pulls the gun and waves it at her.

"Mrs. Lancaster gets scared, having been beaten up on nights like this in the past, takes the gun away from him, and bam! He's dead. Jim, maybe there's a BWS case here, after all."

"Maybe. Don't think so," Fields said. "This old lady, Clara Sullivan's her name, says he told her he falls asleep when he gets drunk. Has to be brought home and poured in bed. He was a bit embarrassed, but she thought a little boastful, too. Happened every time. Doesn't sound like he was violent at all."

"Sure, that's what he'd tell her. Wife beaters don't usually go around bragging to their neighbors about it. You know, like, 'hey did I tell you I beat the snot outta my ol' lady last night?'"

Fields shrugged, knowing she was right. He held his notebook in his left hand and flipped the pages with his thumb. A one-handed marvel.

"Something even more interesting. Apparently Mrs. Sullivan reminded him of a paternal aunt by the same first name. He took to her in a motherly way. Hinted around several times about some sort of trouble between himself and his wife. He was never very specific."

"Physical?"

"Don't think so. He never hinted at a physical confrontation, according to Mrs. Sullivan. Money trouble."

"Money?!" Benton said. "He was rolling in it."

"Yep, but apparently Anna Lancaster didn't feel she was getting her fair share. Lancaster told Mrs.

Sullivan that his wife complained constantly about the lack of spending money.

"One morning, right after an especially ugly Saturday night, he told Mrs. Sullivan that his wife could go through money faster than even he—he emphasized the word *he*—faster than even *he* could make it.

"Said if he hadn't been thinking ahead, there'd be nothing left for his estate after he died. She didn't know what that meant, and the subject never came up again. That was about two or three months ago."

"Okay, that's interesting, but I'm not sure it adds much," Kathryn said, "since money doesn't seem to be a problem for them."

"I agree," Fields conceded. "Anything on the blood tox report on Lawrence?"

"We haven't got it yet. I'll call Doc Nelson and rattle his cage a bit. It'll be interesting to see what his B.A. level was." The blood tox she asked Morgan Nelson to run would determine the level of alcohol in the victim's blood at the time he was killed. "Anything else?"

"Lots. When I reviewed Granz' file, I saw he had scheduled interviews with ten people at Lancaster and Young. Never made them. So, I called them all Saturday night. Leaned on them a little bit . . ." He grinned at Benton. "You'll probably get a couple of complaints about my attitude. I got a little pushy."

Benton spread his hands palms down in front of him and made a safe signal, like a baseball umpire. "I'll handle them. Go on, please."

Fields continued. "Dave's list had ten names, five attorneys and five secretaries—administrative assistants, they call them. All five of the lawyers are partners in the firm, three men and two women. The secretaries were two men and three women. All the men had women secretaries and vice versa. Figure that one out and you've got a good master's thesis." He took a deep breath.

"I figured if Lancaster was sharing deep dark personal secrets, it would be with a man, so I talked to the female attorneys and their secretaries first. I was right, none of them knew anything helpful. Nor did two of the male attorneys or their assistants.

"But the last guy I talked to and his secretary were both very helpful. He's the senior partner now that Lancaster's deceased—guy named Philip Hyler.

"It took a bit of convincing, but eventually he told me that he, Lancaster, and two other guys played all-night poker every six months or so. Always played at his house, 'cause he's the only one who isn't married. Also, he doesn't drink; he's a recovered alcoholic. They usually play till four or five in the morning; then he drives everyone home. The other guys live near his place. Lancaster's the only one of the four that lives on this side of the Hill."

Kathryn picked up the inconsistency immediately. "That doesn't wash. If he'd driven Lancaster home Sunday night, Lancaster's car would have been at Hyler's house the following morning. But Anna Lancaster drove it on the Fourth."

"Yep, I thought of that, too. Turns out one of the other guys decided he was drinking too much, so Hyler sponsored him in A.A. a couple of months ago.

"The guy was stone-cold sober the night of July 3.

He followed Hyler in Lancaster's Beemer, then rode back over the Hill with Hyler. It checks out. I called the other two guys. They confirm Hyler's story."

"Gotta get that B.A.," Kathryn said again. "What about his secretary? You said you got something from her, too?"

"This guy Hyler really knows how to pick women." Fields, a happily married man and devoted father, grinned. "That is, if you're one of those sexists that finds women attractive just because they're beautiful, brilliant, charming, and have great bods. That's his secretary. She's a knockout and nice as hell, besides. Married to a San Jose cop. She says most of the single women who work for the firm look elsewhere for romance. Single guys, too. Almost half the firm's partners and senior associates in line for partnership are women.

"Says she doesn't know how, but word is the firm has some way to prevent someone from marrying into the firm's money."

"Didn't seem to bother Anna Lancaster," Benton observed.

"Maybe, maybe not," Kathryn said softly, as if speaking to herself. "Remember, apparently she wasn't happy with her spending money."

"What about her medical records?" asked Benton.

"An interesting development there," Kathryn replied. "No indication of recent physical abuse, but they show that she visited her doctor several times complaining of chronic pelvic pain, headaches, back pain, and gastrointestinal problems. Cramps and diarrhea."

"So, what does that tell us?"

"Maybe nothing, but often women who are not in need of emergency-room treatment don't seek medical attention right after an acute battering incident. But, they do seek help during the calm period afterward when they experience all the aches and pains that are often associated with high stress. Chronic pelvic pain, headaches, back pain, gastrointestinal problems—they're all frequently reported after physical abuse."

Benton shook his head skeptically. "That's not much to work with. Anything else?"

She nodded. "The X rays turned up several rib fractures and a broken arm. I asked Nelson to look at them. He can age the fractures. As a fracture heals, it develops a bony callus which looks like a small marble. He can tell how old the fracture is from the amount of calcification in the bony callus. It's easily detectable in X rays."

Benton was interested. "So, how old were they?"

"According to Nelson, they're a lot older than five years. He says they could be ten years old or even a little more."

"Well," Benton mused, "that means she didn't get them from Lancaster. So how did she get them? Too old for childhood injuries. Maybe an accident of some kind?"

"Maybe, but I don't think so. When Earheart and I interviewed her a couple of days after she shot her husband, she remarked that a woman's greatest danger is from family members. I asked her what she meant, but she wouldn't tell me. But she did tell me she was married once before, years ago, before Lancaster. My guess is it was about the time she received those old injuries."

"Jesus. So maybe she was a battered woman."

"Yeah, but not by Lawrence Lancaster, and he's the one she killed."

After Fields departed, Kathryn gathered her own belongings. "We'll keep digging, Hal, but we may not come up with anything to conclusively validate, or for that matter, to invalidate her BWS defense. I'll let you know if anything breaks."

"Thanks, Kate. I'll be here when you need to see me, and it doesn't have to be about the case."

"I know. See ya later."

23

"PLEASE BE SEATED. GOOD MORNING, EVERYone."

At eight o'clock, Tuesday, July 19, Judge Jemima Tucker convened court to hear a special motion in the Anna Lancaster murder trial. Kathryn Mackay, Defense Attorney Bickell, and defendant Anna Marie Lancaster were present, and the gallery was packed to standing-room-only capacity.

"The media has filed a motion requesting camera

coverage of this trial," Judge Tucker began. "I have scheduled this hearing for the purpose of permitting the prosecution and defense to state their positions before I render my decision."

She turned to the defense table. "Ms. Bickell, what is the defense's position?"

Bickell stood to respond. "Your Honor, my client does not object to camera coverage of her trial, and in fact welcomes it."

Judge Tucker turned toward the prosecution table. "Ms. Mackay, please state your position."

"There is no evidence that cameras adversely affect witness testimony, Your Honor. The District Attorney's office believes that unless camera coverage endangers the safety of the participants, or the integrity of the proceedings, they should be permitted."

Judge Tucker was silent for a moment, then announced, "This issue is by no means new before the courts. I agree that the media has a right to be in the courtroom and tell the public what it sees. I also agree that banning cameras in the courtroom in criminal proceedings would deny technology as it currently exists and would run contrary to the judiciary's goal of making the courts accessible to everyone."

Tucker removed her reading glasses. "The circus atmosphere that developed outside the O. J. Simpson courtroom concerns me, but I am convinced that it was not created by the cameras. It resulted from the extraordinary circumstances surrounding his celebrity status and will not be repeated in this court.

"The motion is granted."

24

"WHAT'S ON YOUR MIND, KATIE? IF YOU don't mind my saying so, you look awful."

"Just tired, Morgan, but thanks for the compliment," Kathryn Mackay answered with a feeble smile. "I just need to go over your testimony in the Lancaster trial. I know it's late, especially for a Tuesday, but the trial starts next week. I'm going to be pretty busy, so I thought I'd better see you as soon as possible." She laid a thick manila file on his desk in front of him, which he glanced at but didn't touch.

Nelson leaned back in his chair, put his feet on the corner of his desk, and crossed his ankles. Then he clasped his hands behind his head and said, "Kate, we've done this dog and pony show a hundred times. We've discussed my report twice already."

She looked down at her lap and her long, dark hair fell over her face. Then she looked up. "I know, Doc, I just thought maybe I'd better . . ."

"Katie, what's this about? What's really on your mind? You didn't come here to talk to me about the Lancaster trial. You could've used the phone."

Abruptly, Kathryn stood. "I'd better go, Morgan. I shouldn't have come. I'm sorry. It's late and you probably want to get home."

"Sit down, Kathryn, please. It's never too late for me to talk with you, you know that. Besides, five o'clock in the afternoon on a weekday is early. And what do you imagine I'd be going home to?" He smiled kindly. "Tell me what's bothering you."

She sat on the edge of the chair. "I talked to Dave Sunday night."

"Yes, and? I would expect the two of you to talk about what's happening."

"Benton ordered us not to."

He flipped his hand as if to shoo away a pesky insect. "That's ridiculous. Stupidest damn thing I ever heard. Tell me about it."

Kathryn's eyes filled with tears, which she dabbed at with a tissue, but she did not cry. "He picked Emma up Sunday morning and took her to Monterey for the day. We agreed he would say good-bye. They had a great time, according to Em, but she knew something was wrong. He told her he was going out of town for awhile on an investigation. That seemed to satisfy her for the time being."

"Sounds like a reasonable approach. So, what's the problem?"

"I told you he and I talked—when he brought Em home."

"Benton'll never know. Besides, what could he do about it, anyway? Dave didn't tell you anything about the investigation, did he?"

"No, not about the investigation."

"So, no harm, no foul, right?"

She dabbed at her eyes, again. "Not exactly. He denied raping Soto."

"Sounds right to me, Katie. Hell, he didn't rape

that woman, I'm sure of it. He told me the same thing. He didn't even know her. There's some kind of mistake, that's all."

"I wish it were that simple, Morgan. He did know her. They were involved years ago, before he and I met. He told me they had sex."

"Consensual sex?"

"That's what he said."

"Well," Nelson said slowly, dropping his feet to the floor and leaning forward with his elbows on the desk, "if that's true, the DNA results are going to fry his ass, because they're going to confirm the presence of his semen in her vagina. Jesus Christ!"

"No, that's the funny thing, Doc. He said he had sex with her on Tuesday, but that he was nowhere near her the night she claims he raped her. If he was trying to cover his ass, he'd have claimed he had consensual sex with her on Friday. I believe him."

Nelson shrugged and sat back in his chair. "Me, too. So, what did the two of you work out?"

Suddenly, tears started to flow and Kathryn sobbed. She placed a tissue over each eye and lowered them onto her fists. Nelson fidgeted in his chair. Like all men, he had no clue what to say or do when a woman cried. "Kathryn, please . . . I . . . you . . . ," he stammered.

"It's okay, Doc, you don't need to say anything. I didn't mean to blubber. That's the first time I've done that in front of anybody since this whole shitty mess unfolded. The only crying I've done has been in the shower," she said. "It's just that suddenly I felt so overwhelmed, and you're the only person I feel comfortable with. I'll try not to do it again."

"Katie, Katie. You're so accustomed to denying your emotions and putting on a show in court that you no longer think you're allowed to act like a human, never mind like a woman. It's me, remember?"

She recovered, although her eyes were red and moist. "Thanks, Morgan. Maybe I'm not so tough after all, huh?"

"Maybe. So what did you and Dave decide?"

"He thinks we can work it out, but we can't. I can't see him again. I told him so. It's over."

"Is that what you want?"

"God, I don't know what I want! Maybe I made a mistake. Maybe I'm wrong; maybe I could forgive him. We never actually promised to be faithful to each other, not in so many words."

"But it was implied?" Nelson asked.

"Of course."

"So, how does that make you feel?"

Kathryn laid her head back on her chair and was silent for a moment. Baring her soul didn't come easily. It was a struggle. When she spoke, her voice was soft and her eyes were fixed on the ceiling. "Betrayed. Angry. Unloved. Christ, I'm not sure. The only thing I'm sure of is I loved Dave more than any man I've ever known. Probably more than anyone I'll ever know. That's what scares me most, thinking that I'll never feel like that again. I took it for granted that he'd always be there when I needed him, when I wanted him. And he always has been until now. Did I make the wrong decision, Morgan?"

He shook his head sadly. "I wish I could tell you I

think you could work it out. You're my two favorite people, you know that. But I can't. It's not in your nature to be forgiving. Maybe it's a personality flaw, maybe not; it doesn't matter. You expect perfection from yourself and everyone else. When you or they don't deliver, you take it hard. You may have to live with your own transgressions, but you don't have to live with Dave's. And you won't be able to. I think you did what you had to do."

Kathryn dabbed at her eyes with the tissue, which was soaked. "I've been that way all my life, even as a little girl. I never had very many friends; I was too intense. When I did make a friend, eventually something would happen. They didn't call when they promised, or they flirted with my boyfriend, or whatever. Then, I'd decide they weren't worth the effort, and suddenly I didn't have a friend anymore. I only have two girlfriends from my hometown that I still talk to, and I lived there my whole childhood. Not much to show for it, is it?"

"You beat on yourself too much," Nelson said kindly. "Give me a choice between an ordinary friend or one like you, I'll take you every time. I don't have many friends, either, but you're one. And I wouldn't trade you for a busload of the other type."

"Thanks, Morgan. So, what does this all mean? Can I forgive Dave and move forward? I don't think I can. You're right, probably, that it's a flaw, but I've got it and have to live with it. I've never forgiven anyone for anything that I can recall. Except Emma."

"Well, there are a lot worse things to be than a good mother and friend to an ancient old pathologist. But I don't think you and Dave can ever work it out. You need to let it go while you can both walk away with your dignity intact."

"I know. I needed to hear you tell me, but I know you're right."

"How about what he told you about Soto?" Nelson asked. "Has he compromised you professionally?"

"I've thought a lot about what my ethical obligations are, Morgan. Dave's denial of the rape charge is just self-serving hearsay. It's inadmissible evidence."

"How about his statement about having sex with her?"

"Well, if it were an admission, it'd be admissible evidence, unlike a denial. But an admission has be a statement that ties him to the crime or tends to prove his guilt. Maybe I'm splitting hairs, but when he says he had sex with Soto at some prior time, he hasn't admitted anything relevant to the rape charge. I'm not going to tell anybody about it, at least for the time being."

"So, then wait and see what happens," he counseled.

Kathryn picked up the Lancaster case file, which Nelson hadn't looked at, and dropped it into her briefcase. "Guess I didn't need to bring this, did I?" she asked sheepishly. "Next time I'll try to remember you're my friend and not use subterfuge. Sorry." She stood up to leave.

"That's okay, Katie, I understand," he replied. He walked around the desk and laid his hands on her shoulders in a unusual display of affection. "Would a hug be of any assistance?"

Kathryn threw her arms around him. "I'll say it would. Thanks for being here."

Nelson returned the hug. "I'm here anytime you need me."

25

AMERICAN AIRLINES FLIGHT 833, WHICH ORIGI- nated in Dallas, Texas, touched down at Aeropuerto Internacional in Mexico City exactly on time at 8:30 A.M., Wednesday, July 20. "Excuse me, please, excuse me," the passenger in seat 6F said to the woman in the center seat and the man in the inboard seat. He lifted the leather carry-on bag over his head and shoved his way into the aisle, eager to deplane. The customs declaration in his hand was simple; traveling on personal business, no checked baggage, no food, no liquor, nobody traveling with him. He would be in Mexico no more than two days.

It took an hour to clear Mexican customs, although he was lucky—when he pushed the baggage- inspection button, he got a green light; his single bag was not inspected. Proceeding directly through the gigantic terminal, he identified himself at the Hertz counter. "Yes sir, your car is waiting in area H-17," the Hertz representative told him in perfect English.

"Gracias," he answered and picked up the keys to the rental car. Locating the green Ford Taurus with no problem, he tossed his bag onto the backseat, climbed in, started the engine, and turned on the air-conditioning full blast. He studied the Hertz courtesy map and, satisfied he knew which route to take, pulled into the early-morning traffic.

The car was spotlessly clean but reeked of cigarette smoke, the air freshener being no match for thousands of cigarros and puros. The trip through a grimy industrial section—along a four-lane divided expressway whose median consisted of a narrow sidewalk which no one used for fear of instantaneous death—took about a half hour.

Along Paseo de la Reforma, the city was more attractive. Landscaping gave way to extravagant gardens fronting international business hotels. "Ah, there it is," he said aloud to himself, and steered the Taurus to the valet station of the Maria Isabel–Sheraton Hotel, where he relinquished his keys to the valet. He required no assistance with his single bag and was checked efficiently into his plush suite.

Immediately, he requested and received from the conserje a directorio de teléfonos para Ciudad Cuernavaca, Estado de Morelos.

He found what he was looking for, showered quickly in cool water, dressed in light cotton trousers and a short-sleeved shirt, and retrieved his Ford Taurus from the valet, whom he tipped fifty new pesos. Delighted, the valet graciously saluted and responded, "Thank you very much, sir. If I may assist you when you return, please ask for me personally.

My name is Ramon." The man gathered that he had just bestowed a very generous gratuity on the valet, although he had no idea how much fifty new pesos was in American money.

At about 1 P.M., he pulled the Ford Taurus into the city of Cuernavaca and began his search for Verada a la Sombra 26. It was not difficult to find with the map he obtained at the hotel; Cuernavaca is not a large city. It was a beautiful, tree-lined, cool, shady street with crumbling sidewalks, worthy of its name.

Parking in front of the small, neat, freshly painted house, he turned off the ignition, brushed his hair back from his face, sighed deeply, and opened the car door. He was greeted by a blast of hot air which contrasted ominously with the air-conditioned coolness of the car's interior.

Then, Dave Granz walked up the path and knocked firmly on the door of Roberto Soto's home.

All the way from San Francisco to Dallas, from Dallas to Mexico City, and from Mexico City to Cuernavaca, Dave studied his English-Spanish dictionary, attempting to recall his high-school Spanish. He hoped he would be able to communicate, at least enough to express himself.

The door opened, and a small, dark Mexican man in his early seventies stood behind a screen door. Pleasantly, he asked, "Si?"

Summoning up his courage and high-school Spanish, Dave said, "Buenos días, Señor. Mi nombre es David Granz. Lo siento, no hablo Español. ¿Habla usted Inglés?" Dave could hear Patsy Cline singing "Crazy" in the background.

Señor Roberto Soto stood motionless, then, without removing his eyes from the man at his door, he called, "Rosa, venga aquí, por favor."

Momentarily, a thirtyish Mexican woman appeared at the door. There was a family resemblance, no doubt about it. She was Julia Soto's sister. Short and petite, she was prettier than Julia but lacked her sister's sensuality.

She spoke briefly with her father in Spanish, then turned to the man at the door. "Señor Granz. I am Rosa, Julia Soto's sister. My father does not speak English. I know of you, of course, as does my father. He is not happy to find you here. He has instructed me to ask you why you have come to his home."

"Ms. Soto—"

"My name is Rosalia María Soto Martinez," she said. "I am married."

"I'm sorry, Señora," he said. "Something has happened. I need very badly to speak with you and your father concerning Julia. May I come in, please?"

Rosa and her father spoke again in Spanish. The only words Dave Granz understood were "Julia" and "importante." He waited.

Rosa nodded to her father and turned to Dave. "My father does not wish to speak to you regarding Julia. However, it would be impolite to turn away a guest. He asks that you come in, please." She stood aside and opened the screen door.

The house was clean, dark, and cool inside. Rosa and Señor Soto led Dave into a den at the rear of the house. The den window faced into the large, shady rear yard, in which two small boys played with a mongrel dog. A happy family, he observed to himself. After they were seated, Rosa said, "My father wishes to be polite but is distressed by your presence. He requests that you conduct your business as quickly as possible and then leave."

Dave turned to the old man. "Gracias, Señor," he said with genuine gratitude.

A half hour later, Dave knew little more than when he arrived. Julia came home to attend the family when her mother was ill. After her mother died, she became increasingly restive and dissatisfied. She had become an Anglo, rejecting traditional values.

After awhile, she returned to the United States. That was the last time her father saw her. It was not acceptable for the elder sister, if she were unmarried, to leave her father alone and unattended. As far as he was concerned, he had only one living daughter—Rosa.

Rosa asked, "Was there anything else you needed, Señor Granz? If not, my father would appreciate it if you returned to the United States and did not attempt to contact the Soto family again." Mr. Soto excused himself and disappeared.

Rosa looked at Dave apologetically. "I am sorry, Mr. Granz. Had you called me, I could have told you this would be the result and saved you the trip to Cuernavaca." She paused, then said simply, "Julia loved you very much."

Dave rose and walked slowly to the front door. "Maybe if I spoke with your father again . . ."

"No, Señor. I cannot permit it. He is not well, and although he appears to be under control, he is extremely upset by your visit. I am afraid you must leave. I do not mean to be rude, but you must go now."

Just as Dave started the engine in the Taurus, Rosa ran down the path from the house. She opened the passenger door and sat down, closing the door behind her. She was crying. "I am sorry, Mr. Granz. My father has retired to his room. He would be very upset with me if he knew this, but I must speak with you before you leave. It will only take a few minutes of your time."

Dave rolled the windows down in both front car doors, then turned off the ignition. He looked at Julia Soto's sister but did not speak.

She began slowly. "Mr. Granz, you must understand that the Mexican culture is different from your own. Although I have never been in the United States, I know a great deal about your culture; all young Mexicans do. My sister talked with me a great deal and even encouraged me to emigrate. As you observed, I have found a happy life for myself here."

Dave began to speak, but she stopped him with an upheld hand. "Julia had become Americanized when she returned to attend our mother. Although it may seem unimportant to you, invalidation of the traditional female cultural values by Anglo-Americans is greatly feared and despised by older Mexican men such as my father. I wanted to attend to our mother myself, but our father would not allow it; she was the elder sister, and it was her duty.

"After our mother passed away, Julia became restless, she dated. She did not follow the traditional ways of being escorted by our father or another male family member. She sometimes met men elsewhere so they would not need to come to Father's home. He was displeased with this behavior, as you might imagine. He feared she was sexually active and warned her against such inappropriate behavior. In our culture, female sexuality is reserved for the marital relationship.

"I knew, of course, about your relationship with Julia. I knew she was not . . . this is very embarrassing, Señor, I apologize . . . I knew she was not a virgin. She was a beautiful thirty-five-year-old woman, and she loved you very much. She was disappointed that you did not accompany her or come to meet her family. She told Father about you, expecting that you would eventually come here and meet him and receive his approval to marry Julia. But you never did. She was embarrassed."

"I never knew . . . ," Dave groaned.

"Yes, I know that. She began to see men who were, even in my opinion, not suitable. She began to frequent—how do you call them—nightclubs alone.

"Occasionally, she came home late. She and my father fought. Our father considered virginity to be essential to respectability for a single woman. He tended—tends—to view all women either as 'Madonna' or *puta*—whore. There is no in-between.

"One evening she went out alone. On the way home—it was about midnight—she was confronted by a group of young men. There were three of them. They were very drunk and belligerent. They made indecent comments to Julia, which she attempted to ignore. She was only a few blocks from our home here at the time."

Rosa hesitated, then continued. "This is very difficult. I am sorry. She was raped by those men, Mr. Granz. All three of them."

Although he knew what she was leading up to, the words were shocking, nevertheless. Gang-raped, my God, he thought. No wonder . . .

"When she arrived home, my father was waiting for her. She could not deny what happened. She knew the young men; they lived nearby. My father knows their families."

"What did he do? Did he call the police?"

"No, Mr. Granz, you do not understand the Mexican culture. When a sexually active single woman is raped, it is presumed there is something in her past or present behavior that provokes the assault. Even in her own mind, even as Americanized as Julia had become, this belief is powerful.

"My father contacted the families of the young men and confronted them, naturally."

"And . . ."

"As expected, the men claimed it was she who provoked the incident, that she wished to have sex with them. Both Julia and my father feared reprisal, so they did not notify the police."

"So, that was the end of it? Nothing more was done?" Dave asked.

"Not quite; there is more. It is impossible for you to understand, Señor, but our family honor was destroyed. I was, fortunately, already married. My father strongly suspected she was sexually active with you, although Julia would never have told him so. He felt ashamed and was no longer able to face his friends. He became a recluse, rarely leaving his home. Julia herself felt stigmatized. She was no longer asked out by the nice young men she knew. I believe she may have become promiscuous, although I do not know this for a fact.

"It is only fair to tell you, Mr. Granz, that both Julia and my father blamed you for what happened to her."

"I don't understand."

"Well, you see, being unmarried, the only way her sexual involvement with you could be accepted was for you to marry her. That way, the only man she would have been with was her husband. When you did not come to meet the family, even for our mother's funeral, it was obvious that you had no such intentions. That was why she began seeing other men."

"I still don't see—"

"Let me continue, please. You see, in their minds, if you had come and met the family, she would not have been out that night and therefore could not have been assaulted. In their minds, it was your fault. After awhile, Julia and my father's relationship became so poisoned that she returned to the United States."

Rosa sighed. "Mr. Granz, I do not know the truth of all these matters; no one except Julia knows it. But, my sister was . . . is an honorable woman. She was no whore. She did not have sex with those three men. They raped her, I am sure of that. I am equally certain it was not your fault. I know you were not to blame. I do not know if that helps or not, but you should not blame yourself."

Dave sat back in his car seat, stunned, realizing he

had listened to this story hunched forward, grasping the steering wheel tightly in both hands.

"There is one more thing, Mr. Granz. One night not long after Julia was raped, one of the three young men disappeared. His family has not heard from him since. The police have stated that he is probably dead, although no body has ever been recovered. I am not absolutely certain Julia was responsible for his disappearance, but there is one thing I am certain of," Rosa concluded.

Dave could only stare at her.

"Julia cannot return to Cuernavaca. There is nothing for her here."

On the way back to Mexico City, Dave played and replayed the story he had heard from Julia Soto's sister. When he deplaned at San Francisco International Airport at 10 P.M., Thursday, he was still replaying it. It seemed he had aged years in the past day and a half, and perhaps he had.

26

"HAL, SINCE LANCASTER'S PHYSICAL EXAMI-nation and X rays showed no signs of recent abuse, there's no physical evidence that she was in mortal danger when she shot her husband."

"You're right. Those ten-year-old fractures aren't

relevant to this case. On the other hand, the absence of recent injuries doesn't mean she wasn't abused, either."

"Of course not, but if there had been signs of recent abuse, they would certainly validate her claim. We can't ignore their absence. We've got to decide based on what we've got, and what we've got is nothing to support her self-defense claim. And now we can factor in his blood-alcohol level."

Kathryn Mackay and District Attorney Hal Benton met in Kathryn's office late on Thursday, July 21. Four days hence, Anna Marie Lancaster would be tried for murder, manslaughter, or not at all.

"How the hell did Nelson obtain blood to do a tox screen? I thought the Lancaster body was burned to a crisp."

"I prefer to describe Lancaster's body as charred. But you're right that when a body is burned badly, it's sometimes impossible to obtain blood from the usual larger blood vessels. The heat bakes the blood, causing formation of what he calls a 'blood cake.' It's generally unsuitable for analysis, so he has to get blood someplace else."

"So, where does he get it? He can't just send out for it like pizza." The more gruesome the subject, the more it provoked morbid humor as a defense mechanism.

"He can usually squeeze blood from congested organs like the liver, kidney, or lungs. In extreme cases like this one, he obtains it from bone marrow."

"So, after all that, did we learn anything worthwhile?"

"Lancaster's blood-alcohol level was .29."

Benton whistled softly. "That must've been some poker game."

"My guess is that he continued drinking after he got home. The body starts metabolizing alcohol immediately after consumption ceases, even metabolizes it while the person continues to drink. If they weren't drinking and driving, it would have been even higher before they left Hyler's place to still be .29 an hour later."

"So," Benton suggested, "he gets home, drunk and belligerent. They fight, and he has a few more drinks. He gets nasty. Punches her out, maybe in the stomach or someplace that doesn't leave marks or bruises. She isn't submissive, so he pulls the gun and threatens her. In mortal fear of immediate death, she relieves him of his weapon. Slam-dunk self-defense."

"I don't buy it, Hal."

"Okay, convince me," Benton challenged.

"To claim self-defense, she's got to believe she's gonna die right now, not later. She can't kill her abuser to escape a previous threat or a danger that might arise. Not good enough. It's got to exist at the precise time she killed him."

"Go on," Benton encouraged.

"It follows that if the victim was incapacitated at the time the fatal shot was fired, the imminence requirement isn't fulfilled."

"Okay."

"The victim's blood-alcohol level was .29. Nobody can function when they're that drunk. So," Kathryn continued, "she killed a man who was so drunk he couldn't possibly pose a threat of death or great bodily harm. What's more, she could easily have escaped."

"You're sure?"

"Sure enough that I don't think we can avoid going forward. I'll check with Nelson to see just how incapacitated he would have been with a .29 B.A. But I think I already know the answer. If I'm wrong, we'll reconsider."

"Okay, so what about the gun?"

"You said it yourself. In the worst-case scenario, she takes it from him. How does he pose an imminent threat of death if she's got the gun? Anna Lancaster shot and killed an incapacitated man who posed no threat to her whatsoever when she killed him. We have no choice but to try her for first-degree murder."

Benton looked at her. "I agree."

27

KATHRYN STOOD IN FRONT OF THE FULL LENGTH mirror and surveyed her appearance. "Emma, can you come in here for a minute, please?" she shouted.

"I'm in the bathroom, Mom, I can't," Emma shouted back.

"It's really important," Kathryn said.

Emma walked into her mother's bedroom in her pajamas. Exasperated, she asked, "Okay, Mom, what is it? If I'm late for school, this time it'll be your fault."

"How does my outfit look?" Kathryn asked, turning from side to side so Emma could evaluate her navy linen jacket with a matching pleated skirt and low heels.

Emma scrunched up her nose and considered. "I don't think so, Mom. You look like an old lady."

Kathryn sighed. "That's what I thought, too. Thanks, honey. I'll try something else. Run back to the bathroom and finish getting ready. But give me a kiss first."

"I wish this were as easy as the weekend," she said aloud but to herself. "All I have to decide on Saturdays and Sundays is which pair of jeans and which T-shirt to take out." She returned the original outfit to its hangers, slipped out of her shoes, and reconsidered her wardrobe. Finally, she selected a black wool-gabardine double-breasted suit, a white poplin shirt, and black leather pumps. She resurveyed herself and nodded with satisfaction.

Then she went back into her bathroom and completely redid her makeup for the second time. Thank God, she thought, Emma and I don't share a bathroom.

It was Monday, July 25, the opening day of the Anna Lancaster trial. By the time the alarm sounded that morning, Kathryn had already been out of bed for an hour and a half drinking her second cup of coffee. To her surprise, she had slept soundly, her mind so focused on the trial that she was able to keep thoughts of Dave Granz and her disastrous personal life at bay.

For opening statements, she always paid particular attention to her appearance. Her first direct communication with the jury since voir dire called for a special look. Jury selection is difficult on everyone, often creating animosity between the attorney and the jurors. It is crucial that rapport be reestablished before they are asked to consider testimony.

Kathryn fully realized the important role that appearance and perception play in the minds of a jury. She once tried a case in which the defense attorney, a meticulously and expensively dressed man, showed up in court once or twice each week without socks in his expensive wing-tip shoes. On those days, while she examined witnesses, he crossed and uncrossed his legs, making certain his pants leg rode up over his hairy calf, and swung his foot back and forth. The tactic so distracted the jurors that Kathryn found it virtually impossible to maintain their attention. Despite repeated requests, the judge refused to order him to wear socks.

Similar issues might arise in the Lancaster trial, Kathryn realized. Angela Bickell was a gifted and flamboyant attorney who was unlikely to alter her behavior, despite Judge Tucker's prior admonishment.

At 7:30 A.M., Kathryn drove to the Government Center after dropping Emma off at the bus stop. Bypassing her assigned parking spot, she drove her Audi directly to the side of the building, pulled into space 119, and stuck a special permit on the dashboard.

The previous Friday, anticipating a mob scene at the courthouse, Kathryn lobbied the building services director for, and received, a VIP parking permit. The special permit allowed her to park in the single row of spaces reserved for elected officials and visiting dignitaries along the west side of the building adjacent to the park. It was commonly referred to by county employees as "The Lineup."

She guessed right about the mob scene.

Gleaming stainless-steel, motorized cafeteria vans were set up at each entrance to the parking lot, doing a land-office business in coffee, bagels, rolls, juice, and breakfast burritos.

Broad sound trucks and mobile TV transmitters supporting roof-mounted antenna dishes from local channels five and seven, along with units from San Jose Channel Two and San Francisco Channel Eight lined up shoulder to shoulder in front of the court building like offensive linemen on a pro-football team.

A spider-web maze of tangled cables, wires, tubes, and giant umbilical cords connected the trucks to portable generators, light poles, amplifiers, video cameras, and microphones.

Soldier-ant workers scurried from unit to unit dragging mysterious equipment, preparing for an invasion but inescapably trapped in the spider's web.

Not yet attracting national attention, the Lancaster trial was of tremendous state and local concern. An advocate for women's rights in general, and abused women in particular, Kathryn was stunned when she approached the steps leading to the main entrance to the government building.

At least fifty women, along with a handful of men, paraded back and forth across the steps, chanting in unison, "No, No, She Won't Go." What they lacked in numbers, they compensated for in volume. Most carried handmade signs. Some were hastily and carelessly prepared, while others were more professional in design. One read "Anna Lancaster, Our Hero." Several simply stated the group's unanimous purpose: "Free Anna Lancaster." Some expressed individual thoughts like: "Jail the bad GUY, not the victim" and "Where were you when she needed you?"

One sign was carried by a small Hispanic woman whose head was wrapped with clean white bandages. Her broken left arm hung in a sling, and her lips were puffy and bruised. She carried a sleeping infant in her right arm. Her sign was tucked under the broken arm and rested on her shoulder. In blood-red letters on white cardboard, the hand-painted sign read simply, "Kathryn Mackay, Traitor Bitch."

Kathryn dodged the crowd before they recognized her by dropping through the below-ground entrance to the disaster center and riding the private elevator to the second floor.

Hal Benton waited for her outside the door to her office. Coincidentally, he also wore a black suit, white shirt, and black oxfords. Good choice, Kathryn thought to herself.

"Good morning, Hal. Did you see that demonstration on the main steps?"

"I saw it. That's why I'm here. I want to be sure you're okay with this. This is a tough case. I also know that as the founder of the Domestic Violence Commission, you know many of those people. If you take this case to trial, you may never be able to work with some of them again. If you think you will be compromised, or can't handle this thing, say so now."

She looked at him thoughtfully. They stood in the hallway outside her door, where other attorneys gathered to chat before their workdays began. "Come inside, Hal, please," she said, then closed the door behind them.

Sitting at her desk, with her boss in one of the leather chairs facing her, she gazed at him intensely, then spoke solemnly. "Hal, you know I have had serious reservations about this case. We have discussed it at length, and I've told you everything that concerns me."

She paused, pensively. "We decided that Lancaster ought to be tried for murder, and that's what we're doing. If I doubted that we should go forward, or that I'm capable of prosecuting it to the best of my ability, I would have told you so. Don't worry about me. I can handle the crowds and the trial and all the trouble that goes along with it."

"I knew that, Kathryn. I just wanted to hear it from you. If you say you're okay, that's enough for me. If you need anything, just holler." Benton stood up and walked to the door, where he paused and turned before twisting the handle.

"And Kathryn? Not that you need it, but good luck."

28

"GOOD MORNING EVERYONE," JUDGE TUCK-
er said when she convened court at precisely 9 A.M.,
Monday, July 25. "The record shall reflect that the
defendant Anna Marie Lancaster and her attorney
Angela Bickell are present in the courtroom, as is
Kathryn Mackay, representing the People." She nodded at Kathryn and said, "You may proceed with your
opening statement, Ms. Mackay."

As she rose from the prosecution table, Kathryn
noted that nearly every participant in the judicial
proceeding was female, unlike the early days of her
career when she was one of a handful of women
prosecutors and not a single female judge sat on the
bench. In those days, she was invariably the lone
woman at law-enforcement briefings. How things
change, she thought; I hope for the better.

More importantly, she considered the jury of ten
women and two men with mild trepidation. She
normally preferred a better gender balance, and in
this case a predominantly female jury probably fa-
vored the defense. But she was unable to dismiss any
of the female jurors for cause and was extremely
reluctant to use a peremptory challenge to excuse a

juror based on her sex. So, she would play the hand she was dealt.

She walked purposefully to the podium, situated so that while she spoke, the jurors could see only her, the American flag, and a bookcase full of law books. She gazed intently at the jury, making eye contact with each individual member.

"Good morning, ladies and gentlemen. As you know, my name is Kathryn Mackay, and I am an assistant district attorney for the County of Santa Rita. My job is to represent the People of the State of California, who have charged the defendant Anna Marie Lancaster with the crime of murder."

She permitted the importance of her words to sink in a moment. "This will be my last opportunity to speak to you directly until all the evidence has been presented. From now on, I will speak to you through questions I ask witnesses who are called to testify.

"Please pay close attention to both the questions the witnesses are asked as well as their answers. You, and you alone, will decide what significance to assign the testimony you hear, and it is you alone who must determine the defendant's guilt."

Kathryn followed three simple rules with respect to opening statements: one, speak without notes; two, never speak for more than one hour; and three, address potential weaknesses in her case before the defense does.

Rule three is especially important in "unpopular victim," or "sympathetic defendant" cases. The defendant in this case, Anna Lancaster, was impeccably dressed, beautiful, believable, and very sympathetic.

"During this trial, you may be asked to believe that

it was the victim who committed the crime, and the defendant who was victimized. Such arguments can be compelling, and it may be difficult for you to separate your emotions from your intellect. Please don't confuse the two.

"Set aside your hearts, and judge the evidence with your heads. Separate fact from fiction; extract the truth from the rhetoric. Remember: the victim in this case, Lawrence Lancaster, is dead.

"As jurors, each of you solemnly promised to be fair and impartial. The People cannot ask more of you than that, nor shall the People accept less. A criminal trial is a search for the truth; it is you who will determine what that truth is."

Kathryn interwove her fingers and placed her hands on the podium in full view of the jury. Although she appeared to speak contemporaneously, she had rehearsed her opening over and over until it was right.

"Any civilized society recognizes the supreme value of human life and excuses or justifies the taking of a human life only in cases of absolute necessity. Any lesser standard is repugnant to civilized men and women and must be rejected as an affront to our humanity.

"The absolute necessity contemplated by this lofty standard, the justification for the taking of a human life, is called self-defense. Self-defense occurs when the taker of life kills out of a reasonable fear that she is in imminent danger of her own death or great bodily harm.

"The fear of danger she experiences must, as I said, be imminent. If it is not—if the danger exists only in the future, no matter how soon that future might arrive, it is not imminent, and the killing cannot be excused or justified. Her claim of self-defense must be rejected.

"Imminence is of such crucial importance in this case that I would like to spend a moment defining that concept as it is contemplated by the law. In common terms, imminence means that the threat of death or great bodily harm facing her is immediate and absolutely inescapable by any means other than killing the person who poses the threat.

"Let me provide an example, if I may. Suppose I am in the kitchen of my home with my daughter, who is, say, two years old. A toddler.

"We're mixing up a batch of brownies, as mothers and daughters often do."

Kathryn smiled at the jurors and noted with satisfaction that they all smiled back.

"It is a warm summer day here on the central California coast, so we have opened the sliding door to the patio. As we stir our brownie mix, I hear a vicious snarl and turn to see a pit bull charge through the patio door straight at my daughter. This pit bull is growling and salivating, and I know of this dog's vicious reputation.

"As he rushes to attack my daughter, I pick up a butcher knife and plunge it into his body, killing the dog and saving my daughter's life. Had I not acted instantly and with deadly force, my daughter would have been killed.

"That was an imminent danger, ladies and gentlemen, which clearly justified my instinctive and deadly response.

"If the dog had simply been clawing at the screen

door, however, and if we could have fled to another room to call an animal-control officer, the danger I perceived would not have been an imminent one.

"My example illustrates that, to support a claim of self-defense, the perceived danger must be substantially more than a fear that a life-threatening situation will *become* imminent; it must *be* imminent.

"The law, then, ladies and gentlemen, does not justify the taking of a human life on the basis that the taker of the life believed a danger would become imminent sometime in the future. It must be immediate and inescapable at the precise instant the fatal shot is fired.

"Likewise," Kathryn continued, "a defendant cannot be excused from guilt of murder when she kills the one who threatens her with death or great bodily harm, unless she actually and reasonably perceives that the victim is about to attempt, or is attempting, to fulfill that threat.

"Now, I recognize that applying such a strict rule in some cases is difficult because of our sympathy for the plight of the battered woman. However, it is fundamental to our concept of law that there be no discrimination between sinner and saint solely on moral grounds.

"Abusers of women, while they deserve punishment for their acts of violence, nevertheless are entitled to the same protection of their lives by the law that is afforded to everyone. Any less-exacting standard fails to protect every person's right to live.

"It is that right to live, guaranteed by law to each and every one of us, that I will ask you to preserve and protect in this trial."

Kathryn paused and glanced at her watch. Right on schedule. She continued, "So, you might ask, how does the battered woman obtain relief from her abuser?

"If, as it does not, the law does not permit Anna Lancaster to shoot her husband; if, as it does not, the law of self-defense does not provide an alternative means of resolving a battered woman's problem, what does?

"For resolution of her problem, the battered woman must look to other means of escape or relief provided by her family, her friends, or by society in general such as restraining orders, shelters, and criminal prosecution of her abuser.

"Yes, these means are sometimes difficult, and while they have proven tragically inadequate in some cases, the solution is to improve those means, not to diminish our standards of protection against the unjustified taking of human life."

Kathryn glanced once more at the jury, gratified to see that she held the undivided attention of each person. She preferred to finish on a high note and wrap it up quickly.

"I would like to conclude by reminding you that, as horrible as an abuser's behavior might be, the law of the State of California would not condemn to death a person for a murder he merely *threatened* to commit, even if he had threatened and had committed other murders in the past, and now threatened to murder the defendant.

"It follows then, ladies and gentlemen, that the law will not even partially excuse a *potential* victim's slaying of her *potential* attacker unless more—much more—than mere threats and a history of past assaults is involved.

"During this trial, you will hear evidence that will establish conclusively that Anna Lancaster could not have perceived an imminent danger of death or great bodily harm from her husband, whom she shot to death, because such an imminent danger did not exist.

"She was, therefore, not justified in shooting him and is guilty of murder.

"Thank you for your attention."

Kathryn returned to the prosecution table, swallowed a sip of ice water, and prepared to call her first witness.

29

THE DRIVER OF THE SAN FRANCISCO–SANTA Rita Airport Express dropped Dave Granz off at the driveway to his apartment a few minutes after midnight Thursday.

Before he exited the airporter van, he and the driver spotted a huge white and pink, heart-shaped, helium-filled balloon floating from the rear bumper of his Ford Explorer.

"Man," the driver said with genuine admiration in

his voice, "you've got some way with the ladies. How do I get me one like her?"

Dave tipped the driver five dollars and said, "You don't want one like that, trust me," then climbed out the sliding passenger door of the Econoline van.

"Damnit!" he muttered. He yanked the balloon free of its silver mooring twine and read the bright blue metallic printing: "I love you."

Another balloon, identical to the other, except metallic silver, was tied to the front bumper with a gold string and inscribed with the words "I'm sorry."

It took Dave only a few minutes to remove the balloons, pop them with his pocketknife, and toss them in the dumpster.

When he reached the front landing, he spotted two dozen long-stem red roses wrapped in green paper propped against the hinge side of the front door of his apartment. The envelope stuck in a plastic holder was from Jerry's Floral. Dave removed the card, whose message read "I'm sorry."

On the light brown apartment door, written in dark green paint was the single word "PUTA." The paint was still wet.

After tossing the flowers in the dumpster, Dave located an old quart can of paint thinner in his broom closet and removed the wet paint. The apartment door would need repainting, but he would not ask his landlord to do it; he would do it himself.

After tossing his leather bag on the bed, he glanced at his answering machine. The message light blinked rapidly four times.

He grabbed a Corona Light from the refrigerator, carried it into his bedroom, sat on the edge of his bed, swallowed a mouthful of cold beer, then reluctantly pressed the play button on his answering machine.

The first message was time and date stamped at nine-thirteen Tuesday night, July 19.

"Dave, Morgan Nelson here. Just wanted to see if you're okay." A pause. "Don't do anything stupid. Give me a call if you need to talk." Another pause. "Okay, Dave. Gotta run; my patients are waiting. Take care of yourself."

The second message, also late Tuesday night, was a hang-up. The line remained open for several seconds before it was disconnected, during which time Dave could hear breathing and soft instrumental music in the background.

Message three came in shortly before 1 P.M., Wednesday, July 20. At that time, 3 P.M. Cuernavaca time, he had been talking to Julia Soto's sister. The only voice he heard was Whitney Houston's, singing "I'll Always Love You."

The last message, at 5:45 A.M., Thursday, July 21, was another hang-up. Once again, Dave heard breathing and soft background music.

Dave erased all the phone messages, chugalugged the Corona Light, unplugged his telephone, checked the locks on his doors, and went to sleep.

At nine-fifteen Friday morning, he called Jerry's Floral. If he was going to prove that Julia Soto was harassing him, they might be able to help by identifying who bought the flowers.

"Good morning, Jerry's Floral," a woman's voice answered brightly.

"Good morning, my name is David Granz, I wonder if—"

"Oh, good morning, Mr. Granz. My name is Rebecca Timmons. I am the owner of Jerry's. You're with the District Attorney's office, aren't you?"

"Yes," he answered, thinking it wasn't strictly untrue, since he was only on administrative leave. "I was wondering if you might help me."

"Certainly, sir. Did you enjoy those two lovely assortments of roses? I filled both orders myself."

"That's what I called about. They were, they are beautiful. I wonder if you can tell me who sent them."

"No, I'm sorry I can't."

"Mrs. Timmons . . ."

"Miss Timmons."

"I'm sorry. Miss Timmons, I must tell you I'm mystified. I've never had a secret admirer before. I'm dying of curiosity. If you won't help me—"

"I didn't say I won't, Mr. Granz. I said I can't, because I don't know."

"You don't know? But I thought you said you sent them yourself."

"I did. But both times—the lovely arrangement I sent to your office a week or so ago, and the one delivered to your home yesterday—they were ordered anonymously."

"I see. How were they paid for? If you took a credit card, maybe you could check for me."

"No, they were both paid for by cash. Last week, a—shall we say—a homeless man, came in. He told me a woman stopped him on the street and paid him twenty-five dollars to place the order for her. It was late in the afternoon; that's why they weren't delivered until early the next morning. We're open until seven each evening, you know.

"Then, yesterday afternoon a young boy, I'd say junior-high-school age, came in. He told me the same thing—that a lady paid him twenty-five dollars and gave him the address and the money. I'm afraid I don't know who your secret admirer is, but I'd say she's very persistent."

"Yes, I'd say so, too," Dave said. "Miss Timmons, I wonder if you could possibly do me a favor. If someone else comes in and orders flowers for me, could you ask them to wait? Then call me and I could come to the store. I can't stand not knowing. You can understand that, I'm sure."

Miss Timmons chuckled. "I certainly can, sir. I'll be sure to call if it happens again. And, Mr. Granz?"

"Yes, ma'am?"

"If you find out who she is, I'd suggest you marry her. You don't find women like that every day."

"You're absolutely right about that," he agreed. She did not detect the sarcasm in his voice. "And thank you so much for your help."

Dave checked his car just before midnight Saturday. Between that time and dawn the next morning, someone scraped deep grooves in the paint with a sharp object.

Monday morning at 8 A.M., Dave Granz called the San Jose Police Department.

"San Jose Police. How may I direct your call?"

"Sergeant Belovik, T.M.U., please."

"Certainly, and your name, sir?"

"Dave Granz."

The receptionist clicked off and a moment later a man's voice answered. "Very funny, Granz. If this is a T.M.U., I'm the Budweiser frog."

"Hi, George. You told me you were head of the new Threat Management Unit."

"Nope, what I said was that our department wants to start a T.M.U. and model it after the LAPD unit. LAPD has the only functioning T.M.U. team in the country. Right now I'm a one-man show. I'm still trying to get up to speed on this stalker stuff. The only real progress I've made is that I bought a brand new computer program called Mosaic that's designed to assess the likelihood that someone's a stalker.

"Anyway, what's this crap I hear through the grapevine that you're on paid administrative leave? How the hell do I get a little duty like that?"

"You don't want to know, George. But it's true. Ran into a little trouble. That's what I called about. To see if you could help me out."

"What kind of help?"

"I need you to run a name for me through your files. No DOJ or NCIC inquiry. See if she's got a local rap sheet or field interrogation cards. Anything. This has gotta be on the Q.T., though. Just between you and me."

"Jesus, Granz, I can't go poking around without authorization. I get caught, and they'll have my ass in a sling," Belovik complained.

"We go back a long way, George. I wouldn't ask if it weren't important. And I'd do it for you."

Belovik thought for a minute. "Whadaya need?"

After Dave outlined the scenario—the phone calls, the vandalism, the threatening notes, and the charges against him—Belovik whistled. "Jesus, man, that's heavy-duty. Sounds like you've got a stalker after your ass. Gimme an hour or so to dig into this and keypunch this shit into that new computer program, see what kind of profile it spits out. I've been wanting to try it, anyway. Meet me here at my office. I don't want to do this over the phone. ¿Comprende?"

"See you in about an hour, buddy. Thanks."

30

WHEN DAVE GRANZ SETTLED INTO THE CHAIR facing George Belovik's desk in the San Jose City Justice Center, his friend looked at him, shook his head, and tossed a single-page computer printout on the desk, which Dave picked up. "Read it and weep. According to Mosaic, your friend scores eight and a half on a ten-point scale as a likely violent stalker. You've got yourself in some very deep shit, my friend."

"Talk to me," Dave said.

"Well, let's start out with what you already told me. You were involved with this Julia Soto a few years back. She runs off to Mexico and returns a couple of years later. While she's in Mexico she gets gang-raped, and shortly thereafter one of the guys that assaults her turns up missing and probably dead. How'm I doin' so far?"

"So far, so good, except I don't believe she killed the guy. She's not that crazy."

"Oh yeah? Don't bet on it," Belovik challenged. "Statistics say you're probably wrong. These nuts are violent, almost all of 'em. Anyway, you don't know she's back until she pops up in an investigation. You go to her place and start the relationship up again." He raised his hand to cut off Granz' protest.

"She's carrying this monster torch for you, and now she thinks you just relit the fire. You've ridden in on your white horse with your trusty Zippo lighter to save her; exactly what she thinks you shoulda done in Mexico."

"Whadaya mean, what I shoulda done in Mexico? I wasn't even in Mexico."

"Exactly the point, Sherlock, at least as far as she's concerned. Just like her sister told you. Way she sees it, if you'd a gone on down to meet Daddy like you should have, the two of you'd a got married and lived happily ever after. She wouldn't a had any reason to be on the street the night she got assaulted; she'd a been tucked warm 'n cozy in your marital bed. Safe 'n sound. But what th' fuck do you do? You leave her on her own to go out 'n get gang-banged."

"Bullshit!" Granz protested.

"Hey, I'm not sayin' it makes sense or that it's rational. I'm tellin' ya how she saw it. That's the whole point, man. She ain't rational. If she was, she wouldn't be doin' this shit. So, she starts sending you flowers, gives you cards, leaves intimate, suggestive messages on your phone machine. You tell her maybe you're involved with somebody else. You've got to think about it. You made a mistake. You blow her off.

"Let's assume you didn't rape her, like she says you did. Let's say that she just sees it that way. As far as she's concerned, you use her and toss her in the scrap heap, just like you did the first time. Metaphorical rape at the least."

"George—"

"Lemme finish, for Chrissake. You asked! Far as she's concerned, you raped her. End of story. By the way, did you keep any of those tapes or any of the cards or other stuff?"

"No, should I have?"

"I don't think it matters. By the time enough shit's gone down that you could make a case against her, it's probably too late. Besides, none of it's incriminating. No law against making phone calls or sending flowers. That is, if you could even prove she sent them, which you can't. And you can't prove she did the vandalism, either. I'd a done the same thing you did. Ignore it as long as possible and hope it goes away so nobody'd know. Then, if that don't work, handle it myself." He grinned and lit up a Marlboro, leaned back in his chair, and blew the smoke at Dave. "Little embarrassing for a hairy-ass macho cop to admit he's bein' picked on by some skirt, ain't it?"

Dave waved the smoke away with his hand. "Fuckin'-A. I thought you couldn't smoke in here. Signs all over the damn place."

"You can't. Screw 'em. It's my office. Why, 'dyou quit?"

"Yeah, a year or so ago. I can handle it. Go on."

Belovik blew another cloud of smoke Granz' direction. "Good. So, she gets nasty. Damages your car. Threatens you. It's escalating, and you don't know what's goin' on. You scared?"

"Damn right."

"You oughta be." Belovik pushed a case file across the desk. The file tab contained a case number and the name, SOTO, JULIA. "Lemme summarize it for ya."

He took a deep drag on the Marlboro. "About a year ago, I catch a call from this guy; Watts was his last name. Says he's been in a sexual relationship with this woman but broke it off. She wanted to get married, he didn't.

"He begins to get love notes in the mail, sweet messages on his phone at home and at work. He tells her in no uncertain terms he's not interested, so she starts getting a little nasty. Actually, a whole lot nasty. Trashes the front of his house. Torches his car—brand new Lexus, no shit, tosses kerosene on it and burns it to the ground. Follows him around day and night."

Another cloud of blue smoke drifted from Belovik's desk. "Finally she calls him up and says, 'You've dishonored me. I'm no longer suitable for marriage. If I can't have you, nobody can.' The next day, she's waiting for him at his office. Waves a gun at him, says she's gonna blow his head off. He's a CPA. Probably messed his pants when she pointed the piece at him.

"So, I go out and talk to her. Lived on your side of the Hill. Nice digs. She denies it all, naturally."

"Why the fuck didn't he have her arrested?" Granz asked. "Sure would have saved me a lot of trouble."

"Hang in there, I'm getting to it. He's too damned scared to testify against her. He splits, transfers to Littleton, Colorado, of all goddamn places. Big CPA firm, they've got offices all over. Who the hell knows what CPAs actually do. Do you?"

"Nope. Go on, for Chrissake."

"Yeah, yeah! Anyhow, I talked with Watts later by phone. He says she called him for awhile after he moved but eventually gave up. I suppose she lost interest. That's typical for these types."

"What types? What do you mean, 'types'?"

"That's what this Threat Management Unit is all about. Law enforcement has traditionally dealt with violent crime *after* it occurs. But stalking has become so widespread in recent years that in 1990 stalking itself became a crime in California; Penal Code Section 646.9. The idea is to intervene before the perp becomes violent instead of after.

"It's really complicated," Belovik said, lighting another Marlboro. A heavy purple cloud hung from the ceiling.

"I sure as hell don't understand it completely. But, in a nutshell, the shrinks have figured out that stalking is a symptom of the delusional obsessive disorder. By obsessional, we mean an abnormal long-term pattern of threat or harassment directed at a specific individual. The target can change, but it's always only one victim at a time.

"Usually these wackos are referred to as 'erotomaniacs,' but that's a little misleading. There's really three different disorders. Each nut-case has his or her own special lovable qualities.

"Real erotomaniacs stalk a celebrity or media figure—somebody they don't know. They usually aren't dangerous, although we all know about the John Hinckley/Jodie Foster case and others where they did get violent.

"Another, called 'love obsession' also usually involves someone the stalker doesn't know personally.

"Your friend Ms. Soto is what's called 'simple obsessional.' Almost half of these nuts are women. They target someone they've had a prior relationship with, usually an intimate one. It's almost always triggered by a single event that causes the relationship to go sour, or a perception that they've been mistreated.

"What follows is a systematic campaign to, first, rectify the schism; then, when that doesn't work, to seek retribution. They almost always destroy their victims' property, like she did your car and apartment door. It's gonna get worse before it gets better, too, pal. Count on it."

"Oh, great, thanks, I'm glad I asked," Dave said.

"There's more. They are by far the most likely to become violent. Deadly violent, sometimes. Almost half of them who threaten bodily harm follow through. I think Soto's a loose cannon."

"Is there any good news?"

"Yeah, but it's sorta like saying the good news is you busted your left arm 'cause you pick your nose right-handed. Simple obsessives like Soto don't last very long; a few months at most. No stamina. Guess they've got limited attention spans, or they can't maintain that level of rage for too long."

Belovik stared at Granz with serious concern, then fired up a fresh Marlboro off the lighted butt and dropped the old one in a half-empty Coke bottle. The Coke bottle looked like the leftovers from a sewage treatment plant.

Belovik didn't notice. "You've got a problem, my friend. Sounds like your Ms. Soto has been delusional obsessive in the past—in Mexico, maybe, although who's to say the asshole didn't deserve whatever he got. Watts was her second victim. Looks like you're her third."

"Jesus Christ," Dave exclaimed, then sat back to look at his friend. "So, what do I do?"

"Protect yourself. Wait it out until she runs down. If she's a typical simple obsessive, she'll either give up or find another lucky guy to pay attention to."

"I don't think I'll count on that," Granz answered. "Thanks. I'll let you know what happens."

Belovik looked Granz in the eye as he stood up to leave and grinned. "Thanks for what? We never had this conversation. I don't know what the hell you're talking about."

31

D<small>R. MORGAN NELSON STRODE TO THE WITNESS</small> stand, raised his right hand, swore to tell the truth, and sat comfortably in the witness chair.

"Please state your name, sir, and spell your last name for the court reporter."

"Morgan Nelson, N-e-l-s-o-n."

"And what is your occupation, sir?"

"I am a forensic pathologist."

"For whom do you work?"

"I work for the Sheriff-Coroner of Santa Rita County."

"I see. Would you please describe for the jury your education, training, and experience that qualify you to be a forensic pathologist."

Angela Bickell rose from her chair at the defense table. "Your Honor, the defense stipulates to Dr. Nelson's qualifications as a forensic pathologist. It is not necessary to bore us all with redundant and tedious detail."

Before Judge Tucker could react, Kathryn Mackay turned to the bench. "Your Honor, the prosecution does not consider Dr. Nelson's qualifications boring, redundant, or tedious. If the jury is to weigh his testimony, they must be allowed to consider his expertise. Therefore, we do not accept the proffered stipulation of the defense. Furthermore, the prosecution requests that any further proffers be made outside the presence of the jury."

"The prosecution is within its rights to not accept your stipulation, Ms. Bickell," the judge stated. "The next time you make an offer or a speech, you will do it at the bench. Would the court reporter please reread the question?"

After the question was reread, Kathryn returned her attention to the witness stand. "Doctor?"

"I have a doctorate in medicine. I completed six years' post-graduate training in pathology. I am Board Certified in Anatomical Forensic Pathology."

"Can you please explain for the jury and the rest of us exactly what forensic pathology is?"

"Certainly." He smiled at the jury, to whom he addressed his responses. "Forensic pathology is the science of interfacing with law-enforcement agencies in assessing traumatic injury and conducting autopsies."

"I see. How many autopsies have you conducted?"

"Over eight thousand. I perform between three and five hundred per year."

"Have you ever qualified as an expert witness in California courts?"

"Oh yes, several hundred times."

"Doctor, are you ever asked to conduct forensic examinations, perform autopsies, consult with other forensic experts, or teach seminars in other states?"

Angela Bickell jumped to her feet. "Your Honor, really! Is this necessary? Must we now be subjected to a travelogue? What could possibly be the point?"

Judge Tucker glared. "The point, Ms. Bickell, is that the jury is to hear and evaluate Dr. Nelson's qualifications so they might better determine the level of credibility to assign his testimony. Be seated."

Judge Tucker turned to Nelson, whom she knew well and respected. "You may answer counsel's question, Doctor, if you can remember what it was."

Unperturbed, Nelson turned to the jury. "Thank you, Your Honor. I remember the question. I have consulted with law enforcement and other forensic experts in more than forty states and twenty foreign countries. I regularly conduct seminars and teach courses in forensic pathology and firearms examination for schools such as Stanford University, the University of California, and various police academies."

"Thank you. Now, can you please tell the jury about your education, training, and experience that qualify you as an expert in firearms and ballistics?"

"I am a member of the Association of Firearms and Toolmark Examiners. I trained at the FBI Academy at Quantico, Virginia, and Forensic Science, Incorporated, a private firearms and ballistics laboratory in Northern California. I have authored and published numerous scientific articles in the Harvard University *Journal of Law and Technology* and the *Journal of Forensic Science.*"

"Have you ever qualified as a firearms and ballistics expert for the purpose of rendering forensic opinions in California courts?"

"Yes, on approximately fifty occasions."

"Dr. Nelson, on the morning of July Fourth of this year, were you called to the county morgue to examine the body of Lawrence Lancaster, which was recovered from the scene of a fire?"

"I was."

"What time was that?"

"It was late morning. Before noon."

"And did you examine the body?"

"I did. It was severely burned by the fire."

"Were you able to determine the cause of Lawrence Lancaster's death?"

"Yes. He died of a gunshot to the brain."

"Given that the body was so badly burned, how could you locate a gunshot wound?"

"The head X ray of the deceased revealed a foreign metallic object which I removed. It was a twenty-two caliber bullet."

"Doctor, is it possible that the victim died from injuries sustained in the fire, or from smoke inhalation, and was shot after he died?"

"No, that is not possible. If an air-breathing animal such as a human being is even barely alive during a fire, smoke and other particulate matter will be found in the lungs or the windpipe, which I can discover upon examination of the body. There was no evidence of smoke or other fire-produced matter in either the victim's lungs or trachea."

"So . . . ," Kathryn dragged the question out, "this means what, Doctor?"

"It means Lawrence Lancaster was dead before the fire started."

"Were you able to determine the distance from the victim that the fatal shot was fired?"

"No, I wasn't," Nelson answered.

It was a minor weakness in her case that she wanted to reveal before the defense. "Can you tell us why?"

"When a gun is fired within approximately three feet at a human body, tiny particles of gunpowder are expelled from the muzzle and imbed themselves in the victim's skin. It's called 'tattooing' or 'stippling.' The victim's body was so badly burned that, even if stippling had been present, it would not have been detectable."

"So, from this would you necessarily conclude that the shot was fired from a distance greater than three feet?"

"No, it simply means that I cannot establish the distance from which it was fired."

"So, in this case, is it possible that the fatal shot was fired from close range, within three feet of the victim's head?"

"Yes, it is possible."

"Is it possible to determine the direction from which the fatal shot was fired?" Kathryn asked.

"Sometimes we can tell by the position of the body, the location of ejected cartridge casings, or other external evidence. It was not possible in this case."

"When a body is badly burned, is it possible to recover blood for forensic testing?"

"Yes, I recovered blood from Lawrence Lancaster's body."

"And you ran certain forensic tests on that blood?"

"I did."

"What did you find?"

"There were no drugs in his blood. His blood-alcohol level was .29."

Kathryn asked, "Is .29 high?"

"Yes. It is almost four times the legal limit for intoxication, which is .08."

"Is there a level at which there would be so much alcohol in a person's blood that he would be at risk of death from the alcohol itself?"

"Yes."

"Was Lawrence Lancaster's blood-alcohol level high enough that he might have died from alcohol poisoning?"

"No, it was not high enough for him to have been at risk of death, but he was quite drunk."

"Would the victim have been functional, or was he

so impaired that he would not be aware of his actions?"

"His mental functions were impaired."

"Doctor, does the blood-alcohol level continue to rise after death?"

"No. Blood circulation ceases at the instant of death, so additional alcohol cannot be transferred from the stomach to the bloodstream."

"So, if the victim's blood-alcohol was .29 during the autopsy, it was .29 at the instant he died. Is that correct?"

"That's correct."

"And I believe you said that at .29 the victim would be mentally impaired. How severely impaired were Lawrence Lancaster's mental functions at the time he was shot and killed, Doctor?" Kathryn knew the answer to this question long before she asked it.

"Unconsciousness occurs between .25 and .28. Lawrence Lancaster was unconscious when he was shot and killed."

Bickell jumped from her chair and charged toward the bench. "Objection, Your Honor. Sidebar!" Kathryn followed quickly.

"Your Honor," Angela Bickell whispered loudly enough to be heard in the hall outside, "I object to this witness's testimony and ask that it be stricken. The prosecution never disclosed that Lancaster was unconscious—"

"Lower your voice, Ms. Bickell. State your objection so the jury cannot hear."

"The prosecution is required to turn over all of its experts' reports to the defense, Your Honor. The prosecution produced no reports that stated Lancaster was unconscious. I move for an immediate mistrial and sanctions against the prosecutor."

Tucker turned and scowled at Kathryn. "What about that?"

"Your honor, the prosecution complied with Penal Code Section 1054 discovery requirements." Her slight smile could be best described as smug.

"Don't test my patience, Ms. Mackay. Did you disclose to the defense that Lawrence Lancaster was unconscious when he was killed, or didn't you?"

"There is no such report," Kathryn replied. "However, the results of the blood toxicological screen were appended to the autopsy protocol and clearly showed the victim's blood-alcohol level to be .29. Defense counsel had every right and, I suggest, a duty to have that report examined by her own expert, who would have confirmed what Dr. Nelson has testified to."

"Damnit, Judge, I'm going to—" Bickell blustered.

"Watch your language, counselor," Tucker warned. "She's right and you know it. If you failed to have the numbers interpreted, that's your own fault. Your objection is overruled, and your motions for a mistrial and sanctions are denied. Now, step back, both of you."

The two lawyers returned to their respective tables. Fields handed Kathryn a yellow legal pad, which she studied briefly to regain her place in Nelson's direct examination. Then she turned back toward the witness.

"Doctor, I believe you stated you removed a twenty-two caliber bullet from Lawrence Lancaster's head. Is that correct?"

"Yes."

"Did you examine the bullet closely at that time?"

"No, it was immediately submitted to the Department of Justice lab for analysis. Later, I examined the bullet microscopically and compared it to a gun that was provided by the lab to verify the criminalist's examination results."

"The process you applied to compare the bullet and the weapon is the science of ballistics. Is that correct?" Kathryn asked. Whenever Nelson provided a lengthy explanation, Kathryn recalled a story Nancy Reagan told. She said whenever someone asked the president what time it was, he explained how the clock worked. She had asked Nelson to not explain how the clock worked.

Nelson smiled. "That's essentially correct."

"I see. And this scientific procedure is capable of conclusively establishing that a bullet was fired from a specific gun. Is that correct?"

"Yes, that is correct."

"Can you explain for the jury, please, Doctor?" Kathryn asked.

"The metal in a gun is extremely hard, so it etches a pattern on the bullet as it is expelled through the barrel. The inside of a gun barrel contains spiral rifling which makes the bullet rotate in flight for stability. The rifling is peculiar to various brands of weapons; clockwise for certain weapons, counterclockwise for others. The barrel also has minor manufacturing imperfections. The combination of unique markings makes it possible to positively match a particular bullet to the gun that fired it."

"And you were able to do that in this case?"

"Yes. The bullet recovered from Lawrence Lancaster's brain was fired from the gun I test-fired."

Kathryn retrieved a gun, marked by an evidence tag, and handed it to Nelson. "Is this the gun that killed Lawrence Lancaster?"

"Yes."

"Are you certain?"

"Yes. The evidence tag contains my signature, which I inscribed after conducting my examination."

"Doctor, is this a complicated gun to use?"

"Not really. But you must manually cock it before it will fire."

"Could you demonstrate for us, please, Doctor?"

Nelson attempted to pull the trigger. "You can see that unless it's cocked, pulling the trigger has no effect," he said. "It won't fire."

Holding the weapon in his right hand, he inverted his left and slammed the slide backward, then allowed it to release. In the silent courtroom it sounded like a cannon. "There is no mistaking the sound of a semiautomatic pistol being cocked. The weapon would now be ready to fire if it were loaded," he said.

"So, a person can't simply pick up a weapon like this and fire it without thinking?"

Bickell was on her feet instantly. "Objection, Your Honor. That calls for speculation on the part of the witness."

"Overruled," Tucker responded. "Dr. Nelson is testifying as an expert on firearms. As such, he is permitted to speculate on matters within his area of expertise."

Nelson did not require the question to be repeated.

"It is impossible to fire this weapon without cocking it, and it cannot be cocked accidentally."

"Is it your opinion, then, that for a person to fire a weapon such as this one, the person would be required to think about what he or she is doing, however briefly, before doing it?"

"Yes, that is my opinion."

"Did you ascertain the owner of this weapon?"

"Yes, it is registered to Lawrence Lancaster."

"Lawrence Lancaster was killed in his own home with his own gun?"

"Yes."

Mackay turned to the bench. "No further questions for this witness at this time, Your Honor."

32

ANGELA BICKELL EXERCISED THE PREROGATIVE of the defense to defer her opening statement to the jury until immediately before presenting the defense witnesses. She smiled, stood, and walked to the end of the counsel table, where she placed her hand on the defendant's shoulder.

"Good morning, ladies and gentlemen. You all know that I am Angela Bickell and that I represent the defendant in this case, Anna Marie Lancaster. What you do not know are the most important facts about this case.

"If I may be indulged, I ask each of you to look carefully at my client." Lancaster was dressed in a conservative dark suit with low-heeled shoes. She wore virtually no makeup.

"The woman you see here is no killer. Oh, she shot and killed her husband, all right; the defense does not wish to deceive you about that. But she is no killer. Why did Anna Lancaster fatally shoot Lawrence Lancaster? The reasons are not so simple as the prosecution would have you believe.

"Anna and Lawrence Lancaster were husband and wife. Their romance was short and intense, and they married slightly over five years ago. But the dream became a nightmare very quickly. Within a few months, he became violent. Eventually, he became deadly violent.

"During the next five years, Lawrence inflicted untold violence on his wife. He intimidated her. He threatened her. He berated her. He hit her. He beat her. Repeatedly. Over and over. Lawrence Lancaster beat Anna Lancaster time and time again for five years, and time and time again, she came back to him.

"Yes, she came back to him after each humiliation, after each beating. You might ask why an intelligent, educated, competent, beautiful woman would return time after time to her abuser, only to be beaten again and again and again? It's a fair question. It's a simple question.

"And there is a simple answer. She loved him. That's right, she loved him. He was her husband, and she loved him. So much so that despite overwhelming abuse, she held onto the dream they shared when they promised to spend the rest of their lives together. She wanted it to be as he had promised and she had hoped.

"They had it all: wealth, beauty, love. But Lawrence Lancaster had something else, something he never told my client about before they were married. He had a violent and uncontrollable temper.

"But when she discovered, to her horror, the extent of her husband's rage and violence, did she blame him? No, she blamed everything except him. She blamed his violent behavior on alcohol. She blamed his violent behavior on financial worries. She blamed it on stress. Yes, and worst of all, she even blamed it on herself.

"So, she tried to change; to make it better. She became a better, more compliant wife. She was certain that if she could just figure out what she was doing wrong, she could make it right.

"But she couldn't make it right for one very simple reason; she wasn't doing anything wrong. She was an innocent victim of his uncontrollable violent fits of temper.

"She hid in the closet, but that didn't help. He simply broke the door down. He strangled her; he tried to run over her with his BMW; he sat on her and pinned her against the floor; he beat her; he choked her. My God, ladies and gentlemen, he even raped her. Some day, she knew he would do more than that; she knew he would kill her.

"That day arrived on July Fourth. On Independence Day, Lawrence Lancaster's violent behavior reached unprecedented levels. He was drunk. He was abusive. He was mean. He threatened to kill her, and he meant it. He had the means; he kept a loaded pistol in the house.

"My client reasonably feared for her very life last Independence Day. She did not believe she would be allowed to live until evening. So, she waited until he passed out from alcohol.

"She found his handgun. She had no alternative; either he would kill her or she must kill him. It would be even worse when he came to, and he might come to at any moment. When he did, he would kill her. That was when Anna Lancaster shot her husband one time in the head while he was passed out on the couch.

"I will introduce you to an expert on domestic violence and battered women. She will confirm that Anna Lancaster was in mortal fear for her life at the time she shot and killed her husband. She will testify that such beliefs are widespread and well documented among battered women. She will demonstrate to you the reasonableness of my client's fear.

"This expert will demonstrate to you beyond all doubt that Anna Lancaster killed her husband in self-defense.

"And, ladies and gentlemen, as the prosecutor herself confirmed, a person who kills in self-defense, as my client most certainly did, is guilty of no crime whatsoever."

Then and only then did Angela Bickell remove her hand from the shoulder of her client, who was weeping silently, and resume her seat at counsel table.

33

Kathryn slept fitfully the night before the defense expert was to testify. She knew her sleeplessness wasn't due to the trial, but because she had dreamed repeatedly of Dave Granz during the night, dreams that alternated between idyllic picnic lunches on the cliff overlooking the ocean and ugly ones in which they beat each other with their fists. Both were equally distressing, and both tested her powers of concentration to the limit.

Nevertheless, she opened the afternoon session in Department Six of Superior Court. "Your Honor has before her a motion I filed during the noon recess with the court clerk. I am requesting that the court limit the testimony of the defense expert on Battered Women's Syndrome to battered women in general, not the specific state of mind of the defendant at the time she shot and killed Lawrence Lancaster."

Judge Tucker considered the motion quickly before ruling. "The prohibition against testimony concerning the defendant's specific mental state does not exclude Dr. Houston's opinion as to the reasonableness of defendant's acts in claimed self-defense. Reasonableness is not a question of mental state but about the acts themselves. The prosecution's motion

to limit Dr. Houston's testimony is therefore denied."
The judge then turned to the bailiff and said, "Will
the bailiff bring in the jury, please."

When the jury was seated, Judge Tucker instructed
Angela Bickell to call her first witness.

Bickell rose. "The defense calls Lauryl Houston."

A woman arose from the gallery immediately behind the defense table, pushed open the swinging
gate, walked to the court clerk, and raised her hand to
be sworn. She was dressed in a pale blue suit and wore
her gray hair short. She wore faintly tinted plastic-
framed eyeglasses and had a large nose and thin lips.

"State your name and spell your last name, please,"
Bickell asked.

"Lauryl Houston, H-o-u-s-t-o-n."

"Please tell the court what you do for a living."

"I am a psychologist."

"You are a psychologist, not a psychiatrist?" Like
Mackay, Bickell recognized minor weaknesses in her
case and sought to minimize them by exposing them
herself.

"No, I am a psychologist, not a psychiatrist."

"Can you explain the difference to the jury,
please?"

"Certainly." Houston was a very experienced witness and fielded questions easily. "A psychiatrist has a
degree in medicine, while a psychologist's extensive
professional-training program is dedicated to psychological studies. A psychiatrist treats personality disorders, often by discussing a person's childhood and
prescribing drugs. Psychologists treat the person's
entire psyche, what I like to call a 'holistic' approach."

"Thank you. Can you outline your professional and academic background, please? You needn't go into too much detail, or we'll be here all evening." Bickell smiled.

"I earned an undergraduate degree from Southern Oregon State College in Ashland, and a master's degree in psychology from Portland State University in Portland, Oregon. I have a Ph.D. in clinical psychology from the University of Oregon in Eugene. I have been a practicing psychologist for fifteen years."

"Very good. Now, during your studies and in your private practice—I'm assuming you are in private rather than government practice. Is that correct?"

"Yes, I have my own practice in Salem, Oregon, the state capital."

"Okay, as I was saying, in your studies and in your private practice, have you studied about or treated women who have been physically abused by their husbands or domestic partners?"

"Oh, yes, many times. I realized early in my career that battered women would be my area of practice specialty. There is a severe need for professionals trained in this area."

"And have you determined there to be similarities among these women as to their outlook toward their problems, and their mental states?"

"Yes, it is referred to as Battered Women's Syndrome."

"Is that a term that is widely recognized among professional psychologists?"

"Definitely. It is now accepted as a personality disorder with common, predictable, and treatable characteristics among its victims."

"Is it true that most battered women are educationally and economically deficient—perhaps poorly educated and poor is a better description?"

"Oh no, that is a myth that only perpetuates the problem. Battered women come from all walks of life. They can be your neighbor, your mother, even your closest friend, and you may not know about it."

"Then, any woman could be a battered woman, even one who is young, pretty, smart, wealthy, and married to a successful lawyer. Is that correct?"

"Absolutely."

"These women must be docile or submissive, though—correct?"

"Another myth. In fact, I have treated over five hundred women, many of whom are what we would consider assertive personalities."

"How do battered women cope with this problem, Doctor?"

"Two of the most common strategies employed by battered women are flight and counterviolence. Flight unfortunately does not occur frequently enough. Counterviolence involves verbal or even physical resistance and reciprocal violence on the abuser. It is the least effective approach and also the most likely to stimulate the batterer to greater violence."

"So," Bickell summed up, "submission doesn't work, flight doesn't work, and fighting back doesn't work. Is that about it? Is there anything else about counterviolence as a strategy available to battered women that we should know?"

"Yes. It is common for women to not recall severe beatings they receive. They often suffer memory lapses. It is a common way for them to block out and minimize the danger they feel, to justify continuing in a relationship with the battering partner. An abused woman usually views her batterer as far more powerful than she; counterviolence is seen as futile. But counterviolence is not mutual combat. The fact that a woman does make an ineffectual attempt to defend herself, what we call counterviolence, she is no less a battered woman, and no less in danger of being killed."

"You mentioned that many battered women are killed by their batterers. Are there any statistics to back that up?"

"Yes, there are. Every year in the United States, four thousand women are killed by their partners. Twenty percent of all adult female suicides result from being battered. According to the FBI, six million women each year are beaten by their husbands or boyfriends. It results in more than thirty thousand hospital emergency-room visits. More than half of the women in this country are battered at some time in their lives. Worst of all, one out of four men and nearly as many women think that sometimes it's proper for a man to hit his wife. Domestic violence is a deadly epidemic of unprecedented proportion."

Bickell drew a deep breath and expelled it slowly. "So, a woman stands a high chance of being battered, and if so, she's likely to be killed?"

"That is correct."

"And are these statistics buried in some obscure scientific publication, or are they available to the general public?"

"Oh, they are quite public, I assure you. In fact, the

San Francisco newspaper ran an article with these statistics just recently. Any woman who reads the newspapers, watches television, listens to the radio, or talks to her friends knows she is in immediate mortal danger."

"In your professional opinion, Doctor, is a battered woman's fear of being killed or gravely injured by her batterer a reasonable fear?"

"Such a fear is not only reasonable, it is common sense. To ignore it would be foolhardy and suicidal."

"Is there any way to reliably predict when a battered woman might snap and become violent toward her abuser, in your opinion?"

"Not really. A battered woman is amazingly resilient. To use a metaphor, she is much like a bough on a willow tree that is repeatedly battered by heavy winds over a period of time. She bends but does not break under each storm, but each weakens her imperceptibly. Like the willow tree, she has a limit. Eventually, she will be forced to the ground once too often, and when that happens, she will break; she will become violent. Nothing violent happens until the bough breaks. There is no way to predict when the bough will break for any particular tree or any particular woman, but it will inevitably occur."

Bickell returned to the defense table and studied her notes. "Dr. Houston, I'd like to discuss my client, if you don't mind. Were you asked to evaluate Anna Lancaster to determine if she possesses the characteristics you have described as being common to women suffering from Battered Women's Syndrome?"

"Yes, I was. I spent several hours evaluating Mrs.

Lancaster. She exhibited many of those characteristics. In my opinion, she suffers from Battered Women's Syndrome."

"Doctor, you previously testified that the fear of being killed that a battered woman experiences is reasonable under the circumstances, and that Anna Lancaster is a typical battered woman. Was the fear that my client felt on the morning of July Fourth that she was about to be killed by her husband, whom she shot to death, a reasonable fear?"

"Yes, in my opinion, it was a reasonable fear under the circumstances."

Angela Bickell turned to the bench. "No further questions, Your Honor."

34

"THIS CAME IN THIS MORNING'S MAIL. CELL-mark Labs." Walt Earheart walked into Kathryn Mackay's office Thursday morning and dropped a stack of papers unceremoniously on her desk. His solemn look didn't change as she picked up the report. Cellmark was a private laboratory in Maryland that specialized in DNA testing.

Kathryn flipped through the two-page report, blanched, looked up at Earheart, then reread it carefully. "This can't be right. According to this report, the semen recovered from Julia Soto the night she was raped belonged to Dave Granz. He told me—"

"I know what he said, and I don't want to know what he told you. Benton ordered you not to talk to him about it. And I know what that report says. That's why I'm here. No one has seen this except you and me, yet."

"I appreciate that, Walt. What do we do?"

"What do you mean, what do we do? I've got to get this to the sheriff. I shouldn't have even showed it to you, but I knew you had to hear it from me. Give you some time to prepare yourself. But it's time and date stamped today. I can't sit on it."

"I didn't ask you to sit on it, Walt; I just want to talk to you about it." Kathryn was stalling for time to think. "Damn, Cellmark's one of the best. Still, it's possible they made a mistake."

"Anything's possible, Kate," Earheart said. "What sort of mistake are you thinking about?"

"Well, for starters, it's possible for two people to have the same DNA pattern."

"Christ, Kate, that's virtually impossible."

"No, it's not. The random match probability is no better than one in a million. Assuming there are fifty million adult men in the United States, there are at least fifty with the same DNA pattern."

"You're getting pretty defensive here. I heard it's as high as one in a billion. But, even assuming the smaller number, how many of those fifty men were in Santa Rita the night Julia Soto was raped? That was Dave Granz's semen."

And how many admit to having consensual sex with her within seventy-two hours of when she says she was raped. Dave's admission could cut both ways, Kathryn thought. "Maybe, maybe not. Labs make mistakes, too. Samples could have got mixed up. They might have tested the wrong blood."

"Spoken like a true defense attorney," he said.

"Damnit, Walt, you know when you take the one-in-a-million probability and compound it by the possibility that the lab got their samples mixed up, you've got significant room for error. That also doesn't take into account the possibility that someone intentionally planted the evidence."

"This sounds like the O. J. Simpson police-conspiracy theory. Are you serious? Who would set Granz up? And maybe you can tell me how someone could get Granz' semen and plant it in Soto's body. Whadaya think, someone'd just walk up to her and say, 'Excuse me, ma'am, would you mind pulling up your skirt and taking off your panties. I have this little glob of semen I'd like to put up there for safekeeping. I'll come and get it as soon as I have a permanent location for it.'"

"Walt, the DNA report says there wasn't enough semen recovered for RFLP testing, so they had to ID it by a PCR test. That's not nearly as accurate." Kathryn stopped for a deep breath, and when she drew in her breath, it caught in her throat as a sob. "There's another thing."

"I thought there might be. What?"

"Well, a DNA match is only one aspect of a rape investigation. Lots of other factors have to be proven, too."

"For instance?"

"For instance, you've got to prove intercourse was accomplished by force or fear. It's just her word against his."

"True, counselor. Most rape cases are her word against his, as you've said yourself in any number of jury trials. But you'd make a lousy defense attorney. Dave can't prove he wasn't there, either. Says he was driving and walking on the beach alone that night. Pretty convenient, wouldn't you say?"

"What did the lab come up with when they examined his clothing?"

"Sand, but that doesn't prove he wasn't there earlier or later or that he didn't rape that woman."

"Read the Constitution, Walt. He doesn't have to prove he didn't; the government has to prove he did. And he didn't," she said with more conviction than she felt.

"Kate, you're grasping at straws here. I've been doing the same thing ever since I saw that report. But we can't be blinded to the facts. That was Dave's semen in Julia Soto."

Kathryn nodded. "You're right. But there's got to be some explanation besides rape. I'm sure of it."

"Well, maybe so, but I've got to get this report up to Purvis." He rose to leave.

"Walt?" Kathryn asked.

"Yeah?" he answered at the door.

"He can't face this. I know him."

35

A<small>T</small> NINE O'CLOCK ON F<small>RIDAY</small> THE TWENTY-ninth, Kathryn Mackay began cross-examination of Dr. Lauryl Houston, who was reminded she was still under oath.

"Doctor, after completing your review of the reports and documents presented to you by the defendant, did you prepare a written report containing the findings and conclusions to which you have testified in this court?" Kathryn remained seated beside her investigator, James Fields.

"No."

"Did you prepare a written report detailing the precise information upon which you based the opinions and conclusions that you expressed in this court?"

"No."

Kathryn rose and walked toward the witness chair. "Doctor, are you familiar with what is called the 'scientific method'?"

"Yes, I am familiar with that term."

"Isn't the scientific method the cornerstone of objective scientific proof?" Kathryn asked.

The witness did not respond.

"I'm sorry, I didn't hear your answer," Kathryn urged.

"Well, yes, but it doesn't . . . ," she began hesitantly.

"It doesn't what, Doctor?"

Bickell stood. "Objection, Your Honor. Counsel is not allowing the witness to answer the question."

Before the judge could rule, Kathryn said, "Excuse me, I didn't mean to interrupt. I thought you were finished. Please continue."

The witness squirmed slightly in the witness chair. "I was saying that not all scientific activities must adhere to the scientific method to be valid."

"Okay. Would you agree that the primary principle underlying the scientific method is that a scientist publishes her findings and conclusions so that other independent and objective experts can examine them to see if they are valid?"

"Yes, that is the underlying principle."

"Thank you. Now, you are also familiar with the concept of 'peer review' as it applies to your scientific field, aren't you?"

"Yes."

"Please explain to the jury what the term 'peer review' means."

The witness looked at the defense attorney, but there was no basis for an objection. "It means that your work is reviewed by other people."

"It's more specific than that, isn't it? Peer review means that a professional such as yourself provides written reports so other experts in the same scientific field can evaluate her work. Isn't that true?"

"Yes, I suppose you could define it that way."

"In fact, virtually everything of scientific import ever developed in the field of psychology has been written up and subjected to the peer-review process. Isn't that correct?" It was more a statement than a question but demanded an answer.

"Yes, you might say that."

"Yes, I might. Isn't this an application of the scientific principle?"

The witness grew increasingly uncomfortable with each question.

"During your training, Doctor, didn't your instructors teach you to write up and report your data, your findings, and your conclusions such that other professionals could review them?"

"Not always," she answered sullenly.

"I see. Is it true that scientific discoveries and conclusions are generally disregarded by the scientific community as unproven until they have been subjected to the rigors of the scientific principle, including peer review?"

"Generally."

"Is that a yes or a no?"

"It's a generally," she snapped.

Kathryn looked at the judge, who instructed Houston, "The question requires a yes or no response. Please answer the question."

"Yes."

"In this case, however, you did not prepare a written report, in contravention of both your training and the scientific method. Isn't that true?"

"It's true that I didn't prepare a written report in this case."

"You have been appointed by the court on many previous occasions as a forensic expert, haven't you?"

"Yes."

"You were required to provide a written report on your examination findings and the conclusions you drew from them each and every time, were you not?"

"Yes."

"And were you aware that those reports would be made available to all the parties involved, including the other side, before trial?"

"Yes."

"And you have been thoroughly cross-examined in the past concerning those written reports. Isn't that correct?"

"Yes."

"Doctor, have you ever been retained as an expert for the prosecution in a criminal trial?"

"Yes, I have," she answered warily.

"Has any prosecutor ever asked you to not prepare a written report?" Kathryn emphasized the word "ever."

Houston seized the opportunity to shift the blame to the defense attorney. "No, never."

"Yet, you did not produce a written report in this case. Who asked that you not prepare a written report?"

"The defense attorney."

"Did you inform Ms. Bickell that her request was in contravention of both your training and the scientific method?"

"No."

"No? Did you tell Ms. Bickell here that an ethical,

reputable, and truly unbiased psychologist would not hesitate to report her findings and conclusions in writing so a proper independent review could be made?"

"No," she answered warily.

"Are you saying that you went against your own professional training and violated the scientific principle simply because the defense bought you with money?"

"Objection, Your Honor, the prosecution is badgering the witness."

"Overruled," Judge Tucker said, "I'd like to hear her answer. Answer the question, Dr. Houston."

"No, that isn't the reason," Houston answered.

"Then were you simply afraid to report your work in writing because I would have time to review it properly before cross-examining you?"

Immediately, Kathryn said, "I withdraw the question, Your Honor." She studied her legal pad before continuing. "In arriving at your diagnostic impressions of the defendant and their behavioral implications, which you did not report in writing, you relied on numerous sources of information. Is that correct?"

"That is correct."

"Was one of the sources you relied on a face-to-face interview with the defendant?"

"Yes."

"And I presume you received information concerning the defendant's social, educational, and medical background from friends, school records, physicians, and so forth."

"Yes, Ms. Bickell provided me with those records."

"Doctor, did you use any other information or sources in forming your opinion?"

"A diary. I was given her diary."

"A diary?" Kathryn had heard nothing of a diary. "Do you mean the type of diary people often keep in which they record very intimate and personal thoughts and experiences? That kind of diary?"

"That's right," Houston answered. "Diaries are extremely valuable as diagnostic tools. Often, more revealing than hours of clinical interviews."

"In what form was this diary kept, Doctor? Is it in the defendant's own handwriting?"

Bickell objected. "That's two questions, Your Honor. Perhaps the prosecution could ask questions one at a time so the witness can answer."

In a breach of court protocol, Houston interrupted, "That's all right, Your Honor. I can answer the questions simultaneously."

The judge nodded her consent.

The witness smiled at Kathryn Mackay. "This is the computer age, Ms. Mackay. The diary is not in the defendant's handwriting; it is on computer disk."

"Do you have a printed copy of that diary with you in court today?"

"No, but I have the computer disk."

Kathryn asked for and received Tucker's permission to approach the bench, out of the jury's earshot. "Your Honor, this is unconscionable! The defense attorney is playing games here. By directing her expert to not prepare a report, the prosecution is at a disadvantage. I need the diary so I can study it. I request a week's continuance to prepare for additional cross-examination."

Bickell interrupted. "I'll print out a copy of the diary and give it to the prosecution."

"Your Honor," Kathryn said, "the best evidence is the disk itself, and the People are entitled to it. I'm concerned that it might be inadvertently damaged or accidentally erased. Therefore, I request that the Court order Ms. Bickell to immediately turn the disk over to the Court for duplication by the County Computer Services Department."

"So ordered," Judge Tucker said. "I will direct Computer Services to have a copy of the disk in your hands this afternoon. You have until next Monday morning to examine its contents. The Court will be in recess until then. Now, step back."

36

"WHAT'S UP, COUNSELOR? ENJOYING YOUR tiptoe through the tulips of Anna Lancaster's psyche?" Jim Fields asked.

Kathryn Mackay sat hunched over her desk studying Anna Lancaster's diary. Dating back several years, the first entry was less than a year after the Lancasters were married. Kathryn was amazed that some of the physical violence she described had not shown up as recent injuries on the X rays.

"Jim, there's something wrong here. This thing is typed perfectly. Grammar's perfect, spelling's perfect. Hell, there aren't even any typos. Did they locate a personal computer in the ruins of the Lancaster fire?"

"Don't think so. I'll check." He made a notation in his book. "Why?"

"I don't recall one, either. Where would she have access to a computer with WordPerfect software?"

"At work, probably; she was a secretary at the law firm. I still don't get it."

"That's because you're not a woman and have, therefore, never been a teenage girl."

Fields grinned. "Thank God! That'd be the most spectacular metamorphosis in the history of humankind, scientific principle notwithstanding."

"Well, sexism aside, when girls or women are so influenced by something that they record it in their diaries, they usually don't wait until they get to work the next day and type it into a computer."

"So, sexism aside, what do they do?"

"They pull out a nice leather-bound diary, unlock it with a tiny key they keep secreted where nobody can find it, and they write in it. In their own handwriting. That's what they do."

Fields's face lit up. "Okay-y-y-y," he mused, "that makes sense. Where does it get us?"

"I'm not sure, but it bothers me. And there's something else." She paused while Fields watched expectantly. This was woman stuff.

"How could someone, even a professional typist, sit down the next morning at work and key in something so traumatic and vicious as those beatings she described and not be upset enough to screw up a few words here and there, misspell a word, or make a grammatical mistake. Sounds too . . . that's it, Jim."

"What?"

"Maybe they weren't written contemporaneously. Maybe she just sat down at the computer and keyed them in all at the same time."

"Why would she do that, and what difference would it make, anyway, if they're true?"

"Well, maybe she was asked to by her attorney. That might explain the why. As to what difference it makes, done that way they're not a diary at all, and they're not admissible to establish the truth of the matter.

"Let's see." Kathryn retrieved a dictionary from her lower-left desk drawer and flipped it to the Ds.

"Yeah, here we go. A diary is defined as a daily record or journal. That means it's written shortly after an event while the details are fresh in the mind. That's why diaries and journals are considered valuable in establishing personality characteristics. But, if events are recorded significantly after the fact, recall is diminished. When they write about it later, people tend to write what they wish happened, or what they imagine happened, not what actually happened."

"Okay, I'm with you. In that case, she certainly wouldn't want to do it in her own handwriting. That's too easy to detect."

"Explain."

"Document examiners like forensic accountants use this technique to discover fraudulent business records, tax records, and the like, that have been transcribed all at the same time. Entries into a ledger should be made incrementally, over time, as the transactions occur. Recorded properly, they will vary from each other considerably in appearance. The color of the ink will be different, for example, and so will the quality of the writing, because the same writing instrument won't be used every time. Not possible.

"Also, handwriting varies slightly for the same individual, too, due to temperature—you see how good your writing is when you're cold—and other factors. Writing surfaces also vary, creating variations in the quality of the writing made on top of them."

"Go on, this is very interesting."

"If a person writes what purports to be a series of sequential items that occurred over a long period of time, all in one sitting, the only way it could be disguised is by going to elaborate lengths to change all those factors constantly. An overwhelming job. Couldn't be done."

"Or," Kathryn joined in, "by doing it on a computer, whose printed product looks the same every time, anyway."

"Right. But even then, we might be able to tell, if we could access the computer itself."

"How?"

"Whadaya mean how? I thought you were a computer guru, the way you carry that laptop around and whip it out at the slightest provocation," Fields kidded.

"I know how to run 'em and that's it."

"Ah, the secret is out. Anyway, computer records

are really electronic files. Every time they're saved or updated by the program that's being used, like Word-Perfect, it time and date stamps the file. If I can locate the files, I can see when they were created."

"Can you tell that from the floppy disk we have?"

"Maybe, maybe not. Some copy and transfer programs don't transfer anything except the data. Safest thing would be to look at her computer at work. Besides, who knows what else we might find."

"Right. I'll draft a search warrant for Tucker's signature. Let's get rolling on this. We need to access that computer before someone erases those files. Jim, while I type up the search warrant, do me a favor, will you?"

"Sure, name it."

"Just so we don't leave any loose ends, would you run up to the County Recorder's office? Check the public filings and see if anything has been recorded in either of the Lancasters' names over the past five years."

"No sweat. What am I looking for?"

"Don't know. Maybe a property sale, a vacation-home purchase, a big loan with a perfected lien, passport photo, divorce, anything. Who knows? I'm playing a hunch. Hell, it doesn't even rise to the level of a hunch. I'm fishing."

"Okay, I'll have them run an alphabetical search on the entire data base. It'll take a few minutes, but it should give us anything that's under either name, no matter what kind of document it is."

"Good idea. Run her maiden name, too, okay?"

"Gotcha. What is it?" Fields prepared to write the name in his notebook.

"Don't you have that? It would have been in her personnel file at Lancaster and Young. Granz was going to look at those along with the others."

"Jesus, Kate, I never looked at them. I'm sorry, I knew something would fall through the cracks when we transitioned from Granz to me. What now?"

"Not your fault, Jim. I'll add them to the listing of property to be searched. How long on that records check?"

"Half an hour, tops."

"All right. I'll have the search warrant and affidavit ready when you get back. See ya."

When Fields returned, Kathryn had the search warrant and affidavit ready to fax to Judge Tucker. "Find anything?"

"Naw, routine stuff. Building permit for a small improvement to the house. Mortgage. A prenuptial agreement, a—"

"A what?!"

37

KATHRYN MACKAY AND JIM FIELDS approached the top of the hill near Crest Road in his new Mercury Cougar. "So, what's the big deal about a prenuptial agreement? And why would he record it? They don't have to be," Fields said.

"No, but he could've recorded it without her knowing about it. Most people just sign them, stick them in a drawer someplace, and forget them. But he's a lawyer. They're so common, just about everyone has one nowadays, especially people like the Lancasters."

"Yeah, I think it takes the romance out of a marriage. Sorta like, 'Okay, darling, I'll slip into something sexy as soon as you sign off on the shopping mall, and I'll trade you for the rental property.' Makes me glad I was married while we were young, broke, and stupid."

"I know what you mean. But think about it. Anna Lancaster comes along and marries this rich attorney who's older than she is. She'll probably outlive him, then what? It gets really messy from a business point of view. She steps in after he dies and demands her community-property share of the law firm. Very ugly. The partners in that firm aren't going to let that happen. I'll bet they make everyone execute prenups when they marry."

"Makes sense," Fields said, "Matter of fact, Hyler's secretary told me the single women and the single guys, too, look outside the firm for romance, that the firm has some way to keep outsiders from marrying into the firm's money. I'll bet she was talking about the prenups and didn't know it. Probably not widely advertised; it sounds a little sleazy. But so what?"

"I'm not sure. We were just assuming she would inherit a ton of money if his death looked accidental. Hence the fire to cover up the fact that she shot him. Maybe we were wrong. If there was a prenuptial agreement, what she got on his death, even if it were accidental, would be determined by the terms of the agreement. Don't know where that takes us, but it sure puts a different slant on things."

Traffic was heavy past the reservoir, through Los Gatos and Campbell, but light on El Camino Real, and they arrived at Lancaster and Young before closing time. Philip Hyler, who had been called and forewarned that the search warrant was to be served, met them. He was a tall, slender, very Aryan-looking man, impeccably dressed and meticulously groomed. "Good afternoon, Mr. Fields," he said, shaking Jim's hand.

Then he thrust a well-manicured hand at Kathryn. "Ms. Mackay, it's such a pleasure to meet you. I only wish it could be under more pleasant circumstances. I often wished I were a trial attorney, but I'm afraid I don't have the killer instinct."

Kathryn shook his hand, not certain whether she had just been complimented or insulted. "The grass is always greener, Mr. Hyler. I've often wondered what it would be like to practice law in an environment like this rather than back-alley crime scenes and tiny un-air-conditioned offices. Neither of us will ever know, will we?"

Hyler chuckled. "That's for sure. If you'll follow me, I'll show you Mrs. Lancaster's office."

As he led them through a large, open space that comprised the work stations of two dozen or more secretaries and other clerical workers, he said over his shoulder, "I appreciate how sensitively this is being handled. This is very disruptive for the firm and disturbing to our staff, as you can imagine. Ah, here we are."

He led them into a spacious, well-appointed outer

office with a closed door which Kathryn assumed connected to the office of deceased partner Lawrence Lancaster.

"This is—was—Mrs. Lancaster's office. I put her personnel file and Larry's on the desk. Her computer keyboard is under the desk where the pencil tray would normally be. You can see the monitor on her desk. The CPU is on the floor to the left."

"Thank you," Fields said. "You left the computer off, as I asked?"

"Yes, of course. It hasn't been turned on since Anna was arrested, as far as I know. Now, if you'll excuse me, I'll leave you to your work. My extension is 2888, if you need me. Please contact me, rather than the staff, if you require anything."

As soon as Hyler departed, Fields pulled the secretary's chair up to Anna Lancaster's desk. "Grab a chair and watch," he told Kathryn.

Fields withdrew a floppy disk from his shirt pocket and inserted it into the disk drive of the minitower Compaq computer. "Boot disk," he told Kathryn.

"Can't you just turn it on? That's what I'd do," she said.

"Yeah, and it'd probably be okay. But she could've sabotaged the computer, wrote a little program that trashes everything on the disk drive if it's started up at the wrong time or on the wrong day of the week. Highly unlikely, but better to be safe than sorry. This will bypass the usual start-up procedure. When the computer boots up, it'll be on the floppy rather than the hard drive, and I can look at the hard drive's directory. See what's on it."

"All Greek to me," Kathryn said. "Go for it."

"This is all real basic stuff, believe me. If I run into a start-up password, or if the files are encrypted, we'll need somebody who actually knows what they're doing. Interesting, though, most computers have little or no security built in. Here goes."

The Compaq started up, buzzed as it searched Drive A for a floppy disk, found it, and asked for confirmation of the system's internally maintained time and date. Fields tapped the Enter key twice and received an A:\>_ prompt.

"All right!" he muttered, "Let's see what's over on the hard drive." He typed 'C:' then pressed the Enter key. The hard drive answered 'C:\>_'. Fields then typed in 'CD\DOS' and the computer responded 'C:\DOS>_'.

"Okay, let's get an overview of what's on her computer. I'm gonna type in a Tree command for her hard drive. That'll give me the directory and subdirectory setup. There's usually a separate directory for each program, so we'll be able to see what sort of stuff is on there. My guess is we'll find a network, a word-processing program, WordPerfect to be precise, maybe a game or two, and not much else. Big company like this would have most of the stuff on the network server."

"Why wouldn't the word-processing program be on the network, too?" Kathryn asked. Then as an afterthought, "Can you get us on the network?"

"I don't think we need to. She would have typed confidential stuff for her boss, who just happened to be the firm's senior partner and also happened to be her husband. He wouldn't want that stuff out on the network where everybody could read it. My guess is

261

it'd be restricted to her work station. Let's see if I'm right."

Working the enter and pause keys alternately with his left hand, Fields scanned the contents of the computer's hard-disk drive. "Pretty much what I thought. Windows 3.1, a Novell network, WordPerfect, Casino Gambling, and Chess. Couple of surprises, too."

"Like what?"

"Quicken, for one thing. It's a little bookkeeping system. Lets you write checks, balance your checkbook, stuff like that. Great program—I use it myself."

"I don't balance my checkbook," Kathryn said candidly. "I figure if I've still got blank checks left, there must be money in my account. What else?"

"Compuserve. It's a system for sending and receiving e-mail and accessing on-line services like airline-reservation and information data bases."

"I know what Compuserve is; I didn't just fall off a pumpkin truck," Kathryn answered in feigned disgust. "Why would she have Compuserve? Wouldn't that require a direct outside line?"

"Yep, it would."

Kathryn lifted the phone on the desk and started punching buttons. She replaced the receiver and reported, "Direct outside line."

"All right," Fields said, "let's get a closer look." He entered the WordPerfect directory and requested a directory listing. In addition to program files, he spotted three subdirectories. One was named LARRYDAT, one ANNADAT, and the third ANGDAT. Fields started the program and listed files in both the LARRYDAT and ANNADAT subdirectories. Pressing the Enter key, he was able to quickly scan the contents of each file, all of which were routine business correspondence.

"Damn," Kathryn said.

"That's strike two," Fields said absently. "You're not out till strike three. Let's see what's in ANGDAT." Only one file was listed: "ANGELA.BIK 20,214 07-08-97 11:45p".

"J-i-m-m?" Kathryn said, drawing his name out as a question. "That's too close to be a coincidence. ANGELA.BIK has to be Angela Bickell. And look at that date and time. Right after Anna Lancaster hired Bickell and posted bail. That file was typed late Friday night, while nobody else was here. She would've had a key to the building. Let's look at that file."

Fields dropped the red highlighter over the file name, pressed 1, and retrieved the document onto the monitor.

"There it is, Jim. There's the diary. Neat as can be. Look at that, each entry is followed by a hard-page code so it looks like it was written and printed out at separate times. She wrote the whole thing all in one sitting, just like I thought. Can you print it out?"

"Yep, no problem." He pressed the print key and sent several dozen pages of information to the Hewlett Packard LaserJet 5L on the table beside the desk.

When it was finished, Kathryn decided to look into Compuserve. Logging on was simple. Fields simply rebooted the computer normally, and when the Windows screen appeared, he clicked on the Compuserve logo.

"Jim, let me take over here for a minute. Take a quick look in her personnel file and see who she has listed as a next of kin," Kathryn said, sliding her chair alongside his and grabbing the computer mouse.

A moment later, he reported, "Looks like a sister. Elizabeth Flynt. Lives in Redding."

Kathryn clicked the mouse on the Compuserve member directory logo and scrolled through the letters of the alphabet until she located the Fs, then slowed the scroll. "There she is."

Exiting the member directory, she clicked on Lancaster's on-line mailbox and found no waiting mail. She then peeked into the WinCIM in-basket and out-basket which temporarily stores incoming and outgoing mail. "Empty," she muttered. "Let's take a look in her filing cabinet."

"What're you looking for?" Fields asked.

"You can download incoming mail from the Compuserve mailbox into a Windows file called a filing cabinet," Kathryn said. "That lets you save messages and review them at your leisure off-line so you don't run up your access charges."

Fields was impressed. "Wait a while," he said. "You told me you didn't know anything about computers. Now, you sound like an expert. How do you know so much about Compuserve?"

"Got it on my laptop," she told him. "Emma uses it for school projects. And I can access certain legal services and bulletin boards, like the alumni group from my law school."

"Jim, look at this!" Kathryn had just opened an old e-mail message from Elizabeth Flynt, addressed to her sister Anna Lancaster. The letter described a beating Elizabeth had suffered at the hands of her husband several years earlier. Almost all the messages from Elizabeth contained very detailed accounts of abuse she had sustained.

As she read, Kathryn became aware of a striking similarity between the messages written by Elizabeth Flynt and those contained in the diary of Anna Lancaster. The discrepancy was that, where Lancaster's diary was typed flawlessly, Elizabeth's letters were obviously written by an emotionally distraught woman. They contained profanity and were filled with typing and grammatical errors. One in particular caught Kathryn's attention.

"Jim, get that early entry in Lancaster's diary, the one where she talked about being slammed against the refrigerator and chased out into the backyard."

"Okay, got it."

"Now listen to this." Kathryn read verbatim from an e-mail message sent from Elizabeth Flynt to Anna Lancaster three years previous. "Dear Anna. The nightmare never changes. Last night bob (spelled with a small B) and I fought again. When I askd him to leave, he said i just wanted him to leave it all to me. i dont even know what he ment. I thought he was going to kill me. He hit me up against the refrigerator and knock me out. Then he chased me out into the back yard. he knocked me down on the walkway by the house, you know the one that goes to the garage door and the street. He beat my head on the sidewalk and said this time i'll fucking kill you. I think he meant it. The son of a bitch! I think he would have if—"

Fields interrupted. "Let me finish it, Kathryn. I can read it right from Lancaster's diary."

Fields read from the computer printout, "He beat my head on the sidewalk and told me, 'I think this time I'll fucking kill you.' I think he meant it. The son of a bitch! I think he would have if he hadn't been scared off by a police siren going by on the street."

They sat stunned. Tentatively and almost reverently, Kathryn said, "Those weren't Anna Lancaster's experiences in her diary. They were her sister's. Jim, we've got to go to Redding. Immediately."

"I know. As soon as we get back, I'll call United Airlines and book us on a shuttle from San Jose. You call Mrs. Flynt and tell her we're coming."

"I don't think so, Jim. I think we'd better just drop in unannounced. Her husband might not take kindly to all this."

Kathryn thought for a minute as they gathered their files. "One more thing."

"What's that?"

"I want a copy of that prenuptial agreement."

"You'll have it before we take off for Redding if I have to get the County Recorder down to the County Building personally tonight."

38

IT TOOK LONGER FOR JIM FIELDS AND KATHRYN Mackay to drive to the airport than the entire flight to Redding. The flight was smooth, the skies were clear, and the small jet-prop airplane was less than half full.

It was already sweltering at nine-thirty Saturday morning when they stepped off the plane onto the tarmac at Redding airport. The air-conditioning in the rented Toyota was a blessed relief.

"Remind me to never live here," Kathryn said as they drove past the shopping center toward downtown. "Let's see if we can find some decent coffee."

Fields parked the car at the curb in front of Starbucks in the downtown mall. While they sipped their coffees at a sidewalk table, Fields asked, "So where do the Flynts live? Are you familiar with this place?"

"A little. I had a friend who lived here, so I came to visit occasionally. They got transferred to Georgia. The street address looks to me like it's in that nice neighborhood near the Sacramento River," she said. "We'll check there first."

"So, whadawe do, just drop in on them? Damn, it's hot. Why didn't you tell me not to wear a suit?"

"Would you have paid attention?"

"No," he grinned, "but I'd know you cared."

"I thought about this the whole way up here," Kathryn said, oblivious to Fields's attempt at humor. "I think we'll get the best results if we just show up at the door. Don't give him time to intimidate her. Maybe she'll feel secure enough to talk with both of us there."

He nodded.

"All right, then, let's finish our coffee and see if we can find the Flynts."

As expected, the Flynt home was in an expensive neighborhood near the river. A sprawling ranch-style home typical of the area and the era, it's address was 772 Shasta Way. Fields parked the Toyota on the side street, Willow. As they walked toward the corner, Kathryn poked Fields and pointed to their left. "There's the concrete walkway, the garage, and the gate in Elizabeth's e-mail. We're walking along the street she was trying to flee to."

A small woman resembling Anna Lancaster answered the door. She was in a dark blue sweat suit, despite the heat. "Yes?"

"Elizabeth Flynt?" Fields asked.

Cautiously, she said, "Yes, who are you, please?"

Fields held his badge and ID case to the screen door, which emitted a blast of cool air. "I'm Inspector Fields from the Santa Rita District Attorney's office, Mrs. Flynt. This is Kathryn Mackay—she's an assistant District Attorney. We wondered if we might talk with you for a few minutes."

She backed away from the door. "Mackay? You're the woman who's prosecuting my sister."

"Yes, ma'am, I am," Kathryn answered. "It's vitally important that I speak with you. May we come in? Please, it won't take long."

"I don't know; I'm not sure my husband would—"

"Mrs. Flynt, is your husband home? Perhaps we could speak with him," Fields suggested.

"He isn't here. He's at the fitness center. What was it you said you wanted to see me about?"

"Ma'am, if we could just come in for a few minutes?" Kathryn urged.

She hesitated, then opened the screen door and allowed them to step inside. The house was early-to-mid-seventies style, walls covered with walnut paneling, with reddish-brown shag carpets and heavy drapes. The kitchen appliances, including the refrigerator, whose door was slightly dented at about head height, were avocado green.

"Would you like coffee?" she asked.

"No thanks, but I'd love to use the restroom," Kathryn said.

"Through the door to your left—that's the master bedroom. There's a bathroom there."

Mackay knew there are few places to learn more about a woman than her bathroom. Elizabeth's bathroom was neat and tidy, and looked like it belonged strictly to her. The toilet seat was in the down position; her husband probably didn't use it. The medicine cabinet contained the usual toiletries and personal items. It also contained a hospital-sized box of gauze bandages, a huge roll of medical tape, and a giant bottle of generic brand tincture of iodine. A pair of crutches leaned against the wall behind the door.

Kathryn flushed the toilet without using it and rejoined them in the kitchen. "Mrs. Flynt," Kathryn said, "Inspector Fields and I don't want to take up too much of your time, but we do need to speak with you. You know your sister's lawyer claims Anna is a battered woman? That her husband beat her frequently and that's the reason she killed him?"

"Yes, I know that."

"Mrs. Flynt, . . . may I call you Elizabeth?"

The woman nodded.

"Elizabeth, more than half the women in the country are abused each year. Has this ever happened to you?"

"I . . . I thought you wanted to talk to me about Anna Marie. Why do you ask me that?"

Softly, Kathryn continued, "I think we may be

talking about you when we speak of Anna Marie's abuse. Elizabeth, I know that relationships between adults—a husband and wife—are sometimes violent. It's nothing you should be ashamed of. I may have some suggestions for what you can do. What happens when you and Bob fight?"

Elizabeth hesitated, then tears formed in the corner of her eyes. "You can't know about that. I've never told anyone except . . ."

"Except your sister? We know about your e-mail correspondence with Anna Marie. We were allowed to see the messages."

"You don't understand, Miss Mackay. Bob, my husband, is under a lot of pressure at work. He's not mean at all. He loves me. It's just that sometimes he gets upset when things are hard."

"I know he loves you; of course he does. I'm not saying he doesn't. What sort of work does he do?" Kathryn sat on a chair at the kitchen table.

Elizabeth looked for a moment, then also sat, her left leg tucked under her on top of the chair. She leaned forward and placed her elbows on the table.

"He's a foreman for a large cattle company. There are so many problems in his industry right now. They keep taking over grazing range for housing, then there's all the talk about red meat being bad for you. And sometimes I don't make it easy for him at home."

"What do you mean?" Kathryn encouraged.

She glanced at Fields who had seated himself beside Kathryn so Mrs. Flynt could see them both.

"Mr. Fields would understand. Sometimes when Bob gets home I don't have dinner ready. I'm not a very good cook. Sometimes I don't clean the house well enough. Things like that. I try hard, but sometimes I just don't do a good job. He gets angry."

Kathryn had heard the scenario many times; a battered woman blaming herself for the abuse, so she could justify staying with him. "Elizabeth, that's not enough reason for him to beat you. Have you reported this to the police?"

"Well, yes, a few years ago."

"What happened?"

"They came out to the house. By then he wasn't mad any longer. The police asked me if I wanted to press charges, but I didn't."

"Why not?" Kathryn asked, knowing the answer.

Elizabeth Flynt drew in a deep breath and cleared her throat. "I was afraid of what he'd do to me."

Fields asked, "Mrs. Flynt, have you talked to anyone else about this besides your sister?"

"Well, I called County Social Services once. All they said was that we could come in for counseling if we wanted."

"Did you go?"

"Oh, no! Bob would never do that. It wasn't his fault. I told you."

Kathryn shook her head. "How about the pastor at your church, or your doctor?"

"We don't go to church. Once, I went to my doctor. I had a broken nose. He didn't want to get involved, I don't think. I don't think I want to talk about this anymore. I thought you wanted to talk about my sister."

"We do, but can't we talk about you a little bit first? I think it's very important," Kathryn said.

Mrs. Flynt stared at Kathryn almost defiantly. "I threatened to leave Bob once. That was the worst beating I ever got. That's when my nose was broken. Besides, where would I go?"

"There are shelters. I'm sure there's a battered women's shelter here in Redding or somewhere nearby," Fields answered.

"That's easy for you to say; you're a man. And easy for her, too," she said, referring to Kathryn. Her tone was stronger.

"So I go to a shelter, then what? They protect me for a day or two, or a week or two, then what? Where do I live? How do I make a living? How do I care for my son? I have no college education. I haven't worked since right after high school. I was a secretary. I can't make a living, certainly not enough to support my son. And he'd find me, anyway. Then he'd kill me. I know he would."

Kathryn was surprised. "You have a son?"

Mrs. Flynt smiled. "Yes, Scotty. He's eight."

"Where is he?" Fields asked.

"At the YMCA with his father," Elizabeth answered with pride. "They're very close. They work out every Saturday morning together. Sometimes my husband takes him to work with him. Scotty wants to grow up and be just like his father, a cattle man."

"Elizabeth, has your son ever witnessed the violence, seen or heard your husband beat you?" Kathryn asked.

"He's only eight. He's always asleep or in the den watching television. He's too young to know what's happening. Bob has never hit me in front of Scotty."

"Children know a lot more than you think, Elizabeth, believe me," Kathryn said. "Almost every abusive man was raised in an abusive home. If your son continues to see this, he will grow up exactly like his father. He will beat his wife, too. Is that what you want?"

"Of course not, and I don't think how my husband and I raise our son is any of your business. Bob and I love each other, and we love our son. We'd never do anything to hurt him, including get a divorce."

Kathryn was frustrated but sensed she was on shaky ground. "Of course you wouldn't; I wasn't suggesting that. I apologize if I've offended you or poked my nose where it doesn't belong. The real reason we came was to see if you might help with Anna Marie."

"Well, I don't know much. Bob and I liked Larry a lot. He worked so much we didn't see him often, but he was a nice man, always attentive to Anna Marie.

"Anna Marie and I used to talk on the phone a lot, but Bob thought the phone bills were too high. So, Anna Marie bought me a computer for my birthday. She paid for Compuserve so we could exchange e-mail messages without running up Bob's phone bill. Compuserve is accessed through a local phone number so it doesn't cost us anything."

"You and she exchanged pretty personal information by e-mail, didn't you?"

"Yes, we did."

Kathryn said gently, "Did you ever ask her if Larry hit her in any of your e-mail letters?"

Elizabeth looked panic-stricken. Kathryn looked at Fields. "Elizabeth," she said, "if Anna isn't really a battered woman, I can't allow her to claim in court that she is. If you have a letter proving that Anna was never beaten, I need it. I don't want to, but if it's necessary, I'll call the Redding police to stand by here and guard the computer while I have a judge issue a search warrant for it. If I need to get a search warrant, Inspector Fields will have to take your computer, and this will take quite awhile."

"You can't do that. If the police are here when Bob gets home, I'll get in trouble." She thought for a minute. "If I give it to you, will you leave right away, before Bob gets home?"

"Of course," Kathryn answered. "We don't want to get you in trouble. All I want is that e-mail letter."

Kathryn accepted the printout after it was retrieved from the computer. "Thanks. Just one more thing, if you don't mind. What did you mean when you said she'd never let that happen again? She told you Larry never hit her."

"I think you'd better leave now," she said. "I don't know if I should talk to you about this."

"Elizabeth, Anna Marie's X rays showed old broken bones. A broken arm and several broken ribs. How did she get them? Was she in an accident, or was it something else? Anna Marie told us she was married before Larry, when she was very young."

"Well . . . if she already told you, I suppose it's okay. Her first husband was named Benjamin—Bennie, we called him. They were high-school sweethearts. They got married when Anna was seventeen. He drank a lot. One night he came home after a football game, drunk. They got in an argument and he hit her. They had only been married a couple of years.

She fought back and he beat her up really bad. He gave her a concussion and broke her ribs. And . . ." She looked about to cry.

"Elizabeth, if you—" Kathryn began.

Mrs. Flynt sniffed her nose. "No, it's all right. He punched her in the stomach over and over. Anna was pregnant at the time and lost the baby. She was in the hospital for several weeks. When she got out, she took her things and left. She never went back."

"I didn't know," Kathryn said. "And he broke her arm, too?"

"No, I'm not sure about that. It happened right after she married Bennie. She told everyone she fell. But I don't believe it. I think Bennie broke it, and she was ashamed to talk about it. After Bennie, she said she'd never be dependent on another man, and nobody would ever lay another hand on her, either. She doesn't like men very much."

"Small wonder," Fields said softly.

Mrs. Flynt looked at her watch. "I think you'd better leave. Bob will be home soon."

Kathryn tried one last time. "Elizabeth, can we drive you somewhere, somewhere you'll be safe?"

"I'm safe. Besides, like I said, where would I go?"

Kathryn pulled a business card from her wallet and indicated for Fields to do the same, then jotted something on the backs. "Will you take these, please? Just take them and hide them away someplace safe. I've written our home phone numbers on the back. Promise me you'll keep them. Call either of us anytime if we can ever help. Will you promise me that?"

Elizabeth Flynt hesitated, then tucked the two

business cards into the waistband of her sweatpants. "I'll put these in my diary," she promised. "I keep it in my underwear drawer. Bob would never look there. Now, please go. I'm afraid of what will happen if he comes home and finds you here."

Walking down the front walkway, Kathryn asked, "Did you get it all?"

Fields withdrew the cassette recorder from his jacket pocket. It was still running. He flipped it to off. "Yep, turned it on while you were in the bathroom. Recorded every word."

When Fields pulled the rented Toyota away from the curb and headed for the Redding airport, he said to Kathryn, "I hope the next time the Redding Police are called to that house, it's not the homicide unit."

39

FIELDS LEANED ACROSS THE AISLE OF THE SMALL twin-engine jet-prop as it lifted off the Redding runway and said to Kathryn, "You wanted me to remind you to never live there. Consider yourself reminded. Now, you keep reminding me to never so much as drive through that inferno, at least not between April and November. I've never been anyplace so hot! Thank God for air-conditioning." The temperature on the ground was 102 degrees and climbing.

Only one other passenger was on the plane, seated at the rear, out of earshot. Neither had mentioned Elizabeth Flynt or Anna Lancaster since Fields's comment about the homicide unit. Both knew there was nothing more they could say.

"Jim," Kathryn said, "what's the status of your internal affairs investigation on Dave?"

He shot her a quizzical look. "Why?"

"I have a favor to ask. Something personal. It's important or I wouldn't ask."

"Kate, I hope you aren't thinking what I think you're thinking. You know I can't do that. Benton gave strict instructions. You're to remain out of the loop completely."

"Do you have the file with you?" she persisted.

"Aw, Christ, Kate, come on."

"Do you?"

"Of course I do. You know I do. I've got to work on it over the weekend."

"I need to see it, Jim. Please. Don't make me grovel. You're my friend."

He thought. "Yeah, I am. And I'm fuckin' nuts, too," Fields uncharacteristically swore. "Here's all I can tell you. That coffee filled up my bladder. I'm going to go back to that little head and relieve myself. If somebody removed the file from my briefcase on the seat while I'm gone, how would I know? Then I'm gonna close my eyes and catch a few winks the rest of the flight. I'll need to take another leak just before we land. Got a bladder-control problem. If somebody slipped the file back into my briefcase, I'd never know about it. Now don't ask me about it again, 'cause I can't let you see it."

After Fields went to the bathroom, seated himself across the aisle, and closed his eyes, Kathryn took a deep breath and slowly opened the thick manila folder, her hands shaking visibly. The tab read GRANZ, DAVID A. 5348688.

Opened, each side of the folder was hole-punched at the top, and the papers secured by Acco fasteners. The left side held background and personal information. On top was a five by seven shoulder-up photograph, which Kathryn recognized as Dave's police ID photo. On the right, loose-leaf fashion, was another stack of papers, the DNA report on top.

Kathryn flipped through the papers one page at a time, not knowing exactly what she was searching for. She stopped when she located a transcription of the interview Walt Earheart had conducted of Julia Soto at the SANE room the night Soto reported she was raped.

This was Kathryn's first contact, even indirectly, with the woman who accused Dave Granz of raping her, and with whom he admitted to having sex. She felt angry, conflicted. She had spent most of her professional life defending the rights of rape victims who frequently had no one else to stand up for them. On the other hand, she loved and cared for Dave Granz and could not believe he was capable of such a thing. She took another deep breath, expelled it slowly, and began to read the transcript.

She skimmed the report, picking out only the salient points:

EARHEART: Did you agree?

SOTO: No, of course I did not. . . . He removed a

twenty-dollar bill from his wallet and threw it on the floor.

EARHEART: What happened then?

SOTO: I told him to leave, but he would not.

EARHEART: . . . Then what happened?

SOTO: . . . He kept shouting, "Twenty dollars, you fucking bitch, twenty dollars, you fucking whore." . . . Then . . . he stood up and unbuttoned his pants. . . . He said, "Come on, suck on this. Give me some head."

Kathryn was familiar with the different rape-case scenarios. She had heard statements like this before, but something was too familiar here. The language, the phrases, the order of events. . . . She read on.

EARHEART: Okay, then what happened?

SOTO: He threw me against the wall. . . . I must have blacked out. When I came to, I was on . . . the floor. . . . He was ripping off my clothes. I . . . screamed, but . . . He hit me again. . . . I tried to crawl away from him, but he . . . tore my panties off. . . . He kept saying over and over, "Twenty dollars, fucking bitch, twenty dollars, fucking whore." . . . I told him if he would not hit me again, I would do what he wanted.

Kathryn was absolutely certain she had read or heard these words before, but . . . where and when? She read ahead quickly.

EARHEART: . . . What did he say?

SOTO: . . . He said, "Fucking-A you will . . . He told

me . . . "Lie down and spread your fucking legs, you bitch. And lift up your ass."

"Oh, God," Kathryn said aloud, then glanced at Fields, who appeared to be asleep. "I know what this is. I know what this is and where I heard it before, but how, why . . . Am I sure? Absolutely certain?"

EARHEART: Then what happened?
SOTO: . . . He . . . said, "You'd better keep your mouth shut about this."
EARHEART: Those were his exact words?
SOTO: . . . He said, "If you breathe one fucking word of this, I'll come back and kill you."

Kathryn would never forget Francesca Jaramillo, a prostitute who had been raped by a dirt bag named George Zabrowski. Francesca was afraid to appear in open court, so Kathryn persuaded her to testify in front of the Grand Jury. Kathryn was certain she could persuade them to indict Zabrowski despite the fact that Frankie was a prostitute. She was wrong.

Kathryn had prosecuted dozens of rape cases, but this one stuck in her mind because of two or three highly unusual phrases Zabrowski had used. When Jaramillo asked Zabrowski to pay her twenty dollars for sex, he became enraged. As he struck her, causing her to hit her head and, as she had put it, "black out," he shouted, "Twenty dollars, you fucking bitch, twenty dollars, you fucking whore." Then, he had told her, "Suck on this. Give me some head."

Jaramillo told the Grand Jury that she had offered

to do whatever he wanted if he wouldn't hit her again, and Zabrowski said to her, "Fucking-A you will. Lie down and spread your fucking legs, you bitch. And lift up your ass."

Suddenly, Kathryn understood. She remembered seeing Julia's name on the personnel list in the translation department of Lancaster's firm. Somehow, Julia Soto either read the Grand Jury transcript of Jaramillo's testimony, or the police report. That would be easy enough to do. She had been a court translator. She would have known many police officers and court personnel. Police reports and Grand Jury transcripts are public records.

But how could Dave's semen be found inside her the night she was raped? Could he have had consensual sex with her that night and denied it to Kathryn, hoping to minimize their involvement. Or maybe he really had raped her.

Kathryn clumsily slipped the case file back into Fields's briefcase. As the pilot announced the final approach to San Jose International Airport, Kathryn leaned over and nudged her friend. "Wake up," she said.

Fields yawned and stretched. "Man, I slept like a log. We there yet?"

"We're there. Thanks, Jim," she said. Kathryn felt anxious, and a hot streak of anger ran through her body. She had to get over to Dave's apartment right away. She had to tell him she knew. Whatever she felt about Dave Granz, and whatever else he was, he was no rapist, and she had to reach him before it was too late.

40

A<small>T</small> THREE-FIFTEEN S<small>ATURDAY</small> <small>AFTERNOON</small>, Dave Granz turned off the water in the shower and listened. The phone rang again. He pulled a towel off the rack, dashed into the living room, grabbed the TV remote, and muted the sound which he had turned up so he could hear the action in the Giants game. He picked up the extension next to the couch. Drops of water formed a stain on the carpet. "Hello. Granz."

"David, it's Julia."

He paused, then asked, "What do you want, Julia? I told you not to call me anymore."

"I left something for you outside the door to your apartment. I think you'll want to see it. I'm going to hang up now, but you need to check it right away."

"What the fuck did she do, put a bomb on the door?" he muttered to himself. He wrapped the towel around his waist and walked to the front door. When he swung it open, Julia Soto stood on the landing with a cellular telephone in one hand and a revolver in the other. The gun pointed directly at Dave's chest.

"Good afternoon, David, may I come in?"

Dumbfounded, he backed away from the door, which Soto stepped through, closed, and locked, her eyes never leaving his face. "Julia, what's going on? What—"

"Be quiet, please, David. I would appreciate it if you would go back to your couch and sit down. Now, please," she ordered calmly. "I really do not wish to hurt you at the moment, but I assure you I will do so if you do not do as I say."

Dave held the towel while he backed into the living room and sat tentatively on the couch. Julia sat in an armchair beside the television. "Turn the ball game off, please. I would like to talk to you."

"Julia, I don't know what it is you have in mind, but don't do something you'll be sorry for. It isn't too late to stop."

Dave's voice was that of a man calm but afraid. A man experienced in life-threatening situations but not yet accustomed to them.

Nothing. Then, softly she said in barely controlled rage, "It is already too late, David. I am already sorry. Sorrier than you can ever know."

Calmly. "No, Julia, it isn't too late yet." A pause. "Julia, let me put my clothes on. I was in the shower when you came. That's why I answered the door in a towel."

"Yes, I assumed that. Your floor is all wet. By the way, your apartment is not as nice as the one you had before. What happened?"

"It's cheaper. I can't sit here holding a towel over myself. Let me go put some clothes on. Then we can talk."

"I do not trust you. If I turn away, you will take my gun. I cannot allow you to go into the bedroom alone.

And besides," she said, looking at his bare legs, "you are not holding the towel over yourself. The view from here is quite revealing."

Dave pushed the towel down into his lap, and it came loose at the side. "Julia, I can't talk to you while I'm undressed. Let me put some clothes on. You can come with me to make sure I don't try anything."

"All right," she said, standing, the gun still pointed at his chest. "Go into the bedroom slowly. This gun is loaded, I promise you."

He backed into the bedroom. A pair of jeans and a T-shirt were on the bed. He looked at them but hesitated to remove the towel and put them on.

"Put them on. You may remove the towel," she said angrily. "Why would I care? I have seen you naked; I saw you that way just a few days ago. Have you forgotten? It is the way a whore should see you. That is what I am to you, is it not? A whore? That is what you . . . what you and they have made me. A whore."

Dave dropped the towel and quickly put on his clothes, then stood beside the bed. "Julia, I don't think you're a whore. I care about you. It's just that I'm not ready."

"You dishonored me. And then, when I needed you, you were not there."

"Julia," Dave said, "listen to me. I went to Cuernavaca. I spoke with your father; I spoke with Rosa. A week ago. I know those men raped you."

"Damn you, David!" she shouted. "You spoke with my family? How dare you? How dare you go to my home after . . . after . . . Why?"

"Because I had to know. I had to know what happened to cause you to change. I talked with the

San Jose police, Julia; I know about Gary Watts too. Why him? What did he do?"

"He used me, just as you did. Just as they did in Cuernavaca. You think it is different, what the two of you did?" Because you raped me by taking me to dinner and buying me gifts instead of throwing me on the ground? You think that is different? At least the men in Mexico were honest. Not you. Not Gary. You deceived me, you tricked me. You defiled me, and now I am unsuitable for respectable men. I might as well be dead. And I will be, but not before you." Julia's hands shook, but the gun never wavered from Dave's chest.

Dave's voice was strained but calm. "Julia, how did you fool the police, the lab into believing that was my semen they recovered when they examined you at the hospital? It couldn't have been mine."

"But it was, David."

"Julia, it couldn't have been. We didn't have sex that night. We hadn't had sex since the Tuesday before."

"After we had sex that night, I kept you."

"You . . . what? You kept me? What do you mean?"

"After we made love, when you refused to spend the night, I knew you wouldn't return. I retrieved your condom from the wastebasket and removed your semen from it. I put it in a bottle and stored the bottle in the freezer."

Dave speculated, "So, on Friday night, you removed the . . . ejaculate from the freezer and placed it inside yourself? God, Julia, I had no idea you hated me so much."

"How could I not?" she wailed. "It is you who are

responsible for what I have become. You and, and, and that *woman.* Mackay. Yes that is exactly what I did. Then I went to the hospital."

"Jesus, Julia—"

Soto screamed. "I have told you before to not be profane. I warned you! That is not the way you speak to decent women!"

"I'm sorry," Dave said softly. "What did you tell Lieutenant Earheart at the hospital?"

"I was once assigned as a translator at a Grand Jury hearing. Kathryn Mackay forced a poor Hispanic woman to testify. She was a prostitute, a whore, not unlike myself, except she sold herself for money rather than dinner and flowers. I remembered her testimony very well. It was her story I told Lieutenant Earheart. He was not at that hearing and would have no way to know.

"It serves her right. She did not even know I existed. I was never asked to translate during the hearing. She is an evil woman, David."

"No, Julia, Kathryn is not evil. She is a decent and honorable woman like you. She has done nothing to you."

Soto became infuriated. "She has done nothing?! Nothing?! She has taken you from me. If it were not for her, you would have come to me in Cuernavaca when I needed you. I know that."

"I didn't even know her then," Dave told her. "She had nothing to do with it. I just wasn't ready for that commitment."

Soto ignored him. "She was even unable to have the rapist of that poor prostitute indicted! The Grand

Jury did not believe her because she is a whore. Just like they will not believe me. That is why I will kill you, David. Then I will kill myself."

Dave leaned his legs against the bed to steady himself. "Julia, put the gun down, this is crazy. You have to stop now, while you still can. I never meant to hurt you. If I had known, I would have come to Cuernavaca."

"I don't believe you."

41

KATHRYN PARKED HER AUDI BEHIND DAVE'S Explorer and walked up the landing. As she approached the front apartment door, she heard angry voices inside. She recognized the man's voice as Dave's; the woman's, heavily accented with Spanish, she instinctively knew belonged to Julia Soto.

She stood outside the door for what seemed an eternity but was actually no more than two or three minutes. Accustomed to making difficult decisions, she reached into her handbag and silently removed the key to Dave's apartment, which she had not returned. She felt the weight of the small twenty-five caliber semiautomatic pistol she was licensed to carry.

Silently, she swung the front apartment door open and stepped into the familiar foyer that adjoined the apartment's living room. A small puddle of water stood on the tile floor. She had been here many times in the past, stealing precious hours together with her lover. This time was different. Deadly different.

The voices were louder now, easily discernible. Her best guess was that they originated in the bedroom, which entered the living room at the extreme far end.

She took a chance and peeked around the corner of the dividing partition. The living room was vacant.

She heard Dave say "Julia, put the gun down, this is crazy. You have to stop now, while you still can. I never meant to hurt you. If I had known, I would have come to Cuernavaca."

She heard Julia answer, "I don't believe you."

Slowly, she opened her purse to remove the Browning automatic. The safety on the pistol cracked. It sounded like a thunderbolt. Damn, had they heard? She waited, afraid to breathe, but no one moved inside the bedroom. She had no more time. She crept across the living room, took a deep breath and prayed, then stepped into the doorway of the bedroom, her weapon raised to eye level.

Julia Soto's back was to the doorway. Dave stood facing Kathryn. His hair was still wet. His expression never changed. He shook his head imperceptibly, indicating that Kathryn should not fire.

Then he said gently to Soto, "Julia, listen to me." As he spoke, he inched slowly to his right, toward the head of the bed. His eyes never wavered from hers. "I'm sorry you misinterpreted what I did, what I didn't do." He moved another step. The barrel of Soto's gun followed him, but she made no attempt to stop him.

Kathryn knew Dave kept his nine-millimeter Glock automatic service weapon under his pillow when he was at home, except when he slept. His weapon was within an arm's length.

"No," Julia said. Her voice was deadly calm. "No. I have listened to you enough." She steadied the barrel of her gun toward Dave's chest.

"Stop! Julia Soto, stop! Now!" Kathryn shouted.

Soto whirled, her eyes frantic. Then she recognized Kathryn and backed up against the wall. Her pistol still pointed at Dave, but uncertainty showed in her eyes. "Bitch," she hissed at Kathryn. *"Puta."*

Kathryn saw Soto's finger tighten on the trigger, then she heard a deafening blast. The barrel of Soto's gun jerked upward as it recoiled from the explosion.

Dave was hurled backward onto the bed, blood spurting from a gaping wound in his side. He shuddered, then lay still.

Before Kathryn could react, Julia Soto placed the gun to her right temple, whispered *"Puta!"* and pulled the trigger.

"Oh, Jesus, oh Jesus," Kathryn said aloud, at the same time punching 9-1-1 into her cell phone with trembling fingers.

As soon as the dispatcher took the information, Kathryn threw the cell phone on the floor and rushed to the bed. She felt Dave's neck and located a weak pulse. Blood continued to ooze from the wound, but there was nothing she could do but wait and pray.

"Stay alive, damn you, Granz! Don't die, goddamnit, I need to talk to you." He was still alive when the paramedics loaded him on a gurney and wheeled him away to the ambulance.

Kathryn sat on the floor and didn't move until Walt Earheart arrived and took her statement.

42

"How are you holding up, Kathryn? If you aren't up to it after yesterday, I understand. I can come down."

"Thanks, Hal, but if I don't keep busy, I'll go crazy. Let me handle this."

"Okay. You know, if Bickell introduces Anna Lancaster's prior history of abuse by her first husband, the jury might not convict her of First Degree murder," Benton said.

"I can move to exclude that evidence, Hal. Technically, it's not relevant to the murder, but it's anybody's guess whether the judge would rule in our favor."

"What do you recommend we do?"

Kathryn pulled the telephone headset away from her ear, closed her eyes, and massaged her temple, then replaced it. "If I can get her to plead to a lesser charge, that's what I'd like to do. She may not have been abused by Lawrence Lancaster, but she's still a battered woman."

"Your call, Kate. I trust your judgment. Do what you think is best," Benton advised her and hung up.

Kathryn left her office and entered the DA conference room, where Jim Fields, Angela Bickell, and Anna Marie Lancaster waited. Both Angela Bickell and her client were dressed in their Sunday casuals: jeans, cotton T-shirts, sandals. The similarity ended there. Fields wore a summer suit.

"Kathryn," Bickell began, "I certainly hope this is important, being called down here at two o'clock on Sunday afternoon."

"I believe it will be worth your trouble," Kathryn said, "as well as your client's."

"Well, I sure hope you haven't dragged us down here to talk some sort of a deal. If so, you can tell me now, and we can all stop wasting our time. My client isn't interested in a deal."

"Assuming I were prepared to offer a compromise of some sort, would you mind telling me why you wouldn't be interested in listening?"

"Well, it's perfectly clear to me, even if it isn't to you," she said. "You're losing this case. You have no chance of convicting my client of manslaughter, much less murder. To be blunt, I'm kicking your ass all over the courtroom. If you think I'm going to take a deal so you can save your reputation, you're mistaken. Now, if that's all you wanted to see us about . . . ?" She rose from the leather chair as if to leave.

Kathryn smiled, unperturbed. "Ms. Bickell, I can

understand your enthusiasm and desire to impress your client. But be realistic. Dr. Nelson's testimony established your client's premeditation and deliberation beyond a reasonable doubt. She killed an unconscious man. Do your client a favor and listen to what I have to say. If you don't, she's going to be convicted of First Degree Murder. And that's a fact."

Kathryn looked directly at Lancaster. "You don't want to leave yet, Mrs. Lancaster." She reached into her top-right desk drawer, removed a stack of papers, and shoved them across the desk.

"You might want to look at this first."

Bickell glanced at her client, then put on a pair of glasses and scanned the papers quickly. She snorted and tossed them contemptuously back on Kathryn's desk. "Big deal. That's it? So, you printed out her diary from the disk. So what?"

"Well, you're partly right and partly wrong," Kathryn answered. "That's what your client calls her diary, all right, but it wasn't printed from the disk you gave us. We thought it best to go right to the source, if you know what I mean. That diary was printed from the hard drive on your client's computer at Lawrence and Young."

Anna Lancaster sat bolt upright. "You what; how did you know . . . ?"

"Quiet," Bickell instructed her client. Then to Kathryn, "What do you mean from her computer at work? How did you get into it?"

"Got a search warrant. Inspector Fields and I served it Friday afternoon. Mr. Hyler was most helpful. We were able to start WordPerfect right up. And that was the least interesting thing we found. Your client has adapted nicely to the electronic communication age. We found Compuserve, too, so we checked her in-basket."

"This is outrageous. . . . I'll—" Lancaster shouted.

Bickell put her husky arm on her client's and pushed her back into her chair. "Be quiet, please. Her in-basket?"

"Correct," Kathryn answered, then turned to Fields.

"Inspector Fields, will you show Ms. Bickell those messages, please?"

Fields deftly opened his briefcase with his left hand, extracted a stack of perhaps forty typed pages, and handed them to the defense attorney. She read them slowly while Kathryn and Fields waited.

When she finished, Bickell did not speak but turned and handed the pages to her client. Lancaster read quickly and handed them back.

"Quite a coincidence, wouldn't you say, Mrs. Lancaster?" Kathryn asked.

"This doesn't prove a thing, and you know it," Bickell said. "Where are you going with this?"

"I'll tell you where I'm going, counselor. That wasn't your client's diary on the computer disk you gave us."

Kathryn considered the situation. "I'll give you the benefit of the doubt and assume you didn't know your client had plagiarized another woman's account of being brutalized, and that you turned the disk over to us in good faith. However, since those weren't Mrs. Lancaster's experiences in her so-called diary, then your expert witness has been deceived."

"That's—"

"Let me finish, please," Kathryn said. "I'd be happy to recall your expert and ask her whether she could opine as to the reasonableness of Mrs. Lancaster's sense of imminent danger given that the diary she was provided wasn't a diary at all—it wasn't a day-by-day recollection—and, as a matter of fact, didn't represent your client's battering experiences at all."

Bickell tried to hide her surprise. "This is so much crap and you know it, but go ahead. We're listening." It was a show of bravado Bickell did not feel, intended to demonstrate the strength of her advocacy for her client.

Kathryn addressed her comments directly to the defendant. "Well, it occurred to us, Mrs. Lancaster, that you just might hide other important information from us as well. So, I added your personnel file to the search warrant. I was curious about who in your family might be close enough to you to validate your claims of abuse. Very few battered women keep it strictly to themselves. They almost always tell somebody. I wondered who that somebody might be. And what do you think we discovered, Mrs. Lancaster? Right there in your personnel file."

"My sister," Lancaster whispered. "Oh God, Elizabeth."

Bickell was either genuinely surprised and confused, Kathryn thought, or she ought to be nominated for an Oscar. "Your sister? What are you talking about? Who the hell is your sister?"

"Tell her your sister's name, Mrs. Lancaster," Kathryn urged.

Bickell glared at her client.

"Elizabeth Flynt."

"Don't say another word," Bickell ordered. "So what? This is all circumstantial. It proves nothing."

"So, yesterday," Kathryn continued, "Inspector Fields and I flew to Redding. We were fortunate to find Mrs. Flynt home alone. Seems her husband is abusive."

Anna Lancaster looked faint. "You . . . you spoke with Elizabeth? I can't believe she talked with you."

"Believe it," Kathryn said. "She spoke with us for almost an hour. She's very fearful. Her husband beats her regularly. But you knew that didn't you? You knew because she e-mailed you detailed accounts of her husband's battering her over the past five years. And you saved them.

"We figure you concocted your story about being a battered woman. Your lawyer wanted something—anything—to prove it.

"So, you told her you kept a diary on the computer at your office. Ms. Bickell is a very good lawyer. She knew your diary would be very persuasive with the BWS expert. They often work with diaries.

"So, she asked you to print it out and put it on disk. You drove over to your office the Friday night after you were arrested. You typed the entire diary in one sitting. Copied your sister's private e-mail letters to you word for word. Very clever."

Bickell was uncharacteristically reticent. "Ms. Mackay, I didn't know about this. She told me she had maintained the diary for years. When she gave it to me, I assumed it was exactly as she had kept it. I didn't even know she had a sister."

"I believe you, Ms. Bickell. I couldn't believe any woman could be so callous about her own sister, never mind battered women in general. If she succeeded, it would set Battered Women's Syndrome back years. I wouldn't want to see that happen any more than you."

"Still, this doesn't prove my client wasn't battered," Bickell recovered. "I'll request a continuance. Have her reexamined by another expert."

"I'm afraid that won't help, either," Kathryn replied. She slid a one-page letter across the desk. It contained the e-mail letter in which Anna Lancaster wrote her sister that she had never been struck by her husband.

"Is that your letter, Mrs. Lancaster?" Kathryn asked.

Before she could answer, her attorney advised her, "Don't answer that."

"Mrs. Flynt told us your client said that Lawrence Lancaster never laid a hand on her," Kathryn replied.

"You bitch," Lancaster said to Mackay. "My sister will never testify to that in court. She knows I'm the only hope she's got. With Larry dead, I'll have plenty of money. She knows without me, she'll be stuck in that hole with that bastard forever. She'll never testify, not in a million years!"

Kathryn turned to Fields. "Jim?"

He pulled a mini cassette recorder from his jacket pocket and set it on Kathryn's desk, directly in front of himself. "I think you might find this informative," he said. "I recorded it yesterday in Redding."

When the tape finished, the room was silent. "If Mrs. Flynt won't testify, the tape will testify for her,"

Fields said. "But I really don't think she needs that sort of trouble, do you? She has enough problems."

Bickell made one final attempt to salvage the situation. "Motive. You still have nothing concrete to establish why my client would want to kill her husband."

"I thought about that," Kathryn said, "and I believe we've figured it out."

Kathryn withdrew a final document and slid it across the desk to Bickell.

The defense attorney picked it up, read it, then looked at her client in confusion. "A prenuptial agreement? I don't understand."

Anna Lancaster jumped from her chair and grabbed the document. "You can't! You can't have this! I destroyed them. This isn't possible."

"Ms. Mackay, I'd like to speak with my client alone. Would you give us fifteen minutes, please?"

"We'll be right outside in the hall," Kathryn said.

"So, exactly what does all that legal mumbo jumbo in the prenup mean, anyway?" Fields asked Kathryn while they waited.

"Well, I'm not a family law attorney, thank God— you think criminal law gets nasty; it doesn't compare to family law—but it's not too complicated. In a community property state like California, whatever either of them earn while they're married belongs to them both equally. So, any increase in the value of Lawrence's partnership interest in the law firm after they married would be community property. That value skyrocketed during the five years the Lancasters were married. Lancaster's firm won some huge lawsuits. Barring a prenuptial agreement to the contrary, half of that increase would be hers if she divorced him. But, if he died an accidental death, her half would be hers and so would his half. That is, if there was no prenuptial agreement that anyone knew about."

"And it gets more interesting," she continued. "The agreement included standard boilerplate language stating she got absolutely nothing until they'd been married more than five years. It's in almost all of them. That means she had to stick it out at least five years, or it would all have been for zilch, from her point of view."

"Jesus, she's a calculating bitch."

"Yeah, I suppose so, but it's not hard to see how she got that way when it comes to men. I'll bet they executed the agreement in duplicate originals. She trashed her copy; it just worked to her disadvantage. But she needed to destroy his, too. Most men file that sort of thing in their offices. She's his personal secretary. She must've found his original and destroyed it. Only . . ."

"Only," Fields finished, "what she thought was his original wasn't. It was a copy. The original is the one he had recorded."

"Right. The firm wouldn't let that slip through the cracks. They'd require each partner to have them recorded in their county of residence, just in case. She'd have no way to know that since they're no longer required to be recorded by law unless they involved real property. And theirs didn't. The house wasn't mentioned."

The door to Kathryn's office opened. "Ms. Mackay?" Bickell asked. When they were seated, Bickell said, "My client will plead to aggravated manslaughter."

"That's ridiculous," Kathryn retorted. "That's eleven years, max. Even serving 85 percent of the sentence, she'd do only nine years. No deal."

Kathryn looked directly at the defendant. "Listen carefully, Mrs. Lancaster. This is a one-time offer. It is not negotiable. You plead to Second Degree murder. Fifteen to life. You'll serve a minimum of twelve and a half years. Probably more. And you must pay a restitution fine of twenty-five thousand dollars to the local battered women's shelter. If you don't take this deal now, I'll proceed with this trial. I'll convict you of First Degree Murder, I guarantee it. Think carefully. You have one minute to decide. Then the offer is rescinded and this meeting is over. And I will see you in court Monday."

Bickell and Lancaster conferred in whispers. "My client accepts your offer, Ms. Mackay."

"Is that correct, Mrs. Lancaster?"

"Yes."

"Mrs. Lancaster, why? Why did you kill your husband?" Kathryn asked.

Lancaster sneered. "You're not as smart as I thought you were. I needed Larry's money. When I got it, I planned to take Elizabeth and her son away from Redding and that son of a bitch she's married to. Neither of us would ever have to depend on another man as long as we lived. She'll still get my half. I'll have my lawyer see to it."

"But, why kill him? Why not just destroy the

prenuptial agreement and file for divorce. Take your half of the community property and split? You didn't know he recorded that agreement."

"I couldn't take that chance. And half wasn't enough."

43

IT WAS JUST BEFORE DINNERTIME WHEN KATH-ryn pushed the door to County General Hospital Room 428 open slightly and peeked in. She couldn't see anything, so she opened it wider and stepped inside.

The bed occupied the far-right corner of the small private room. Dave Granz lay in the bed with an IV line stuck in his left arm and oxygen tubes up each side of his nose. Monitoring equipment flashed and blinked on a shelf over the bed. His blond hair was matted and unkempt, and one foot stuck out from under the sheet. He looked pathetically small and helpless.

His eyes opened when he heard the door, and he smiled weakly when he saw Kathryn.

"Hi, babe," he greeted her as cheerfully as he was able and waved with his free hand.

Kathryn closed the door quietly, sat tentatively on the edge of his bed, took his right hand in both of hers and squeezed. Tears welled up in her eyes and ran down her cheeks, but for once she didn't deny or hide them.

"How do you feel?" she asked.

He made a weak attempt to dismiss the situation with a flip of his left arm, almost dislodging the IV line, and snorted past the oxygen tubes in his nostrils. "I'll be outta here and back to work in no time."

Kathryn shook her head. "The nurse said you're going to be fine, but that you'll be out of commission for awhile."

"Whada they know? I've been worse. This is a piece-a-cake compared to last time," he retorted, referring to his brush with death at the hands of the Gingerbread Man.

"Men! You're so tough," Kathryn said tolerantly. "No, this time you're going to take enough time off to recuperate properly. You'll be out of the hospital in a week or so, but you'll need looking after."

"I know," he conceded. "I talked to my mom just before you got here. She and Dad are on their way up from San Diego. They're gonna stay at my place till I get out." He grinned at her. "They'll probably check into a motel when she sees what a mess my apartment is. I'm going home with them for awhile. Catch up on some of that good home cookin'."

Even under the circumstances, Kathryn found that grin irresistible. She patted and rubbed his hand, and interwove her fingers with his, but they sat quietly for several minutes while she looked out the window and he stared at the ceiling.

"The doctor said surgery went great," he told her. "They had to remove my spleen, but the bullet missed everything vital. He says I don't actually need a spleen, anyway, but I might be a little more prone to catch colds later." He looked at her and said, "I'd have bled to death if you hadn't been there, Kate. You saved my life."

Kathryn kissed him tenderly on his cheek, which she noticed was damp and salty. "It was the least I could do for an old flame," she said in an ineffectual attempt at humor. Then, more seriously, she added, "You don't owe me anything, Dave."

He pushed her head up gently so he could look into her eyes. "Yes, I do. I owe you a lot. I owe you an apology, and I owe you an explanation. I'm so sorry, Kate; I don't know what the hell I was thinking. You were always so busy, and I didn't have the strength to wait things out. But I'll make it up to you, I promise. It'll be like old times between us as soon as I get back from my folks'."

It was the conversation she dreaded, but once it arose, she had to confront it.

"Dave, we can't be together again. We both know that. It wouldn't be the same, and it couldn't work. If there was ever something special between us, it's been lost forever. I'd never be able—"

"Babe, please, I—"

Kathryn softly touched her fingertips to his lips, and he kissed them. "Shush. I didn't want to talk about this now while you're so sick, but maybe it's best for both of us to get it over with."

He started to say something, but she silenced him with a look. "Maybe I'm too rigid, too unforgiving. Sometimes I wish I could change." She pulled a tissue from the dispenser on the table and wadded it up in her hand, but she was finished crying. "But I can't change, Dave, and neither can you. For better or worse, we are both just whatever we are, nothing more or less. I'd never trust you again. I'd want to believe you were faithful, but I'd always wonder. Eventually, it would poison me, and it would poison you, and it would poison us. We both deserve better than that."

Dave lay his head back on the pillow, closed his eyes, and placed his arm over his forehead. "I know. You're right, but I don't want to let go." His voice lowered to a whisper and cracked. "I wanted to marry you, Kathryn. If only we could go back and start over."

"But we can't," she replied sadly. "We can never go back, only forward. It's the only direction there is."

He sat up slightly and grimaced. "What about Emma? Can I see her sometime?"

Kathryn shook her head. She had thought constantly about it since Dave and Em went to Monterey. It was even harder than ending her own relationship with him.

"She can't keep seeing you, thinking that you'll always be part of her life. She needs a stable family even if it's just with a single mother. If there is a man in her life, it needs to be someone she can count on permanently. If you keep seeing her, it'll never be over for her."

"How about as friends, Kate, can't we all be friends? What could that hurt? I don't know what I'll do if you both just drop out of my life."

"Drop out of your life!? Why didn't you think of that before you got involved with someone, before it was too late?" Then, she added, "It doesn't matter.

What's done is done and it's probably as much my fault as yours. But that doesn't change anything."

They sat in awkward silence for a minute, then Kathryn arose. "I should go so you can rest. Say hello to your mom and dad for me. Take your time recovering. Don't rush it like you did last time."

She walked slowly toward the door and paused with her hand on the doorknob, turning toward the bed. "Dave, I'd appreciate it if you didn't call or write me or Emma. We need to deal with this on our own."

After she closed the door, Dave Granz pulled the sheet over his face and went to sleep.

EPILOGUE

CHESTER AND MARY ENID GRANZ DROVE THEIR son home to southern California as soon as he was released from the hospital. Dave moved back into his old room, which his mother had kept the same since the day he graduated from college. Over the next three months, he gained ten pounds due to inactivity and his mother's cooking, and he thought about Kate and Emma every day.

Philip Hyler arranged and paid for Julia Soto's body to be shipped to Cuernavaca, Morelos, Mexico. Julia's sister, Rosa, and her husband and children, attended the funeral services, but no mass was said and Roberto Soto stayed home. Señor Soto passed away the following week.

On Monday, August 8, Kathryn and Emma Mackay rode the Amtrak train to Truckee, where they rented a car and drove to a friend's condominium at the base of Diamond Peak in Incline Village.

They rented bicycles each day and rode around Lake Tahoe in the clear mountain air. They shopped at antique stores, skipped rocks across the surface of the lake, and ate frozen yogurt for lunch. In the evenings, they hiked through the golf course to the village for dinner.

At night, Emma cried in bed. And after her daughter went to sleep, so did Kathryn. She would never know whether or not she and Dave could have worked things out. The only thing she was sure of was that she and Emma were all each other had and she would never allow anything to hurt her daughter.

Following their week's vacation, they rode the train back to San Jose and took the Airporter to Santa Rita. Emma returned to school and was counseled by Diane Parker once a week. Kathryn shuffled through case files and prepared for trial. Periodically, she scanned the Help-Wanted ads in *California Lawyer* Magazine.

Three months and two weeks after being shot by Julia Soto, David Granz returned to full duty as an inspector in the Santa Rita District Attorney's office.

Printed in the United States
By Bookmasters